"What do you

Luke's eyes gleame
don't think I want to answer right here and now."

The color rose in Charlotte's face. "If you aren't very careful, you'll get caught in the cross fire."

"Which one? The one between our families? Or the one between you and me?"

She couldn't breathe. "There isn't anything between you and me."

He looked at her. Just looked at her. And made her heart stop with the expression in those brown eyes. "You may not be a thief—but you have turned into a charming little liar." His fingers lightly brushed her cheek. "Strange. I thought I hated lady liars. But I don't seem to mind at all when it's you."

Her lips felt full. He was going to kiss her. She wanted to feel his mouth on hers, wanted to feel his hands on her body.

Once she'd trusted him with her life. Could she still?

Dear Reader,

Whether or not it's back to school—for you *or* the kids—Special Edition this month is the place to return to for romance!

Our THAT SPECIAL WOMAN!, Serena Fanon, is heading straight for a Montana wedding in Jackie Merritt's *Montana Passion,* the second title in Jackie's MADE IN MONTANA miniseries. But that's not the only wedding this month—in Christine Flynn's *The Black Sheep's Bride,* another blushing bride joins the family in the latest installment of THE WHITAKER BRIDES. And three little matchmakers scheme to bring their unsuspecting parents back together again in *Daddy of the House,* book one of Diana Whitney's new miniseries, PARENTHOOD.

This month, the special cross-line miniseries DADDY KNOWS LAST comes to Special Edition. In *Married... With Twins!,* Jennifer Mikels tells the tale of a couple on the brink of a breakup—that is, until they become instant parents to two adorable girls. September brings two Silhouette authors to the Special Edition family for the first time. Shirley Larson's *A Cowboy Is Forever* is a reunion ranch story not to be missed, and in Ingrid Weaver's latest, *The Wolf and the Woman's Touch,* a sexy loner agrees to help a woman find her missing niece—but only if she'll give him one night of passion.

I hope you enjoy each and every story to come!

Sincerely,

Tara Gavin,
Senior Editor

Please address questions and book requests to:
Silhouette Reader Service
U.S.: 3010 Walden Ave., P.O. Box 1325, Buffalo, NY 14269
Canadian: P.O. Box 609, Fort Erie, Ont. L2A 5X3

SHIRLEY LARSON

A COWBOY IS FOREVER

Silhouette®

SPECIAL EDITION®

Published by Silhouette Books
America's Publisher of Contemporary Romance

This book is dedicated to Kara, my daughter and good
friend who believes in rainbows, katydids and true
love; to Ed and Dawn, the newest members of the
Larson clan; to Margaret, who can say "I love you" just
when it's most needed; and to Pat—again.

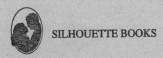

SILHOUETTE BOOKS

ISBN 0-373-24055-4

A COWBOY IS FOREVER

Books by Shirley Larson

Silhouette Special Edition

A Cowboy Is Forever #1055

Silhouette Romance

A Slice of Paradise #369

Silhouette Desire

To Touch the Fire #131

SHIRLEY LARSON

was born on an Iowa farm on April Fools' Day. Her first love was music; she sang in the chorus and played trumpet in the band.

Don Larson played tuba in that same organization. It was on a high school band trip that Shirley decided he'd be a good man to marry. But it wasn't until Don returned from the army and Shirley earned a college degree in music education that they were wed.

Don took a position with Eastman Kodak and, soon after, three children were born: Kris, Kara and Keith. Shirley worked in several positions before deciding that what she really wanted to do was to write a romance. Since then she's published twenty-four books, including two historicals. She lives in the Finger Lakes area of New York, and directs a church choir and teaches voice and piano.

Announcing the Marriage

of

Charlotte Malone

to

Luke Steadman

*Herein lies the end (we hope)
of the Steadman—Malone feud that
has plagued the ranching community
of Two Trees, Montana, for over
two decades*

Chapter One

If there was a smaller, colder, more desolate town on the map than Two Trees, Montana, Charlotte Malone couldn't imagine where it was. Behind her, the Mission Mountains were frosted with snow, even though it was the twenty-sixth of May. The main street was like a wind tunnel, and the arctic breeze rattled a vacant store front window in a forlorn little tat-a-tat. Half the little businesses in town had been abandoned due to lack of interest, money, people, or all three, including a restaurant building Charlotte owned and neglected in favor of her ranch. Saying a prayerful thanks to a munificent heaven that there weren't a lot of folks around to witness her lapse in successful ranching, Charlotte hustled along the deserted street, searching for her straying cow.

"Princess!"

No answer from the cow who would be a free spirit.

The wind reached greedy fingers into the hair Charlotte had tied too quickly and carelessly into a knot, liberating the black, silky strands and tossing them like froth around her head. She shivered and stuck her bare hands as far as they would go into the pockets of her dad's old sheepskin coat. There was nothing like the feel of cold fingers curling into palms to remind a woman she was heading toward hypothermia. If she didn't find Princess soon, Charlotte would freeze, and if that ornery cow *was* foraging in Sam Sandler's trash cans again, the unforgiving owner of the Silver Branch Saloon might just "shoot that straying bovine relic on sight," as he'd promised.

"Princess! Where are you?"

The cow her father, Sean Malone, had raised as a pet knew better than to bawl an answer when away without leave in enemy territory.

A setting sun flashed gold fire on the half block of empty store windows. Ever the optimist, Charlotte felt her spirits buoyed by that glint of gold. It was an omen. Just around the bend, something good awaited her. She'd find Princess. Henry Steadman would call off his suit. She'd find a million dollars lying in the street.

Well, one out of three wasn't bad.

"Princess!"

At least Sam wasn't out loading his gun. Charlotte could see him through the window of the bar, serving drinks to Mike Hallorhan and Harry Foote. Mike's green two-ton Chevy pickup with glistening chrome and four antennas sat parked in front of the saloon, beside Harry's big old black Lincoln. No sneaking around in this town; everybody knew everybody else's car.

The distinctive growl of an expensive motor sounded out of place in the lonely chill of the late afternoon. A sleek sports car, black as the devil's heart, rolled down the street.

Here was a car she didn't know, not in Two Trees, not in this life.

The car came closer, a low-slung silhouette against the orange-streaked sky. The headlights gleamed in the dusky light, popped up and out in that way that was supposed to be European and sexy. The fenders were one long black satiny curve, chrome discreetly and sparingly used. The car cut into a parking place on the opposite side of the street and stopped just short of the high curb, as if the driver had parked in Two Trees a thousand times. The motor died, and dust spiraled up and around the red taillights.

The door opened. The wind stopped and the sun stopped and the earth stopped.

The driver untangled himself from the torturous-looking seat and stood up on legs about as long as forever, dwarfing the car. She knew whose legs those were. She'd have known them if they came walking out of a spaceship.

The chills dancing up her spine doubled, trebled, then were suddenly vanquished by a blast furnace of heated excitement exploding inside her. She was taking a breath to give Luke Steadman a big old Montana hello when he turned his back to her and slammed the car door shut.

His casualness threw her off balance. She'd thought he'd recognize her as instantly as she did him. Obviously, he hadn't.

Recently the town had come to life with incessant buzzing about Luke's divorce. She hadn't believed the rumors. No woman in her right mind would let Luke go. When the gossip had flown a second time, about his dismissal from his father-in-law's legal firm and his loss of his home, Charlotte couldn't take any more. She'd told everyone who'd listen that it couldn't possibly be true. Didn't they all remember what a winner he was? Luke hadn't changed, could never change. He'd always be Luke—honest, steadfast, and totally successful at everything he did.

Now he walked toward her, and she knew she'd been wrong and the townspeople right. The set of his mouth and jaw told Charlotte that Luke Steadman had taken a harder fall in New York City than the one in the Cheyenne rodeo ring that had left him with a broken left femur, tibia and elbow.

He hadn't buttoned his coat, and the wind caught one side of the soft cream-colored suede. He didn't seem to notice the blast of cold that must be slamming against his chest. He strolled toward her with a walk as smooth as silk. He was a good athlete, the town's golden boy, the first quarterback to turn the hometown football team's losing streak into a string of wins. He'd gone to Iowa University on a scholarship he didn't need, graduated with honors from Harvard Law School, and married another law student who was beautiful, rich and smart. He'd had everything . . . till now.

The post office flag snapped and writhed, a sparrow started to sing and stopped abruptly. From the other side of the Silver Branch, Princess bawled. Charlotte didn't, couldn't, move.

He was all grace and manners, and that lean hand came up to whip off his hat the moment he saw her. There was a courtliness in his approach to her that was unmistakably Luke, but when the wind ruffled his hair, his face took on a kind of hard impatience that she'd never seen before. His eyes were the same beautiful dark brown, but there were fine lines of fatigue around them, as if he hadn't had a good night's sleep for a long while.

Not fair. Not fair to see Luke like this, to see his body resonating with a finely drawn tension he held under control with the practice of a soldier home from the wars.

"Hello," he said. His voice was husky, more adult than she remembered it; deeper . . . harder.

"Hello yourself." The throatiness in her own voice unnerved her.

"I . . ." He stopped speaking, his eyes wandering over her face. "Charlotte? I almost didn't recognize you. You've changed. You look . . . older. Very much like your mother."

Nothing she wanted to hear more than that she looked . . . older. "I'll take that as a compliment."

"That's certainly the way I meant it. I . . . Looking at you makes me feel . . . so old. Older. Makes me feel much . . . older."

"When you get to 'ancient,' you can stop."

She smiled at him; she couldn't help it. She hoped he'd smile back at her, but instead, he frowned and began to apologize.

"I'm sorry. That was most thoughtless of me."

"You're forgiven," she said easily. "We'll cut some slack in your rope, since you're from out of town."

He smiled. "Thank you very much."

"You're welcome very much."

This woman he knew and yet didn't know was studying him with blue eyes that looked like crystals lifted from a diamond-clear lake. He'd forgotten the intensity of country people, the instinctive determination to purloin every detail from the surrounding territory and the people in it. Once upon a time, his basic survival had depended on that ability. Now his own keen senses had been dulled by his time in the city. "Do you know if Ed still serves food till seven?"

At the moment, she wasn't sure of her own name. Even big-city cynicism looked wonderful on Luke. He was dressed casually in that suede coat that whispered, "lots of money here," and he wore a black knit shirt with a collar underneath it. No belt on his jeans. *No, don't look at his lean hips, his hard thighs. Never mind. Behave yourself.* "It's not Ed anymore, it's Sam. And yes, I think he might be able to conjure up a burger and fries for you." Luke the lawyer wore brand-spanking-new big-city boots that had hardly been walked on, much less worked in, and it occurred to Charlotte that he probably only ate clams on the half shell these days. "If you want anything fancier, like good food and entertainment with your meal, you'll have to drive to Whitefish."

"A hamburger and fries sounds fine."

In the little silence that followed, she swiped at her hair yet again, and felt the roughness of her work-familiar hands. She must look like a complete mess to him. "I'll say *bon appetit,* then."

"How very continental of you." He lifted a brow, his wonderful mouth slanting in a faintly urbane smile. He thought she was trying to impress him. He should live so long.

"Oh, we're *very* continental here. Now, if you'll excuse me . . ."

"Wait. I didn't mean . . ." Dammit, he'd hurt her. Incredible. He'd known her all his life, until he went away, and now he didn't know how to talk to her. The child he remembered was there, lurking in that lovely mouth and those enticingly beautiful blue eyes, but there'd been too many late nights in the walnut offices of Goodman, Goodman and Harris, too many days of playing maneuver-and-thrust with his father-in-law, for Luke to recall how to handle straightforward honesty. "I didn't realize I'd become such a condescending ass. . . ."

"The things we learn about ourselves are the most valuable."

"I thought I'd had a major education in my own asinine behavior just recently. I guess I need to finish the course.

Maybe you could help me." He smiled, and that smile was no less charming for being deliberate.

"You've never been an ass, Luke. You wouldn't know how."

She'd always been his staunchest defender. Odd, the feeling that gave him. "You'd be surprised what I know," he murmured.

It was obvious to him she was that one-in-a-million person who had no taste for mucking about in his disastrous past. So there she stood, in her too-big jacket, looking self-conscious and adorable all at the same time, standing on those willowy legs and using one of those capable, long-fingered hands to push a floating streamer of that luxurious hair out of her eyes.

"You should wear a hat," he said, and wondered where the words had come from. He'd thought he'd been thoroughly cured of feeling protective toward a woman.

"I ran out of the house before I had time to grab one. I wanted to find my cow before she got herself shot—by Sam. He's threatened to. Shoot her, that is."

"I see." He didn't want her to go. Amazing. He thought he'd given up the habit of wanting a woman's company. "Your cow is here in town?"

"It's her favorite place. Especially the garbage cans behind Sam's saloon. She has—eclectic taste in forage."

"I see," he said again, thinking that he was enjoying himself a great deal, just listening to her, watching her. Now that he thought about it, he'd always liked listening to her and watching her, even when she was a kid.

"It's hard to believe you're all grown up, running your dad's ranch."

"It's my ranch now."

"I know." He had that dark, watchful look in his eyes that made Charlotte feel uncomfortable, as if he could see straight through to her corpus callosum. He said, "I was...very sorry to hear about your folks."

"Your wife sent a card. It was a very nice card. Expensive." Hastily she added, "I thought it was considerate of her, since she really didn't know me."

"I should have written something on it."

"It would have been nice to hear from you. But I knew you must be very busy."

His face darkened. "*Distracted* might be more accurate. Will you forgive me for being so thoughtless?"

She gave him one of those straight, blue-eyed looks that made him realize she'd grown up to be every bit as beautiful as he'd predicted she would. "There's nothing to forgive. Really."

"We'll be friends again," he said, taking his glove off and sticking out his hand, smiling at her with disarming frankness.

She looked down at his hand and then up into his face. A mixture of emotions softened her mobile mouth, gleamed in her eyes, but he couldn't read them. Regret, almost. Friendliness. Not anger. He was thankful she wasn't angry. He'd had enough anger to last him a lifetime.

Luke looked so vulnerable, standing there with his hand out and that careful smile on his face. She couldn't care about the pain he'd suffered, the mistakes he'd made. They weren't kids anymore. She had to be cool, reasonable, calm, and treat him like the stranger he was.

"Oh, Luke," she said softly, and stepped straight into his arms to give him a quick hug that shocked them both. "I'm so sorry you've come home like this...but I'm so glad to see you."

She felt him tense. She'd made a mistake. He didn't move away from her touch, but in that split second, she saw that he'd grown accustomed to having women come on to him, and even more accustomed to putting them off.

She withdrew instantly, a mixture of emotions tumbling through her—regret over her impulsiveness, and something almost like grief. *So much lost.* "I'm sorry. I—thought... I'm sorry."

For Luke, the sense of loss was palpable. He'd been surprised by her embrace and he'd thought no one could surprise him in this world, ever again. His guard had come up automatically, and before he could relax and raise his arms to catch her close, she had slipped away.

Her coat was redolent of all the old familiar scents of home, alfalfa hay, good leather saddles, horses and mountain air. Somewhere deep inside his soul, an emotion stirred that he'd thought was completely dead. An aching longing for something he'd never get back again. "I...just...I keep seeing you as a little kid. It's hard to believe you're... a woman."

He looked more human now and less sure of himself, more like the old Luke Charlotte had known. She smiled. "That's because it happened when you weren't looking."

"I feel like I've been caught in a time warp," he murmured softly, "but believe me, I do like you this way. You're quite... beautiful."

"You must be crazed with hunger. You need something to eat. I'll talk to you later, when you've had your supper and I've found my cow."

"Let me help you look."

She shook her head, her eyes flickering briefly over the suede jacket he wore. "You're not dressed for a cow hunt. You find food, I'll find Princess. Knowing Sam, I'm not sure which of us will have the most trouble."

She was smiling, but she didn't fool Luke. He'd hurt her.

In an instant, she stepped into the lengthening shadows of an alley and disappeared from his sight. The wind whispered past his ear, and the town was as empty as if she had never been there.

Had he conjured up Charlotte Malone out of the food and sleep deprivation and isolation he'd subjected himself to in the round-the-clock driving marathon he'd done to cross the country in a few days? No, he couldn't have. Not in a million years could he have imagined her beauty, her hair, her presence. She seemed as much a part of the land as the mountains behind her. The amazing thing was, her spell was so powerful it made him feel as if he belonged here, too.

That was a hell of a lot of magic.

Luke opened the door to the saloon, and it was as if he had never left. Every sound was familiar, the clunk of heavy glass steins against solid wood as Harry and Mike put their drinks down to look at him, the bass rumble of the jukebox playing an old seventies tune, the crack of a billiard stick hitting the ball. There was even a couple dancing in that small space between the tables, if that full body contact in an upright position could be called dancing. The lady's arms were wrapped around the guy's neck, and his hips were welded to hers.

Not too many years ago, he'd sneaked in here with Richard Malone and a fake ID. The bartender had pretended to accept it, but he'd gone to the phone and called Luke's father. Rich had barely made it out the back door before Henry Steadman came storming into the place, his temper worse than the cantankerous mustang horse Luke used for bucking practice. Strange to think that now Luke didn't know this bartender, and that he was thirty-five and looked it, and nobody in the world would think to ask him for identification. He really was ancient.

Luke ignored Mike's curious look and slid onto a stool at the end of the bar closest to the door. When the bartender, who Luke assumed was Sam, asked what he wanted, Luke said, "Hamburger, well-done. And a beer." The bottle appeared at his elbow, cap off, moist with coolness. Luke drank deeply and was setting it back on the bar when Mike said, "Getting yourself a little fortification before you go home, are you, me boy?"

In the city, those words would have rankled. Here, he knew them for what they were, heavy-handed teasing. Luke glanced up into the bar mirror, saw the reflection of Mike's broad face, his red hair gone grayer than when Luke had last seen him. Mike was twenty years older than Luke, a shrewd hustler who'd never thought twice about beating the socks off Luke at billiards and taking his money. "How are you, Mike?"

The older man's eyes flickered over him. Luke couldn't tell whether Mike liked what he saw or not. Finally Mike said, "Not bad for an old fella. How's yourself?"

"I'm okay."

"Are you now?" Mike murmured, an eyebrow canted.

Did every damn body in town know his business? Luke controlled the flare of anger by turning his head toward the billiard table. "We'll have to have a game sometime."

"It'll be my pleasure," said Mike, his eyes as shrewd as only a half-century-old Irishman's could be. "I won't mind taking your money."

"If you still can," Luke drawled. "An old man like you."

Mike laughed loudly, enjoying Luke's subtle feistiness.

Luke took another swallow of beer, hoping Mike would take the hint that he wasn't in the mood to talk. Damn, he'd forgotten what a small town was like. They must know it all, from the end of his disastrous marriage to the loss of his job, right down to the balance in his bank account. They'd even figured out the less-than-happy reception he'd get from his father.

Mike did take the hint, shifting his attention to ordering another beer with a whisky chaser. Luke finished up his hamburger and his beer and was ordering another mug when a voice beside him murmured, "If you're through eating, maybe you'd like to dance."

She had three layers of mascara on each eyelash, a loose sweater falling off one shoulder, and tight jeans tucked into her boots. And she was young enough to be his daughter. Well, almost. She made him feel...old. Older. He'd stop when he got to *ancient*.

The thought of Charlotte brought the beginnings of a smile—and the local nymphet slid up on the stool beside him. Dammit, he'd encouraged her without meaning to. "Aren't you out past your bedtime?" he drawled.

"Sure I am," she said, surprising him. She sensed his slight interest in her honesty, and her chin came up. "Why don't you make it worth my while by giving me a dance?"

He recognized the vulnerability in the girl. He was conscious, too, of the quiet surrounding them, the waiting. Even the other lady, already engrossed in dancing, raised her head to see what would happen.

A week ago, a day ago, an hour ago, he wouldn't have given a damn if he hurt some strange female's feelings. But out there on the street, Charlotte had understood and been kind to him. Sitting here, warmed by that kindness, Luke found it hard to be rude to this girl. He was filled with a strange reluctance to make her look foolish in front of her friends. But he didn't want to encourage her, either.

Life was packed full of difficult choices, and he seemed to make all the wrong ones. "Don't you have homework to do?"

That got a stifled laugh. Her cheeks flushed. "No, I don't have any homework. I'm not a child."

She might not be a child, but she wasn't grown up, either. What in hell was he going to do with her? "I can't dance, I have a beer to finish. If you'd like something . . ."

"Great. I'll have a gin and tonic—"

"The lady will have a cola," Luke said to Sam.

"I've got an ID," the girl said defensively.

"Made it yourself in your basement, no doubt," Luke said. He turned back to Sam. "The lady wants to live it up. Throw a slice of lemon in that cola."

"I do have a name," the girl said, half sulky, half provocative.

An earthy word echoed in his head. This was all Charlotte Malone's fault, with her mountain-scented hair, her husky voice, and her kindness. She'd revived his old habit of being nice to the opposite sex.

That was magic spell number two.

The girl beside him frowned, knowing she'd lost his attention. "My name's Kim." She waited for him to respond in kind. When he didn't, she said, "You're Luke Steadman, aren't you?" The mascared lashes swept down once, then up in a defiant challenge. "Everybody's been talking about you."

"A fact I don't find particularly cheering . . . or interesting." He cast an indifferent glance on her, with a twist to his mouth that made far more sophisticated women say politely that they'd just seen someone across the room they really needed to talk to.

"You're a celebrity in this town."

"Which says there isn't much for entertainment here," he drawled.

Sam slid the beer along the bar toward Luke, and followed it with a cola and an I-could-have-told-you-so look written all over his face.

Luke drank, thinking he was out of his league. He'd been away too long. He shouldn't have felt sorry for this girl who was determined to hero-worship him, no matter what.

The back door burst open, and a cow clumped in, hooves banging on the wood floor, udder swinging. She hustled past the pool table, past the jukebox, and trotted right up to Luke.

While the dancing couple broke apart and stood there in astonished silence, Charlotte scurried in behind the cow, all annoyance and exasperation. "Princess, you get out of here or I'll send you to cow heaven."

Princess knew an empty threat when she heard one. She just stood where she was, cast big brown eyes up at Luke and slobbered on his arm.

Charlotte lunged for the cow, hair flying. Luke thought she looked like the most beautiful avenging angel he'd ever seen.

"Charlotte!" Sam roared at her. "You'll pay for that door!"

"I know, I know." She flashed blazing eyes at Luke. "You could help me get her out of here before she breaks something else." Charlotte grabbed the cow's tail and used it to come hand over hand down the cow's back, reaching to grab hold of the looser neck flesh. But she wasn't quick enough to deter Princess from nosing over Luke's beer bottle. It turned like a lawn sprinkler, spraying Luke and the girl. Kim jumped back, and Luke grabbed the bottle and set it upright. But not before his jacket was nicely spotted.

Luke said solemnly to the cow, "So nice of you to drop by for happy hour." And to Charlotte, "And you said I'd have to drive to Whitefish for entertainment."

In response, Princess turned her head and began to lap up the beer puddles on the bar.

Kim brushed at her sweater and gestured at the cow. "I don't see anybody asking for her ID."

"Trust me, she's old enough," said Charlotte.

Luke's gaze met Charlotte's. He looked so wonderful, trying to preserve his city facade of indifference while the laughter lurked in his eyes and his mouth twitched with his effort to keep it contained.

"You'll have to send me a bill for cleaning that jacket, if you don't mind getting in line behind Sam." Charlotte leaned on Princess's back. "What's that old song about the drinks and the laughs being on me?"

The man could smile. Oh, yes. About a thousand volts' worth. Charlotte broke into a husky laugh he almost didn't recognize. Princess went on lapping, heading for a lost weekend.

Luke murmured in an urbane drawl, "What's the penalty for serving beer to a bovine in Montana? Are you guilty, or am I? I bought the beer, but you brought the cow."

Sam roared, "Get that four-footed demolition machine out of here!"

With all the mock severity she could muster, Charlotte took a firm hold on the excitement burning like a firecracker inside her. It was sheer heaven to see Luke drop the barrier. "Now that your jacket is ruined anyway, is that offer of help still open, or not?"

"What do you want me to do?"

"Great heaven. Has it been that long since you've punched a cow?"

"Where would you like me to punch her? In the jaw?"

Charlotte flashed eyes that were brilliant with challenge, interest, life. "You know that part of the anatomy that I said you weren't earlier? Well, I take it all back. Throw in *smart*, and you are one."

Princess's tail came up. Charlotte's mock anger dissolved into genuine panic. "Luke! Help me get her out of here before she disgraces herself."

Lightning-quick, Luke shed his city lassitude and reacted like the country boy he was. He grabbed Princess's tail and whacked it down against her body, making her change her mind about relieving herself.

Charlotte began crooning an incomprehensible line of flattery and tugged the cow forward by her ear. Princess moved, albeit reluctantly.

Mike looked at Harry. "Think we should help?"

Harry shook his head. "Naw. Wouldn't want to get sued for getting involved."

Luke gave Princess a good push, while Charlotte went on crooning nonsense and tugging. Step by step, working together, Charlotte and Luke coerced the stubborn cow into clomping toward the front door. They squeezed her through, with some slight damage to the trim on the left side of the door frame. "I know, Sam, I know. Put it on my bill."

"No room left to write on the damn thing!" Sam hollered.

Safely outside, cow in tow, Charlotte breathed in the cold air with a spasm of relief. "I've got a rope in the pickup. I'm parked on the other side."

"Are you going to hang her right here?"

"What a lovely idea. Why didn't I think of it?" And she gave the cow a brisk slap on the back. Princess accepted the mild reprimand with bovine stoicism.

"She's a fence-jumper, is she?"

"She doesn't have to jump. She just walks through."

"We used to send her kind off to the canners."

"She . . . was a pet of Dad's."

"Ah. I see." He studied her, saw the color rise in her cheeks. "Not good to get sentimental about a cow, Charlotte."

"Don't . . . start. Just . . . don't. I've heard it all, from Tex, from Nick. . . ."

Luke raised an eyebrow, and she knew she'd ventured into treacherous waters. "You're seeing my brother?"

"No, I'm not seeing him. We . . . we had dinner together. It was Christmas, time of peace on earth and goodwill to men. It seemed like a good idea at the time."

"It's none of my business, of course."

To Charlotte's ears, he sounded frostier than the ice on the mountains. "Your father and I were having a border dispute. Nick thought the two of us might settle it if we talked. It . . . didn't work out that way. We ended up having a surveyor come out."

"At your expense, I'll wager."

"We settled the argument, anyway."

He wanted to change the subject. He didn't want to think about Nick and Charlotte having dinner together, laughing together. Princess bumped him and lapped at him, giving his jacket another symbol of her affection. "Are you going to load her in the back?"

It was the only time in Charlotte's life she could remember being grateful to that cow. "No. I'm going to make her walk every step of the way, the same way she got here, the old—" she stopped in midsentence and shot a glance at Luke "—darling."

"Don't hold back on my account. I admire a woman who calls a spade a spade."

"I wouldn't want your soft city ears to get bruised with my plain country speaking."

"I think I can stand up to the strain."

Charlotte looped the rope around the cow's neck quickly enough, but she took her time tying the other end to the pickup.

At last, she faced him, her hair blowing wild and free again, long, silky black strands of it everywhere, catching on her sheepskin collar.

Luke said, in that same detached voice, "I owe you an apology. I should have insisted you let me help you look for her. We might have kept her out of the building. I guess I've forgotten how foolish and curious cows can be."

He was carefully indifferent again, more like the Luke she'd seen at first. She shouldn't have mentioned Nick. She wouldn't have, if her brain had been working properly.

"It's okay. I couldn't have gotten her out of there without your help."

She turned to go, knowing she'd blown it. Ten years of thinking of him, and she couldn't sustain a reasonable conversation with him for fifteen minutes. Maybe there was a good reason the Malones and the Steadmans had never gotten along.

Luke reached out and caught Charlotte's arm. She turned, looking up at him with those brilliant, suddenly hopeful eyes, and he knew that he had no more right to encourage her than he had the girl in the bar. "Let's get together soon."

As cool and as subtle as he, she moved out of his grasp. "I'm sorry, Luke. This is a very busy season for me."

There was no mistaking the disappointment in her voice. She hadn't fooled him for a minute. And he felt uncomfortable with her resistance. "I meant what I said, Charlotte. I'd like to see you again."

She faced him, only the Montana wind between them. "I don't think that would be a good idea."

Luke stepped away from her, his face expressionless.

He'd retreated again. She'd sent him back into the chilly world he'd been in when he arrived. Yet how could she feel sorry for him? He was, after all, a Steadman. Show him sympathy and he'd go straight for the jugular. How cold the wind was. "Thanks again for helping me with the cow. I hope you have a good visit at home. Please give Henry my regards, even though I'm sure he doesn't want them."

At the break in her voice, his eyes narrowed. "My father isn't keeping the old feud he had with your dad alive with you, is he?"

She paused, arrested by the tone of his voice. "You don't know?"

"If I did, I wouldn't be asking."

He sounded impatient. And genuine. She said, "I find that hard to believe."

"You're right. I like standing out here in this cold-as-the-hubs-of-hell street arguing with you. It's my idea of a really good time."

"Your father must have told you about—the trouble we've been having."

"I haven't spoken to my father for quite some time. What trouble are you talking about?"

She couldn't tell him. The words wouldn't come.

"Don't be afraid. You used to be able to tell me anything, remember?" He reached out and brushed the hair from her cheek—that was all, just a little gesture of courtesy. His fingertips were cool, but they brought heat to her face...and desire to her body, desire she neither wanted nor welcomed. That was all, just one touch. And she wanted him as she'd never wanted anything in her life.

"I'd never do anything to hurt you, Charlotte."

The power of his presence surrounded her. He was really here, brown eyes shadowed in the darkness, smooth jaw so close, and his mouth dipping towards hers....

"Your father thinks I'm stealing his cows."

His hands, holding her arms, dropped away. Slowly he drew back from her.

"Three of them have been found with the brands altered to look like mine."

Charlotte waited, watching his face go utterly blank of emotion. Oh, this was ten times worse than marshaling her meager financial forces to fight Henry Steadman in court.

Her chin came up. "Say something, Luke. Please. Don't just stand there looking at me like I've sliced you at the knees."

The sun sank lower and disappeared. The flag snapped again, and the breeze sent cold chills over his cheek. Luke saw things he didn't want to see—her fifteen-year-old truck, which he remembered cruising around in with her brother, Rich, the frayed sleeves on Charlotte's obviously hand-me-down jacket, clear indications that she wasn't exactly flush with money. Not an unusual circumstance for a small rancher. And yet... The wind blew her jacket open to reveal a very, very nice pair of breasts filling out a dark knit shirt. He felt the sudden and unwanted clenching of desire. Damn! He'd been living in a fool's world. This lady was a grown woman, capable of all the things an adult was capable of, from lovemaking to larceny. He didn't know her at all. "I must say you don't look particularly...prosperous. It makes a man wonder. Have you come upon hard times, my dear?"

She didn't flinch. "Not till you arrived."

She turned around to the truck, went two steps, then whirled around to him again. She turned a face up to him that was fierce and beautiful. "Let me tell you something, Luke Steadman. It makes a woman wonder why you showed up here, now. Maybe you've come home to ensure that

when your father finally succeeds in taking away everything I own, it's all done legally.''

"I don't know what you're talking about."

Once the floodgates opened, she couldn't stop. Maybe she
didn't want to. Maybe she needed to vent all the worry and
tension that had been keeping her awake nights. "He wants
my ranch, Luke. He's willing to settle out of court if I deed
over the ranch to him."

"I can't believe that."

"I wish it weren't true. But it is." Her gaze locked on his
face. "I didn't steal your father's cattle, or alter his brands.
Somebody else did it, somebody who knows your father
would love to believe I'm stealing from him."

"That's . . . an odd little story. Why would someone go to
so much trouble to frame you?"

"It's an easy way to acquire my land." He looked bland,
and totally unmoved by her story. How could he look any
other way? He was a Steadman, after all. "It's the truth,
whether you believe it or not."

"The truth will out, as they say," he murmured.

"I hope so. And the sooner the better."

She turned away to get into the truck.

God help him, he couldn't let her go like this. He said her
name, and it came out husky and half caught in his throat.
She went still, and for a moment he thought she was going
to ignore him, climb into the truck and slam the door in his
face. But she didn't. When she turned around, her face was
so open, so vulnerable, that he lost the ability to breathe. He
didn't know what she expected of him. He only knew he
wanted to . . . make amends, in any way he could. "You'd
better take my hat," he said, holding out his expensive
Stetson to her.

She was tempted. It would be wonderful to take home
some part of him. A sudden picture flashed, a memory

buried for years. Easter Sunday, she'd been seven, Luke seventeen. She'd been wearing a wonderful child's hat, heavy with pink flowers. After the service, she'd been standing outside with her folks when the wind lifted her beautiful new hat and sent it sailing toward a muddy ditch. Luke had heard her cry out, and he'd jumped and spun with athletic quickness, snatching her hat in midair. He'd walked over and given it to her, and she'd thanked him shyly. It hadn't been until she was older that she understood why Luke's father had frowned at him for his good deed and her own father had scowled in the front seat of the car all the way home.

"Go ahead, take it," Luke said softly, bringing her back to a cold world where her parents no longer existed. "I don't need it, and you do."

Tears stung in Charlotte's eyes. This was a charity hat. The great Luke Steadman spreading noblesse oblige.

"No, thank you, Luke. I don't take things I haven't earned."

It was a direct shot. He felt the irritation rise. He wanted to shake her. "Charlotte—"

"You don't understand how things are here. I really wish you hadn't come back. I liked you better as a memory." She turned her back to him, slid onto the tattered seat and slammed the door.

The truck coughed and sputtered to life and rolled away into the darkness, Princess trotting complacently behind.

Luke stood watching the truck's one red taillight disappearing into the dusk. In the growing darkness, the wind chilled his cheeks with icy cold. He looked up into the endless sky. "Damn fine to be home."

Chapter Two

Night drifted in, turning the sky into an indigo canopy studded by one star, darkening the town with long, empty shadows. Luke got back into his car and drove into the lingering sunset, past the last building in town, past the fence that was Charlotte's, past the hole Princess had walked through, up onto the curving road that led to the corner of Montana sky that belonged to Henry Steadman.

Luke's city car, with its low suspension and wide tires, rattled the cattle guard. A familiar sound. He remembered coming home late at night, knowing there was no way to sneak over the damn thing. Ahead of him wound the narrow lane that led to Henry's pens, where, ten years ago, customers had hoisted a booted foot over a fence rail and scrutinized the sale calves. Now Henry sold calves by satellite in truckload units of fifty thousand pounds.

Apple-tree limbs fat with leaf buds cast spidery shadows over the car's windshield. In the corral next to the barn, three curious Appaloosas jostled for position on the fence to check out the strange car, then exploded into a frenzy of racing. Luke smiled. At thirteen, he'd wanted to breed Arabians, pleaded with Henry to purchase a mare.

It had been a yearlong argument. Then Luke had become interested in Charolais cattle and been wild to begin a small herd on the ranch. His father had said no. That was when Luke had finally realized that any idea he had would be vetoed. His father liked control. And *would* keep it. Luke had known the only thing he could do to save both his and his father's sanity was to give up the struggle. So Luke had withdrawn from the running of the ranch, and concentrated on his studies, football, girls and bronco riding, in roughly that order. Being practical and doing what he knew had to be done to preserve the family peace had earned him his father's exasperation and ire. And, finally, Henry's animosity. Luke had been sorry, but in his youth and hotheaded energy, it had seemed obvious to him that he couldn't be interested in the ranch when he had so little to say about the running of it.

Unfortunately, his father had attributed Luke's lack of interest to indifference and laziness. Luke had taken the easier path and let him think what he would. Nick had been quick to take advantage of the situation, and had become more and more the perfect son, agreeing with everything his father said. Luke had borne it all stoically. He'd had no choice. He'd needed a place in the world where he could make decisions about his life and work. The Lazy S Ranch had not been that place. And so he had left Henry to his undisputed rule of his horses, cattle and land.

Henry had done well, without Luke's help. He had the best of everything.

Others made do with what they had. A frayed sheepskin coat and no hat, black hair flying wild and free. Charlotte, her eyes brilliant sapphires, her lashes a sweep of soot without the mascara his ex-wife, Elisa, applied before she drank her morning coffee. Luke hadn't realized until he saw Charlotte again how much a part of his life her fierce loyalty had been.

Had she been stealing his father's cattle? If she had, why would she tell him about it? To gain his sympathy?

All the lies and mistrust of his past swirled up to haunt Luke. No one was honest. No one was true.

Except Charlotte.

He didn't know what was going on. Until he did, he had to be sensible and stay neutral. He sure as hell couldn't hold on to a memory.

Luke swore and stood on the brake, too hard. He threw himself forward into his seat belt, and thought it was the least of what he deserved.

When he got out of the car and stumbled over the top porch step, his mood deteriorated. Why was it so darn dark? The yard light should have gone on automatically.

It hadn't gone on because it wasn't there. The big old vapor lamp that had kept Luke the child from dodging scary shadows at night was gone.

Disturbed, he turned around to look at the house—and saw that the shutters were gray with weathering. The barn didn't look all that spruce, either.

Henry Steadman had too much pride in his ranch to ignore the upkeep of his buildings. What the hell was going on here?

Luke balled his fist to knock, then shook his head and dropped his arm. This was his home.

Inside, the house smelled of dust. He could see it lying heavily on the top of the old coatrack. It wasn't like Athena to allow a speck of dust to fall anywhere in Miss Laura's house, though his mother had been gone for thirty years.

More uneasy than ever, Luke tossed his hat and coat on the oak settee. In an old habit, he ran a hand around his waist, checking to see that his shirt was tucked into his pants, before he entered his father's presence.

The hallway had two doors, one leading to the mahogany-paneled dining room and one leading to the library den. His father would be there, having his one drink of the day.

The thud of Luke's boots on the pine floor sounded strange to his ears. They carried a man's weight now, instead of a boy's.

His father sat in the old aqua horsehair chair that his mother had hated, a stubby manhattan glass in his hand, the expression in his eyes shielded behind his glasses.

When Luke went to New York and immersed himself in his profession, he'd discovered a frenzied peace of sorts. When his work was stripped away and he was left with nothing except his own resources, he'd discovered there was only one real victory in life, and that was survival.

He would survive this encounter with father and brother.

His half brother, Nick, stood beside Henry, one shoulder butted up to the mantel, those long fingers of his wrapped around the handle of a half-empty beer glass. Nick was the son of the woman who'd made the mistake of taking Henry Steadman into her arms the night his true love, Maureen McIntosh, married his rival, Sean Malone. Henry hadn't married Rose, but he'd taken the baby—and done everything in his power to give Nick a place in his house as his honored firstborn son.

"Hello, Dad."

"Hello, Luke." The high forehead was the same, as was the leonine head of white hair. Henry had Luke's height, but he had lost weight since Luke had last seen him.

His father's eyes met Luke's, gleaming as brown as Luke's own in the firelight. There was no welcome in them.

Calling himself a fool to be disappointed, Luke forced himself to smile as he crossed to his father and held out his hand. "Good to see you."

His father was slow to react to Luke's good manners, but Luke felt it wasn't because his father meant to slight him. His father seemed to be struggling with some emotional upheaval that made it difficult for him to maintain an outward appearance of civility. "It's good to see you, too."

"I hope you've been keeping well, sir." To Luke, Henry Steadman's hand felt cool and papery, despite the heat in the room. It struck Luke suddenly that his father was getting old. He'd never imagined it could happen.

His father withdrew his hand, as if he felt the difference in warmth and strength, too. "Say hello to your brother."

The old resentment rose up, but Luke swallowed it. He raised his head to look Nick in the eye. Nick was still in shadow, his expression unreadable. "How are you doing, Nick?"

"As well as can be expected," Nick said smoothly. He shifted his beer glass to his other hand, moved forward and grasped Luke's hand. His palm was cool, and his fingers were slender but tensile. Luke knew from long experience that Nick was stronger than he looked. Nick withdrew his hand first, a smile of undefined emotion on his lips. He was two years older than Luke, two inches shorter and at least thirty pounds lighter. He'd always had that lean and hungry look. Women liked that look of need, and Nick always seemed to have a current lady, but he hadn't ever brought one home to Henry, as far as Luke knew. Luke wondered what had prompted Nick to ask Charlotte out.

Nick, moving with an economy of motion Luke had almost forgotten, lifted his beer stein and drank deeply. Without so much as a lifted eyebrow, he tossed the glass in the fireplace.

Luke froze. The sound of breaking glass was all the more shocking in the complete silence that followed.

Nick turned to Luke, the picture of composure. "Did I startle you? I'm sorry. I thought a celebration was in order for the return of the prodigal son."

Henry's mouth lifted in a smile. "You'll have to forgive Nick. I'm sure he's feeling a little unsettled. I told him there was no need, that you wouldn't be interested in taking over the ranch."

"Frankly, that's the last thing on my mind."

Another silence.

"What happened to the old yard light?" Luke said, picking the only topic he knew would interest his father. "Must be a lot harder to see down at the stock pen without it."

Carefully, very carefully, Nick shoved his hands in his pockets and faced Luke. "I told Henry this is the way it would be, that you wouldn't be here five minutes before you'd try to start running the place. He said I was wrong. I was . . . but only about the time. It only took you five seconds."

Luke didn't move a muscle. "My comment was a somewhat feeble attempt at making conversation. I'm sorry if it seemed . . . critical." Luke's jaw set. "But as long as you bring up the subject, the buildings look like crap. What the hell is going on around here?"

Nick took a step forward, but Henry Steadman held up his hand. "Leave him to me, Nick. We might have expected this. You know how important appearances are to Luke."

Nick relaxed back against the fireplace, the slightest ghost of a smile on his lips. Luke clamped his teeth together.

Henry Steadman fastened his dark gaze on Luke. "We're doing things rather differently since you . . . chose to leave us.

We're putting more money into improving the herd and less into things like paint and repairs."

Luke's eyes flashed to Nick. "Your idea, I suppose."

"We're in something of a tight squeeze. We need more land to raise more cows. So instead of increasing the number, we decided to improve the herd quality. Your father and I discussed alternatives and arrived at what we thought was a feasible plan. You should come out to the barn and see the champions we've imported from Europe."

"If you don't do something about the barn soon, it will be falling down around your improved herd's ears."

Henry Steadman cast a glance at Nick and then smiled at his firstborn. "Luke has a right to express his opinions, even if they are incorrect. We have to make allowances for him. He's been gone a long time. Sit down, Luke. Have a drink with us."

"If you don't mind, I'd prefer to have a shower and take off the travel dust." He waited, feeling like the interloper he was. "But of course, if you rather I wouldn't stay here, I'll go back into town and look for accommodations—"

"Of course you'll stay here. Your room is ready for you. Where are your bags?"

"In the car."

Nick pulled his hands from his pockets and said, "I'll help you bring them in."

Luke's eyes sliced over Nick. "Don't bother, I'll get them myself."

But Nick followed him out into the darkness and stood beside Luke while Luke hauled his duffel bag out of the trunk. "Pretty nice machine."

Luke didn't reply. When he turned back into the house, Nick stopped him with a hand on his arm.

"What the hell are you doing, coming back here now? Did you need a place to lick your wounds?"

Luke stood very still and met Nick's angry look head on, his own face cool and smooth. "Maybe I came home to see how Henry is doing."

"Henry's fine."

"Is he?" Luke said, looking straight at Nick. "Well, you ought to know."

"I thought once you'd gone, I'd never see you again."

Luke's mouth quirked. "Sorry to disappoint you."

"I never could figure you out. The favored son, the legitimate one. And you just gave it all up and walked away."

"Some guys just aren't very smart. How's your mother?"

"I don't see too much of her these days. She understands that my work keeps me here."

"Too bad. I always envied you your mother."

"I always envied you your name."

"It's your name, too," Luke said easily.

"Well, you may be my brother, but I don't want you here."

Luke's lips lifted. "Is this supposed to be news to me?"

"You'll cause trouble for Henry."

"Don't you mean you're afraid I'll cause trouble for you?" Luke shifted his duffel bag to an easier grip. "I was never able to do that in the twenty-five years before I left. What makes you think I could do it now?"

"I don't want you interfering."

Luke dropped his polite tone and let his voice show what he was feeling. "I'd make trouble in a minute for you, if I could do it without breaking my father's heart. But he thinks you're God's greatest gift to mankind, and I'll be damned if I'll destroy that illusion now."

"You're so noble you make me ill. Don't push me, Luke. I can make you very sorry."

Luke bent from the waist, bowing. "Thank you so much for the lovely welcome home . . . brother." Luke laid a hand on Nick's shoulder, thinking there must be some way to find common ground with the man who was his half brother. "Look, let me set your mind at rest. I don't want the ranch, or anything connected with it. I'm not going to be here very long. How about we call a truce, and try to keep the animosity to a minimum around Henry?"

Nick shied away, like a horse with malice on its mind, but he gave Luke a token smile. "How long is not very long?"

He opened his mouth to say, *Two weeks, three, tops*. But a picture of Charlotte flashed in his mind, black hair blowing, her warm touch. His years of training as a lawyer kicked in, and he decided he'd better not lock himself in to a definite early departure date. "It's just what I said. Not long."

Nick growled and headed off for the barn. Luke swung toward the house, wondering if he'd lost the good sense it had taken him so many years to gain. He couldn't help Charlotte. He had no influence with his father. There was nothing he could do. Unless... he could do a little quiet investigating himself. He was supposed to be good at that. He could ask a few questions, nose around a bit. Asking questions wouldn't involve him in anything.

"Athena, you're going to get in big trouble, sneaking over to the enemy with provisions."

Charlotte shook her head and tried to look stern, but the sight of Athena's familiar broad figure in the doorway, with that wonderful wicker basket covered with a gleaming white towel, made Charlotte's heart leap—and her mouth water. "What if Henry Steadman finds out you're purveying food to the enemy?"

"Pooh," said Athena, shaking her head. Her skin gleamed a wonderful caramel color. She was, according to her own reckoning, part Native American, part Irish and part fox. "If it was his food, which it isn't, it would do his immortal soul good to show a little charity."

Charlotte flashed a look at the kitchen clock—a cat with a wagging tail. It was just after ten in the morning. She should be out checking Lady Luck, overseeing Tex's fence-fixing where Princess had broken through, cutting hay, paying bills. She definitely should not sit down at the kitchen table and enjoy herself. There wasn't time.

"If you have a moment, I'll brew a cup of tea."

Athena's wise eyes darkened, as if she knew exactly what Charlotte's thoughts and worries were, but her face was as cool as river water as she sat down at the table and loosened her shawl around her shoulders.

"How's Mrs. Lettie doing this morning?" Athena inquired.

"I just checked on her about a half hour ago. I knew Tex wouldn't be in a good mood this morning when he left his wife, knowing he had to fix fence. She's soaking her hands in warm water again. As soon as I get out from under this trouble with Henry and I can get my cattle sold, Tex will have the money he needs for the carpal-tunnel operation. But in the meantime, it's really killing her that she can't quilt. She's not a reader, and she hates television."

"She don't like setting around with nothing to do any more than I do, I suspect. What she needs is some young ones to grandmother."

"That will be rather difficult, since she and Tex don't have children."

"They have you."

"Which is no help at all."

"Nothing stopping you from getting married and having babies."

A wry smile on her mouth, Charlotte glanced up at the clock. "You're setting new records, Athena. You've only been in the house one minute and thirty seconds. You used to wait for at least fifteen minutes until you brought up the subject of my marital status.''

''I'm not getting any younger. I want a turn at your children myself.''

''I'm beginning to wonder if there'll ever be any children.''

''Pshaw! Of course there will, and soon, too, if you are as smart as I think you are.''

''First of all, I don't see any men beating down the door for the chance to be my children's daddy. And secondly, I can't do anything until I get Henry Steadman off my neck.''

''Ain't no men around here, that's true enough. But if you get yourself fixed up and go to that dance in town next Saturday night, you might at least put a man in your sight of vision.''

Charlotte grinned. ''Oh, *there's* an exciting list of prospects. Who would it be? Tim, the computer genius, who doesn't ever say a thing I can understand? Or Marris Hollis, who has the Chevy with the front seat rigged to collapse 'accidentally' into a bed and has tried to get every woman in Madison county into it?''

''Mr. Luke single now.''

''For all I know, he's got the seat rigged in that fancy car of his to make a bed.''

''Not Mr. Luke,'' Athena said staunchly.

Charlotte turned away from Athena to pick up the old white enamel teapot her mother had used to have tea parties with her daughter, feeling a little ashamed of herself for being flip at Luke's expense. Athena was right. Luke wasn't desperate like that. He didn't have to be. Women would gravitate to him like lemmings to the sea. ''Oh, there's a fine solution to all our problems. Marry Luke and make Henry Steadman my father-in-law.''

"You wouldn't be the first to marry to stop a war. Used to do it in Europe all the time, before *love* came into fashion."

"Don't you believe in love, Athena?"

"In its time and place."

Charlotte's lips twitched. "I didn't know whether to expect you over this morning or not." Carefully keeping her face away from Athena's, she filled the teapot, giving all her attention to placing it on the burner and turning on the stove before she turned around to Athena again.

"If you're asking whether or not Mr. Luke stayed for breakfast, he did. It wasn't a happy breakfast, even though I made his favorite pecan pancakes and brewed up my best coffee." Athena's eyes were shrewd as they traveled over Charlotte's face. She hadn't said much, but she'd said enough to let Charlotte know what kind of a reception Luke had gotten.

"Sometimes I'm not sure whether I get more angry at Henry Steadman for being so vindictive to me, or for being so stupid about Luke. I just wish Henry would wake up and see what a wonderful son he has," Charlotte said, her cheeks flushing.

"You know Mr. Henry."

"Yes, I know him. The great man took one look at his firstborn and fell in love. People were a bit skeptical about Henry's illegitimate son, so Henry became his fiercest protector and defender. He's bound and determined to make a saint out of Nick. I'd say he's got his work cut out for him." Charlotte smiled at her own attempt at a joke.

"He got heavy going there, but Mr. Henry don't give up easy."

"Isn't that the truth! He's a Steadman." Charlotte smiled at her friend and said, "Nick still holding fast to his policy of reducing your hours?"

"Mr. Nick a little dumb about how much time it takes to clean house. He'll get smarter after he climbs into his dirty bed a few more weeks."

"How do you do it, Athena? How do you keep such a broad-minded outlook on...everything?"

Athena's dark eyes fastened on Charlotte's. "Way I see it, everybody just doing the best they can with what they got. Some of us have got more to do with than others have. I don't mean things," Athena added. "I mean stuff inside their heads, like compassion and intelligence and willingness to suffer a little for somebody else. Mr. Luke, he come out of his cradle with all those things and more. Hard for other men not to hate Mr. Luke. Even his own father jealous of him."

"Is that what it is?"

"That, and a lot of other things. Mr. Luke will be all right, in spite of Mr. Henry. And so will you."

Athena's calm assurance brought a rush of emotion so strong that tears welled in Charlotte's eyes. To cover her reaction, she jumped up and snatched the teakettle, bending her head to let her hair fall forward over her cheek, going about the business of pouring water and dunking in the herbal-tea bags she and Athena liked.

Athena didn't say a word, and the cat's tail swished in the silence. A little more composed, Charlotte brought the steaming cups to the table.

With that economy of movement big women have, Athena reached for the basket and removed a plate covered with a snowy white tea towel. The smell of warm honey-lemon muffins made Charlotte's mouth water. Athena offered the plate to Charlotte.

"You realize where those will go—right to my hips."

Athena made a noise that was pure scoff. "You're going to blow away one of these days if you don't put some meat on your bones. Montana norther will sweep you up and shoot you right down to Wyoming."

"I don't think so," Charlotte said, reaching for the muffin and breaking it open on her plate. She closed her eyes and drank in the aroma of honey and lemon. "Athena," she said, lifting her teacup and looking into Athena's eyes over it, "give me an infusion of your strength and wisdom."

Athena raised her head, a beautiful smile on her face. "You know what my sister say. She say even chinchillas got to have company. She had one once that was so lonesome he started to eat his toes."

Charlotte laughed. "I don't see me doing that."

"My sister couldn't stand him being so lonesome. So she got him another one for company. Next thing she know, she had three chinchillas. That's how things happen. For you, too." She stretched out a hand to Charlotte. Charlotte laid her smaller hand in Athena's, almost—*almost*—believing her. "Especially if you go to that dance Saturday night." Athena's eyes gleamed with humor.

"Athena, you are an incurable schemer. And you've wasted all your energy. I've already told Margaret Murchison that I'd bring the punch and help with the refreshments."

"Did you?" Athena said, and smiled her wise smile.

The sun was high in the sky, friendly today, beaming down on the Montana plains as if it had never heard of a polar-cap wind. The sun was saying, This is a glorious Sunday morning in spring. A year ago at this time, Luke would have been dressed to the gills and heading for the cavernous church where Elisa insisted they go to see and be seen. He much preferred wearing his black-and-red flannel shirt and soft jeans and being mounted on Prince's back, riding across the pasture that abutted Charlotte's land.

He was still a good distance away from the border fence between Steadman and Malone land when he heard Tex talking to a fence post in extremely colorful language. Tex had the barbed-wire pullers clamped on the post, but the post was wobbling. Tex should have set a new post before he started to fix the fence, and Luke had a feeling that Tex knew it.

The sun warmed his back as Luke rode up from his side of the fence, and the saddle creaked as he dismounted. A rake of those faded blue eyes from under a veteran hat bound by a well-used sweatband and a low grumble that sounded suspiciously like "Damned city kid" was Luke's greeting.

"Want some help?"

"Hell, no," Tex growled. "I like coming out here and getting my hands tore apart on fence your pappy is supposed to be keeping up. Makes me as happy as a snake stretched out on a rock in the summertime."

"Got any gloves?" Luke asked, very, very carefully.

"Sure I got gloves. Who the hell can do anything with gloves on? Next you'll be asking me if I got a steel post to shore up this rotten wooden one. Well, I don't. If I did, I'd sure as hell be using it, wouldn't I?"

"How about if I ride back and get one for you?"

That got a reaction. Tex looked up, snatched off his hat and wiped his face with the bandanna that perpetually hung out of his back pocket. "Well, it'd be one miracle in a goshdarn empty row, I'll say that. The first time I ever got any help from the other side of *this* fence."

Without a word, Luke reined Prince around and galloped him back over the field.

When Luke returned, there was Tex, sitting in the bed of the old green truck Charlotte had been driving yesterday, a red thermos lifted to his lips.

Feeling his lack of practice, Luke tossed the iron fence post to the ground and dismounted. He gave his shirt a tug, loosened the snaps and pulled it off. His pale city skin earned a grunt of disapproval from Tex. Luke ignored it and pulled on gloves he'd snatched up. "Hand me that sledge-hammer, would you?"

Tex looked as if he'd like to say a thing or two about loaning the enemy his tools, but he clamped his lips tight and did as Luke asked. He even put himself out enough to hold the fence post steady.

Luke lifted the sledgehammer, felt the pull in his shoulder muscles. Darn thing was heavy, all ten pounds of it. He hoisted it up and drove it home on the top of the post, making sure he didn't slip and hit Tex. His shoulders felt the exertion. He'd worked out in the gym for a while when he first moved to New York, but keeping fit had vanished from his life, the way everything else he enjoyed had, when his job and marriage consumed his life.

"Ain't forgot how to work, then, have ya?" Tex said with grudging admiration, as Luke hammered the post the final two hits that brought it level with the wooden one.

That was as close to a thank-you as he would get from Tex. "Some things you don't forget," he said easily.

"No, I don't reckon you do." Tex unbent enough to pull the two posts of wood and steel together while Luke wrapped the bare wire around the two to make them both more solid.

Luke stepped away and took a swipe at the sweat on his brow.

"Your daddy know you're out here helping me?"

Challenge gleamed in Tex's eyes, challenge that made Luke weary—and wary. "Good fences make good neighbors."

Tex snorted. "Who said that?"

"Robert Frost, I think."

"He never had your daddy for a neighbor. Take more fence than there is in the world to make your daddy a good neighbor to the offspring of Sean Malone."

Luke gazed out at his father's ranch, green pasture bursting with spring fertility under a crystal expanse of sky, red cattle dotting the hillside. "I often wonder if Henry was as crazy in love with Maureen as they said, or whether he just hated losing her to Malone. Do you remember much about it?"

"Don't remember nothing." Almost without pausing for a breath, Tex added, "I got a thermos of coffee in the truck cab. You want some?" Without waiting for Luke's answer, Tex trotted toward the truck. Wondering whether everybody around here was as confused as he was about who was on whose side, Luke used his shirt to wipe his face.

Tex had unearthed a second mug from somewhere—Luke preferred not to think where—and walked toward him with coffee steaming from two cups. Luke took one, thinking no coffee in the world had the deep, dark aroma of a cup savored out in the open.

"Careful, it's hot," Tex warned him.

"I'll be careful," he said. He wondered whether Charlotte had made the coffee. Then he remembered that Tex had a wife. "How is Lettie?"

"Not so good. She's got something wrong with her hands. Carpal-tunnel something-or-other, doc says. Too damn much quilting, I say."

"Does she need that operation they do for it?"

"That's what the doc says. And she'll have it, soon's Charlotte can settle with your daddy." Tex sipped his coffee with a total air of unconcern, as if he hadn't just made Luke's father the complete villain.

"It's a crazy business, isn't it? I don't understand it."

"How you gonna understand anything? You been in the city too long, got your brains scrambled."

Luke suppressed a smiled. "Have you seen anything suspicious on the range?"

"No, I ain't seen anything suspicious on the range," Tex snapped, with a ferocity that made Luke think that just maybe he had. "I got my opinions, but Charlotte says opinions don't count for nothing, we got to have proof." Tex squinted up at the sun, as if checking on its presence in the sky. Then he looked back at Luke, with that same let's-see-what-kind-of-stuff-you're-made-of gleam in his eye. "You pitching for the home team?"

It took Luke a minute to decipher his meaning. *Was he working for his father?*

"I was hoping to fill the slot of umpire."

"Umph. You're gonna have to do better than that."

"What do you think I should do?"

Tex squinted across the pasture to the hollow where Henry's buildings lay. "Maybe you better do like I do. Keep your eyes open and your mouth shut until you can catch the ornery low-down no-good critter in the act of stealing meat off his neighbor's table."

"You think it's a neighbor?" Luke asked, one eyebrow raised.

"Got to be somebody who knows all about the bad blood between your daddy and Charlotte's pappa," Tex said.

"And somebody who's got easy access to both ranches," Luke added, his mind going back to the way Nick had shied away from his touch.

Tex muttered an expletive, emptied his coffee cup onto the ground, grabbed the mug out of Luke's hand, turned his head and spit. "The air's turned real bad around here."

Startled, Luke came out of his thoughts. "What's wrong?"

"You with all your fancy lawyer techniques, I suppose you came out here, all friendly-like, to question me, 'cause you think I got a reason and I'm real close by here."

"You mean motive and opportunity. Yes, I guess you've got that." The idea of Tex stealing cattle seemed so ridiculous to Luke that he smiled.

"Think it's funny, do you? Well, it ain't. Try being accused of stealing once and see how you like it."

Luke had, and he didn't. "Tex, I wasn't suggesting you're the thief. It takes a special kind of mentality to—"

"Oh, so now you're telling me I ain't smart enough to steal no cattle."

"Tex, I'm sure you're smart enough to do anything you want to do—"

"So you do think I did it."

"No, of course not—" Exasperated and annoyed with himself for upsetting Tex, Luke could only watch as Tex stomped around to the front of the truck, opened the door and threw both plastic mugs in, so hard they banged against each other. Luke heard Tex muttering something about a dirty snake and damned if he knew how folks could come back from the city and think they knew every damned thing in the world, and then the truck motor roared, and after a tire spin, he took off.

Luke stood leaning against the handle of the sledgehammer, watching Tex take that old truck over the bumpy pasture with the muffler dangling, knowing Tex must be angry as hell to abuse a piece of old machinery so.

Luke shook his head. Without even trying, thus far he'd managed to convince Charlotte he was here to help his father take her ranch away, make Nick believe he was going to take Henry's ranch from him and convince an old man who wouldn't steal a penny from the street that he sounded like a thief. Three times up, three times out. Nice record. Just dandy. Charlotte was right. He should have stayed a memory.

Chapter Three

Walking out to the barn gave Charlotte the tingling excitement of a ride on a roller coaster. She couldn't tamp the happiness down, no matter how hard she tried. Luke was back, and so the air felt crisper, cleaner, in the morning, and the buckets of feed she carried to Lady Luck were lighter. Shovels of trampled straw flew out of Lady's stall, clean straw floated in.

If she turned her head just that little bit to look over her shoulder, she might catch a glimpse of him riding in the pasture, as she had that day he came to help Tex.

Foolish to hope she'd see him again. Foolish to think she might have a whole conversation with him without having it disintegrate into an argument. Foolish to let the old hopes, the old dreams, rise up and fill her every waking moment. But no matter how severely she chastised herself, she was powerless to stop thinking about him, about his smooth, darkly cynical face, about the way he looked at her and the way he made her feel when she was with him.

He is the enemy.

Why couldn't she remember that?

Because you're a born optimist, that's why.

Saturday night arrived, and with it a thousand sparkles of anticipation that no amount of cautioning from a saner inner voice could dampen. Feeling light-headed with eagerness, she stepped into a steaming hot shower and found herself humming ''Crazy.''

No doubt about it, she was.

She finished with a sluice of cooler water, hoping it would shock her into sensibility. In that timeless ritual of women, she wrapped herself in a towel and stood in front of her closet, trying to convince herself that intuition would help her pick the perfect outfit.

Charlotte ended up reaching for a crisp white shirt with a Western yoke, black denim jeans and Sean's belt with the turquoise buckle, standard dress fare for the Saturday-night dance at the Masonic Hall in Two Trees.

While she combed out her hair, she stood looking in the mirror at her too-plain nose, her too-lush mouth, her too-round hips. If she walked into that big old echoing cavern of a room and Luke was there, she'd need all the self-confidence she possessed to watch him dance with another woman. It seemed she'd spent her whole life watching him with other women, either in her imagination or in reality. Sophisticated, beautiful woman.

She needed eyeshadow. And lipstick, in a deep rose.

Better, but not enough. Instinctively seeking reassurance, Charlotte reached for her mother's jewel box. Nestled in blue velvet lay the Austrian-crystal butterfly hair ornament that her mother had worn only on special occasions. Carefully she lifted it out and up to her hair, plunging the long end of the clasp into the straight, silky strands. Against the black of her hair, the finely faceted gems shimmered like diamonds.

The pain rose anew. If her mom and dad hadn't taken that plane from California to see her brother, Richard, if they had waited for another flight, when the weather was better . . . So many *if*s.

The butterfly sparkled in the light, and Charlotte knew her mother and dad would always be a part of her. For them, she would remain strong. Even if Luke was back and she desperately wanted peace with Henry Steadman, she wouldn't give up the ranch. She'd lost her parents, but she wouldn't toss away their legacy.

Down in the kitchen, Lettie turned around from the stove, her gray hair a bit askew, her eyes bright with interest. In Charlotte's kitchen, Lettie looked like a child playing at mother. She was not quite five feet tall, with tiny arms and hands, and as graceful as a retired ballerina. Lettie and Tex had volunteered to stay at the ranch tonight so that Tex could check on Lady Luck, her expectant mare, at regular intervals.

"Don't you look nice as cherry pie!" Lettie said kindly, her eyes bright and wise. "I bet you don't have time for a cup of tea before you go."

"I don't, Lettie. I'm supposed to be there right now."

"Here, let me help you with that punch bowl. Goodness, did you have to buy all those bottles of ginger ale? You've got enough here for a thirsty army. Now, don't you drive too fast in that old truck, Charlotte, just because you're a tad late."

"I won't, pet." Charlotte leaned over and brushed her lips across Lettie's cheek. "Tell Tex thanks for watching the Lady for me."

"Pooh. That old man would rather be out in the barn than sitting here jawing with me anyday." Her words were practical, but her face softened, the way it always did when she talked about her husband. Charlotte had to believe love was the strongest force on earth when she looked at Lettie's face. Lettie patted her shoulder and smiled. "Now, you just go along and have a good time. We'll take care of everything here. Oh, I wish I were young again and going off to a dance with a lot of handsome young men."

"Me, too," Charlotte said and smiled.

Lettie frowned, displeased by Charlotte's apparent cynicism. "You are young, and don't you forget it. Now, you mind me, Charlotte. You have a good time that you can come back and tell me all about, or I'll be very disappointed in you."

"I'll try my best, sweetheart."

Charlotte drove the short distance into town, and when she alit from the truck, she was feeling apprehensive about more than just seeing Luke. Did the community believe she was a cattle thief? If they did, her reception in the hall would be very cool.

When she reached the hall and climbed to the top of the stairs, laden like a pack-horse with the punch bowl and that box of ginger ale bottles, Marris Hollis gave her the first greeting.

"Hey, Charlotte needs a hand!" he yelled, and started clapping. Several other wags and would-be wits joined him in the applause.

Charlotte was rather glad that Marris's heavy-handed humor covered the awkwardness of her entrance into the hall. Her arms loaded down, she backed up against what she thought was the wall to scan for the tables that had been set up—and bumped into somebody who had the sharpest hipbone in the world.

"How about a real helping hand?" It was Luke who'd bodychecked her, his hip she'd felt on her rear. He leaned over and said softly in her ear, "And an apology? Will you accept both of them from a contrite and obeisant Steadman?" Quiet echoed in that big old cavern of a hall. They had the undivided attention of the town's entire population, ringed around the edge of the room.

She wanted to laugh, she wanted to cry. "There is no such thing as an obeisant Steadman. You're pushing it with contrite."

"How about abjectly regretful?"

"My best advice is to keep it simple. It's more believable that way."

"As in, please accept my humble apology?"

"I'll forgive you if you forgive me."

"Excellent," he said, and smiled one of those knock-your-socks-off smiles.

Seeing the lift of those well-shaped lips made Charlotte's heart melt . . . and drove every resolve to be sensible about Luke right out of her head. "Well, I'm glad that's settled," she said, smiling back at him.

As unconcerned with public attention as only Luke could be, he waited for her to hand over her burden. She stood for a moment, not immediately giving it to him. "I can get this, Luke. You don't have to . . ."

Marris Hollis said something else, but nobody laughed, as Luke reached toward her and, with his eyes dark and zeroing in on hers, slipped the box from her grasp.

"Where do you want me to go with it?"

How do you feel about Mars? "To that table in the back."

Every head was turned toward them as they made that long trek from one end of the room to the other. Charlotte felt as if she couldn't breathe. Her feet didn't seem to be connected to her brain. The silence echoed in her ears.

At the table, Luke turned. "Is this where you want it?"

"Yes." How did he look so unconcerned? He was wonderfully out of place, better groomed, taller, more prosperous, than everyone there, even though his clothes were appropriate, a simple dark green khaki shirt and blue jeans. It must be his hair, still layered in an expensive cut, or his darkly lean face, so well-defined by good bones.

Relieved of his burden, Luke straightened. He seemed totally unaware of the little buzz of conversation that broke the silence and hummed around the room. Charlotte's ears rang with it. "Thank you, Luke." Alone in her room, she'd ached to see him. Now, in the bright glare of light and the community's speculation, she wanted him away from her... and safe. "You're very kind. I can handle everything now."

For one startling moment, his brown eyes darkened, as if he hadn't expected her polite dismissal.

She didn't want to hurt him. In the softest voice she could manage with the wild excitement inside flaring to life, she said, "Don't you know everybody is looking at us." She felt like one conspirator advising the other. "Go away, Luke." And then, daringly, like in the old days, she continued, "your father won't like it."

Luke bent his head slightly, scrutinizing her face, a man with all the time in the world on his hands. "Go away? Is that what you said?"

"That's what I said...." *But I didn't mean it.*

He bent down closer, examining her face with the air of a doctor looking for the cause of an illness. "Is there something wrong with your eyes?"

She wanted to laugh—or cry. She wasn't sure which. Luke always did have a hawk eye for details. "No. I— No. There's nothing wrong with my eyes. I'm just wearing eye shadow. You have seen eye shadow before?''

"Not on you. You don't need it."

"You mean because nothing can help me?" It was something he might have said in the old days, teasing her when she tried to dress up and be adult. She fired the shot back at him, her eyes alight with good humor, her mouth turning up in a smile.

"I mean you're perfect as you are."

Those words, delivered in that husky tone, made her go still with shock. From behind Luke's shoulder, the reflection from Henry Steadman's glasses flashed in Charlotte's eyes. Luke's father stood leaning against the wall, talking to Mike Hallorhan, but he was staring at Charlotte. His mouth pulled hard and tight, and he straightened as if he'd seen the enemy.

What a little fool she was. She *was* in a war. And she was falling for the enemy. All over again.

With that extraordinary intelligence Luke had, he turned around to see what she had been looking at.

"Excuse me," she said in a carefully polite tone. "I have to go to the kitchen to look for a bottle opener." She walked around the table and back through the open archway that led to the kitchen, her knees not quite steady.

Inside the kitchen, with a partial wall between her and Luke, Charlotte yanked open a drawer and searched furiously for a bottle opener. "Why can't he leave me alone? Why can't he have the skin of a horned toad and three heads and look like the back end of a donkey? Why can't I stay angry at him for more than three seconds in a row?"

"Charlotte."

Luke had come up from behind, and now he faced her, leaning his backside against the cupboard. "What?" she said, impatient, not wanting to deal with him or her own emotions, her skin heating instantly at the sound of his voice, her body flaring with excitement that he'd had the interest and the courage to follow her. She refused to look at him and went on rattling utensils in the drawer. "What, what?"

"I'd rather have you talking to me than about me."

"I'm talking about a stubborn old mule my dad used to have." Confused and exasperated, she slammed the drawer shut with a rattle and a bang and flashed him a hot look. "Come to think of it, the two of you are a lot alike."

"We're not children anymore. We don't have to hide our friendship."

"We don't have a friendship. We have a war, and you're on the side of the enemy." Her cheeks flushed, her hair falling forward, Charlotte yanked open the drawer and began turning over eggbeaters and metal serving spoons, searching for the opener.

Luke laid his hand on top of hers, stilling her hand…and her heart. "I'm not the enemy. I'm neutral, like Switzerland."

He sounded amused. She glared up at him. There he stood, easy, relaxed, leaning against the cupboard as if he didn't have a care in the world, his lean face gorgeous, his brown eyes fastened on her with cool preciseness. Who did he think he was, accusing her of being a thief one minute and acting as if he were on her side the next? He must be lethal in the courtroom. "Congratulations. I'll see you at the United Nations."

"You don't think I can be neutral?"

He raised one eyebrow and stood there looking utterly…beautiful. But was he trustworthy? Oh, she didn't know, couldn't think clearly when he was so close and watching her as if her opinion were important to him. She didn't like feeling like this. She didn't like wanting him one minute and distrusting him the next, feeling as if she were talking to her heart's match one moment and a cold stranger the next, even as every nerve in her body tingled with awareness at his closeness. "I don't know what I think."

"I want to be your friend. But I can understand if you'd rather see the back side of my hide. It's your choice, Charlotte."

His hand felt warm and wonderful over hers. Her heart felt as if it were going to jump out of her chest. Irrationally, impulsively, the truth came out of her mouth. "I do want to be your friend, Luke." She kept her eyes away from him, but she could feel him breathing and she could smell his scent, warm, tinged with good male cologne and the aroma of new denim. "But I think it will be much easier for everyone if I'm not."

"I disagree," he said in that soft voice of his.

She looked at him then, wondering if he was playing a game, wondering if she could trust him. Why was he being so persistent? Did he think he could find out something for his father? He was a good investigative lawyer, that much she knew. Was he investigating her?

"What do you want from me?"

His eyes gleamed. "Now there's a question I don't think I want to answer right here and now." When the color rose in her face, he said softly, "I'm surprised at you. You never used to lead with your chin." He reached out and brushed her jaw with a careful fake punch, his knuckles lightly grazing her skin.

Her eyes glowed with a fierce light. "If you aren't very careful, you'll get caught in the cross fire."

"Which one? The one between you and my father? Or the one between you and me?"

She couldn't breathe. She lifted her head, and her thoughts came out of her mouth before she could stop them—maybe because she didn't want to stop them. "There isn't anything between you and me."

There was a silence in the kitchen while he looked at her. Just...looked at her. And made her heart stop with the expression in those brown eyes. "You may not be a thief—but you have turned into a charming little liar." His hand changed position, his fingers lightly brushing her cheek. "Strange. I thought I hated lady liars. But I don't seem to mind at all when it's you."

Her lips felt full. He was going to kiss her. She wanted to feel his mouth on hers, wanted to feel his hands on her body.

But he watched her as deliberately as a hawk with all the time in the world, assessing her reaction like the practiced male he was, not the boy she'd known.

Once she'd trusted him with her life. Could she still? She leaned toward him ever so slightly, and Sean's turquoise buckle pressed into her body, making her remember what she was risking. She shook her head and moved away from Luke.

His hand dropped to his side. In the quiet, his brown eyes seared hers.

She dragged her gaze away from his and looked down at the drawer, pawing through it as if her life depended on her finding that opener. The rattle and clank of metal spoons broke the spell of shimmering quiet and anticipation between them. "I need to find that opener—"

"No consorting with the enemy, eh? Well, don't let me keep you from finding something you need," he said, easing away from the cupboard, "whether it's a bottle opener—or a way to keep your ranch safe."

This Luke wasn't instinctively kind. This Luke could place the knife with the same precise skill with which he dealt out attentive compliments. "You're not being fair," she told him.

"No, I guess I'm not," Luke agreed. "Maybe I've for-gotten how." Mentally Luke cursed himself. He'd bungled it, of course, going for truth. Nothing for it but to get out while he could still keep his hands from burying themselves in her beautiful black hair and pulling her against her will into his arms and doing his damnedest to show her she didn't have a thing to fear from him—at least as far as her ranch was concerned.

Charlotte heard the sound of his boots hitting the floor, heard her heart beating in her chest, heard the clink of utensils as she leaned against the drawer in a sudden relax-ation of tension. The silence that fell on the other side of the wall when Luke went through the swinging door was deaf-ening.

Luke cursed mentally. Everybody was looking at him. Out of the crowd, Mike Hallorhan appeared. "Let me take you to the bar and buy you a drink, me boy. Seems to me as if you could use one."

"When did you take up lifesaving, Mike?" Luke said, turning to fall in step beside him.

"Only since you came to town."

It was the most interminably long evening Charlotte had ever spent in any one place in her life. After an eon, Luke returned from the bar area, Mike Hallorhan beside him. He stayed with Mike and Harry, the three of them lounging on the far side of the room like teenage boys clustering to-gether for courage. Charlotte kept her place behind the re-freshment bar, ladling out punch and trying to pretend he wasn't there, but her eyes strayed to the corner where Luke sat, his head bent toward Mike in attentive listening.

"I don't know why he came to a dance if he isn't going to dance," Charlotte muttered to herself. But tiny tendrils of guilt curled inside her. If she hadn't remembered her father and pushed Luke away, if she hadn't been so absolutely sure that the right thing for both of them was to keep the lines between them sharply drawn, he wouldn't have placed that neat little verbal knife in her ribs. And she might be dancing with him right now, his long-fingered hands holding hers, his hip rubbing against hers.

It was all still there inside her, the curling excitement, the ache—the need. At that moment, he lifted his head and looked at her from across the room. Just looked at her—as if he had read her mind.

"Aren't you tired of working, Charlotte? Come on, let's take a whirl on the floor."

Marris Hollis stood in front of her, smiling that half-defensive smile of his. She'd already hurt one man this evening. She couldn't hurt two. She couldn't lie and say it would be her pleasure, so she just held out her hand and let him lead her to the floor.

His hands were moist, but he had lots of energy, and it was a polka. She held on to Marris and whirled around the floor, the lights and the people gyrating in her vision like a kaleidoscope slipping its infinite colors. She vowed she wouldn't look at Luke, but of course she did. He had his head tilted in the opposite direction, as if there were nothing on the dance floor of interest. She danced faster, and Marris let out a whoop of joy. "You're the first woman tonight that's been able to keep up with me," he said, and gripped her tighter in a mad flurry of turns.

Suddenly the polka was over and the band segued without stopping into a slow tune from the forties, "I'll Be Seeing you." When Sharon Reece, the vocal-music teacher in town, stood up to sing the second chorus, Marris pulled Charlotte close and turned her so he could watch Sharon sing. Which made it easy for Charlotte to see Luke.

Tim, the computer genius, was walking determinedly across the dance floor toward Luke. He began to talk nonstop. Charlotte watched, waiting for Luke's reaction. Tim paused for breath, asked a question. Luke shook his head slowly. Tim began talking again. When the song ended, Tim was still talking. Luke's face was cool and controlled, but he looked at her over Tim's head and she looked at him over Marris's head. As in days of old, those brown eyes gleamed with perception. He knew what she was thinking. He needed rescuing, and so did she. But then, pointedly, Luke returned his gaze to Tim, his mouth controlled, his attitude still one of polite attention, his body still. He would stand there stoically silent and let Tim talk him into an early grave before he'd be rude to the boy. The only gesture of noninvolvement he made was to step back a little. Tim moved forward immediately, eagerly, happy as a kid at Christmas to have found a new listener.

The guilty little voice that had been nagging at her all evening finally had its way. She had to apologize, again, to Luke. And she had to do it now, before the dance was over and she lost her chance. "Would you excuse me, Marris?" Charlotte took him so much by surprise that she was out of his arms before he could protest and catch her closer. Her bootheels clicking on the floor, Charlotte walked over to Luke. "Luke, I believe you promised this dance to me."

"Did I?" He stood there eyeing her lazily, making her suffer, for all of five seconds. "Are you sure?" He waited, giving her the chance to think about what she was doing.

"Yes, I'm sure. Excuse us, won't you, Tim?"

With Tim looking after the two of them forlornly, Charlotte took Luke's hand and walked with him out to the floor.

"I thought you didn't want to be my friend," he said, holding her at a polite and proper distance.

"You needed rescuing," she said, in that moment just before even his polite and proper closeness made her breath catch in her throat.

"Did I?" he repeated, his drawl deepening.

"And I owe you an apology."

He caught her close, then closer. His mouth was at her temple. "No, I owe you one."

"Didn't we just have this conversation?" she said, leaning back and smiling up at him.

"I think we did."

"Your father is watching us," she said.

"I know," Luke said. "It'll do him good to get shaken up a little. He's had things his own way too long."

"Luke, I—"

"I don't want to talk about my father."

"But he's here and he's reality and—"

The hand at her waist dropped lower to her hip and rested on the snug denim. "I like how these jeans fit."

"Luke—"

"Keep talking about my father, Charlotte, and I'm going to pull you so close you can't breathe and cup that sweet little rear end of yours in both my hands, right here in front of my father and God and everybody."

She tilted her head back to gaze into his eyes. It was just like old times, push and dare and shove, testing to see who had more nerve. Except that they were no longer children. They were adults, with adult needs and adult challenges. "You wouldn't dare."

"One more word," he said silkily.

She opened her mouth to give him a blast of common sense, but those brown eyes were so full of wicked enjoyment that she knew he'd do exactly what he said. At the thought of the havoc his hands on her posterior would wreak on her system, she clamped her mouth shut and bowed her head to bump his chest with her forehead.

"There, that's exactly how I like my women," he said, sounding thoroughly smug and self-satisfied. "Docile and silent."

Luckily for him, the music stopped. She stepped away from his arms. "If you ever found a woman like that, she'd drive you stark crazy in no time."

"Maybe so, but we'd have a real blissful two minutes first."

She didn't want to think about a blissful two minutes with Luke, or two hours, or a lifetime. It would always have to be another woman. It could never be her.

He caught her arm. "I was only kidding. What did I say? Charlotte, your face looks like I've kicked you."

"Excuse me. I'd better get back to the punch bowl."

Charlotte managed to avoid Luke for the rest of the evening. She almost succeeded in forgetting he was there by concentrating on the people she knew and loved best in the world: Mike Hallorhan, who'd had the two beers it took him to get courage enough to get out on the dance floor with his raven-haired Delores; Margaret Murchison, dancing with her seventeen-year-old son; Tom Hartley, her lawyer, looking suavely casual in ragged jeans; and Sheriff Clarence Daggett, standing on the sidelines with the benign air of a king observing his subjects, even though he was only two years older than Charlotte.

Henry Steadman didn't dance with anyone, and neither did Nick. Nick had come over to the refreshment table once, but after their eyes met, and hers flashed with anger, she had ignored him, and he'd ignored her.

Clint Everhart, with his saxophone, made a passable attempt at playing "Good Night, Sweetheart." She was relieved, of course. She emptied the punch bowl in the kitchen, washed and recycled the cans and dodged the lingering conversational groups to gather up the remaining paper cups—and tried not to look for Luke. He seemed to have disappeared.

She wasn't disappointed, of course. But it did seem that he might have done the polite thing and told her good-night. After all, *they* weren't enemies.

Most of the cars had pulled out of the parking lot by the time she slid into the truck, her arms full of punch bowl.

The dark figure sitting on the passenger side reached for the bowl to take it out of her arms. Her heart leaped into her throat. "Luke!"

"Didn't you know I wouldn't leave things between us like this?"

"I'm not sure I know you at all anymore."

"Nor I you. But getting reacquainted is definitely…interesting." His hand came out, slid down her hair. "You're as pretty as a Thoroughbred horse," he breathed softly, his husky tone giving the words a slow-burning sexuality.

She reacted as she always did to Luke's devastating magnetism, with fighting words. A good offense was the only sure weapon against his appeal. "That's the kind of sophistication you learned in the city—accost a woman in her own truck and then tell her she's as pretty as a *horse?*" She kept her tone dry, trying to sound like the voice of cool reason, though all the while her heart was rioting in her chest and her body was alive with excitement.

"You're the only woman in the world who would know it for the high compliment it is. I've always been able to say exactly what I think with you, haven't I, Charlotte?" He said it softly, almost wonderingly, as if he'd just discovered the truth of it.

He used his hold on her hair to bring her closer, not roughly, but gently, and slowly, oh, so slowly. His two hands clasped her head to hold her still for his mouth to tease hers. And while he was torturing her with a brush of lips that wasn't quite a kiss, his fingers touched her hair ornament. "You shine like the butterfly in your hair."

Being reminded of her mother didn't quite have the effect of a cold shower, but almost.

"Don't, Luke."

"Don't...what?" His mouth was a whisper away, and he was smiling.

She moved like lightning, tugging away from him. She sat bolt upright and put both her hands on the steering wheel. "I really need you to get out of this truck right now."

Slowly Luke relaxed back against the seat and stretched his long legs out, looking as if he were settling in for the next year. "That wasn't what you needed a minute ago. You wanted to kiss me, then you changed your mind. Why?"

She turned to glare at him, letting the hold she had on her emotions go. She had learned to transform love into temper with him many times as a teenager, and now she would have to do it as an adult. "Never mind what I need. Let's talk about what you need. You need another dunking in the lake."

"Ah, yes, I remember that. It took you and Richard both to get me in."

"Yes, but we did it."

"You Malones are a determined bunch."

"Very much like you Steadmans."

He sat there looking at her with that cool, faintly amused smile that made her want to shake him. Any other man would have taken the hint and left. Not stubborn-as-two-mules Luke. Finally he broke the silence by saying, "If you

want to take a nostalgic drive out to the lake, I'll go along.
Maybe I'll even let you shove me in."

"Oh, don't tempt me, Mr. Steadman."

"I'd like to tempt you, Ms. Malone. I'd like to tempt you
very much."

She braced herself to shut off her feelings, shut off her
mind, shut off her heart. "I'll give you exactly five seconds
to get out of this truck."

He didn't move.

She was playing with fire, she knew, but it would serve
him right if she drove out to the lake and gave him a scare.
She twisted the key furiously, not quite sure whether she
would go through with driving off with him beside her.
When he didn't move or protest, she brought the motor
roaring to life and tore out of the parking lot. On the road,
Luke seemed as poised as Lucifer, that slight smile on his
face saying everything . . . and nothing.

The lake was shimmering, full with spring runoff, crys-
tal-clear, glittering in the moonlight as if diamonds danced
on the surface. It was a deep lake, cold as ice, a forbidden
spot for the kids in town. Frogs croaked like crazy, full of
spring and ready to burst. Charlotte got out of the truck,
and the sight of the water took the fight out of her; but she
knew she would carry the charade far enough along to dis-
concert Luke, if that was possible. She went around to his
side, opened the door and bowed low. He descended and
caught her hand, surprising her mightily, stealing her ini-
tiative, tugging her along over the rough grass.

At the narrow ridge between lake and land, Luke turned
his back to the gleaming, moonlit surface.

"Ready to push me, Charlotte?"

Only one man in the world had ever been her equal in this,
this urge to push heart and soul to the limit to test the stuff
inside. Only Luke had the same need she did to take life to

the edge and see what it held. And while he challenged her, he stood as relaxed as a cat in the sun. Never in her life had she seen a man so worthy of loving.

"Come on, honey. You wanted to drown me. This is your chance." He opened his arms. "Push me in or kiss me. The choice is yours."

Oh, he deserved a dunking in that ice-cold water. But so did she. More than anything else in the world, she wanted to step into his arms and kiss him till his head spun. "Luke, we're not kids anymore. We can't play games...."

"You wanted to push me, now do it." He caught her arms, bringing them both dangerously close to the edge...of life, of love, of sexuality.

"No," she cried, trying to twist away from him. "Let me go."

"Why would I let go of the one woman in the world who makes me feel like I'm alive again?"

Cool air bathed her cheeks, starshine gleamed in Luke's eyes. "I don't make you feel ... old anymore?"

"You make me feel as young as a newborn babe."

"Luke, you're being ridiculous. A week ago, you were a stranger."

"I wasn't a stranger. I was an old friend you hadn't seen in a long time."

"You can't... We can't..."

He put his fingers to her lips. "Hush, hush, sweet Charlotte," he said. It was an old line, but she laughed, and he caught her close and captured her mouth with his. All her resistance melted. She wanted, needed, that warm, wonderful mouth on hers. She wanted, needed, the hard strength of his arms around her. She wanted, needed, to belong to him. Just him. She whirled inside his world, reeling with sensual pleasure: a brush of masculine cheek with the tiniest sting of bristle, a mouth warm and pliant, demanding one minute and teasing her the next, arms that surrounded her, his hands low on her hips, bringing her close, matching her to him, hip for hip, thigh for thigh. He was as cool and clean as the country air that surrounded them, and kissing him was like breathing pure oxygen. Feeling exploded inside her, dreams held inside her head forever coalesced and burst like stars in the night. Her hands came up, slid past the collar of his leather jacket and wrapped around the warm skin at his neck, touched the beginnings of his hair. To touch, to feel, at last. What a wonderful, glorious luxury.

He loosened his hold on her and lifted his mouth, knowing he had to do it now or he soon wouldn't be able to let her go. How long had his body been aching for her? Back into the mists of time, it seemed.

"There's more than one way to drown," he said. He buried his face in the crook of her neck, feeling her hair fall over him while he breathed in her scent. She smelled faintly of the lemon cookies she'd put out on plates, and raspberry ginger ale, and a Montana night stuffed with stars. He wondered why it was that his body was tight with excitement, even while his soul told him he was home at last, caught in the one place in the world where he was safe.

"Luke, we can't do this—"

"Don't move. Not—just yet."

He felt her hand on his head; she was smoothing down his hair as a mother might soothe a child.

He lifted his head, and his eyes caught the starshine. He made a low sound in his throat and moved to pull her close, but she resisted, holding him off with her arms locked inside his. When he pulled back to look at her, his eyes dark, his impatience written all over his beautiful face, her throat felt full. "Luke, we're not children anymore. There's too much at stake now. I can't risk losing everything I have—

Luke, don't look at me that way. You've got to see how it is...."

"Oh, I see how it is, all right. One touch of my Steadman hands, and you'll lose the ranch for sure." He stared out over the water, not looking at her. When he did look back, he might have been another man. "Maybe you're right not to trust me."

"I don't know what you mean."

"You cared for me once...and I went away. You're afraid I might do it again. And you're right."

She closed her eyes. He knew her too well, knew he'd break her heart if he kept on with this. Her head came up, her eyes shone. "So you agree there can't be anything between us."

There was a wicked enjoyment in his dark eyes, in his face, in his stance. "Oh, absolutely. The trouble is, it's too late. There's already something between us. It's called sexual attraction. If you don't believe me, just try kissing me again. I dare you."

She'd loved him for a million years, ached for him to see her as a woman, not a child. Now he had, and it wasn't good enough. She wanted more—and she couldn't have more. She shook her head. "It won't work, Luke." She turned and walked at a crisp pace toward the truck, not running, but not wasting time, her boots sliding on the loose gravel. Inside the truck, she slammed the door shut, her breathing fast. She'd done the right thing. But it hurt so much.

Luke sauntered down the incline, his hair gleaming in the moonlight, his posture telling her nothing of his feelings. She couldn't think about his feelings.

When he was inside the truck, she nearly had herself under control. He turned to her. "You're right to be afraid of me," he said softly.

"I'm not afraid...."

"I can do us both a lot of damage. And you know it as well as I do." His hand came up to caress her head. "Better take me home, honey child."

She turned the ignition key, brought the motor roaring to life. She sent the truck tearing away from the lake, tires spinning.

The silence inside the cab was deafening on the ride home. Too soon, the old truck rattled over the Steadman cattle guard and rounded the driveway to Luke's front door. Charlotte slid the gearshift into neutral and waited for him to get out.

"Thanks for the ride." Luke's tone was noncommittal, his mouth faintly cynical. The double meaning was there . . . and it hurt.

She refused to rise to the bait. "You're welcome."

He opened the truck door, and it squeaked unmercifully, splitting the night with sound. "This is a first, you bringing me home. Too bad it looks like a last, as well."

"Yes, it is too bad," she said, and meant it.

"Good night, Charlotte. Sleep well." His mouth lifted at the corner, the city cynicism written in every line of his face. Then he turned his back and went into the house.

On the way home, she opened the window and let the crisp night air blow in on her face, but even the chill didn't take away the heat—or the pain.

Up in her room, Charlotte lifted her hand to her hair and cried out. Her mother's crystal butterfly was gone. She put her hands to her hot cheeks. She'd lost so much this evening, first her dream of Luke, and now this. Oh, if only it was still in the truck. Surely she would have seen it lying on the seat. She had been upset—perhaps it escaped her notice. She would go and look at once. She would find it. She knew she would.

Luke leaned against the window frame in his old bedroom, gazing out at pasture sheened silver under the moon, at tree shadows tossed by the wind. He felt . . . restless. He opened his hand. The ornament she'd worn in her hair lay on his palm, effervescing in a stray moonbeam. She'd have to come to him for it . . . or else he'd take it to her. Either way, the ornament was his guarantee that he'd see her at least once more before he left. To go where, he didn't know. For the first time in his life, he had no destination, no plans, no goal. He'd thought he wanted it that way. He'd worked hard to free himself of his old demon, ambition. Funny how he'd thought freedom would solve all his problems. Funny how the perfect solution never was perfect . . . or a solution.

He wanted to stay. Damn it to hell. He really wanted to stay. Which meant he couldn't. If he stayed, he'd hurt Charlotte. Better to practice damage control and go now, before it was too late. He'd cut off his arm before he'd hurt her.

Luke padded in stocking feet to his bureau, laid the ornament carefully on top of a white linen scarf and went to the closet to take out his duffel bag, tossing it on the low seat under his window. He'd get a good hot shower in the morning, and then he'd pack and head out. There was nothing he could do here. For anybody.

Chapter Four

The next morning, sun streamed in the bathroom window and steam curled around Luke as he emerged from the shower stall. This was the way he liked to start a morning. Heat energized him. Like Charlotte.

Water beads sparkled on his body, nestled in his dark brown chest hair. He toweled his chest, then took a swipe at the bathroom mirror, misted in the heat.

Out in the hallway, a step sounded. Athena, perhaps? He'd forgotten about living in a house with an unrelated female. He swathed the towel around his hips. When he heard nothing more, he went ahead and spread his toilet kit out on the counter, spritzed on some deodorant and began to shave.

Cool air wafted across his back. He had company. He checked the level of his towel and then the mirror to identify his visitor.

Nick lounged against the doorjamb with a dancer's boneless grace, his hair slicked back with movie-star panache, a hand thrust in his jeans pocket, the other tucked away at his side.

Just what he needed—a confrontation with his brother before nine o'clock. Luke applied razor to jaw, hoping he wouldn't give his old nemesis the satisfaction of seeing him nick his throat. "I'll be done in a minute, if you need the bathroom."

Nick smiled. "Take your time. I'm in no hurry."

Nick in a good mood was bad news. "Sleep well, brother?"

"Passably—considering that you came in rather late—and noisily—last evening."

"I'm sorry if I disturbed your sleep."

"You disturb more than my sleep." Nick raised the hand he'd kept hidden, and in the stray beam of sunlight, Charlotte's crystal butterfly caught fire.

Anger flared quick and hot inside Luke, but he knew better than to show it. He gave his attention to his mirror image, outwardly engrossed in gliding his razor along his cheek, inwardly girding for the fight. "What's the matter, brother? Don't you like my taste in hair bows?"

"The last time I saw this conspicuous little piece, it was in Charlotte Malone's hair."

Luke wiped his mouth with a towel. With careful casualness, he turned completely around to face his brother and leaned his back against the sink. "The last time I saw it, it was on my bureau." Odd, facing off against Nick as an adult. Big brother no longer had the advantage. In the old days, Nick's baiting had put Luke between a rock and a hard place. If he belted Nick, he'd lose what little he had of his father's approval. Nothing to lose now.

Looking slightly less sure of himself, Nick closed his fingers around the butterfly. Despite his careful striving for coolness, Luke's anger flared again. Experienced needler that he was, Nick read the reaction in Luke's eyes and smiled. "I saw your duffel bag spread on your bed. I took a step in to see if you were really packing and planning on leaving us so soon, when this—" he lifted the crystal butterfly "—caught my eye. Made me curious."

"I see the house rules for privacy haven't changed while I was gone. What's yours is yours and what's mine is yours."

The faintest stroke of red touched Nick's cheeks. "This house is going to be all mine someday. Nothing in it will be yours."

"Succinctly put."

Nick said, "Exactly how did you come by this charming little trinket . . . brother?"

"None of your business . . . brother." Luke folded his arms over his chest and kept his face expressionless. "This may be your house in the future, but for right now, I'll thank you to stay out of my room."

"I wonder what this thing is worth."

Slowly, deliberately, Luke extended his hand. "I'd guess its greatest value is sentimental. I seem to remember her mother wearing it."

Nick held on to the butterfly. "You do know Dad's considering taking her into court, don't you?"

He treated Nick to a long scrutinizing gaze. "Yes, I know."

"Then you've got to know he wasn't too happy, seeing you cuddled up on the dance floor with her."

"I'm sure Henry would prefer to deliver his opinions himself."

"How would you know what Dad does or doesn't like? You haven't been around here for ten years. Now, suddenly, you're back, pretending to be all solicitous about his health and welfare. Who are you trying to kid? If you're hoping to impress him and make him change his mind about leaving the ranch to you, you're wasting your time."

Luke felt suddenly cold. "I would hope it will be a long, long while before either of us has to worry about our 'inheritance.'"

"Well, of course. So do I."

In the silence, Luke studied his brother, wondering how this man could have come from half the same gene pool as he. "Nobody's going to supplant you here, least of all me. You've got nothing to worry about. Dad's firmly in your corner, just as he's always been. I'm a temporary aberration in your world, nothing more."

"I can only hope that's true." Nick rubbed his fingers over the edge of the butterfly and raised an eyebrow, looking exactly like a calculating Mordred baiting King Arthur. "You hoping to get a little something on with her, sort of... one for the road?"

"You haven't been around me enough to know what *I* like or don't like, so I'll tell you—very carefully and slowly, so you'll get it. I don't like you maligning Charlotte." Luke didn't realize he'd clenched his fist until he saw Nick's pupils flare.

Shaken, but unwilling to concede, Nick persisted. "What a champion you are for the little thief. I would not advise taking her to bed, however much fun you may think it would be. Dad would not... understand."

"And having my best interests at heart, as you always do, you wanted to clarify it for me." It took all the control Luke had to keep his voice level, to keep from taking that step forward.

"Just trying to be a good elder sibling." An extremely conciliatory smile lifted his lips, and Nick quickly tendered the butterfly to Luke.

Luke gazed down at it, his brain starting to function the way he'd been taught. "I have to be curious about your interest in my relationship with Charlotte." Luke raised his eyes to Nick's face in sharp examination. "I understand you and she went out to dinner a while back. Is it possible you're jealous?"

Nick scowled, as if he wanted to deny it, but, strangely enough, he didn't. "So she told you all about it?"

"Inadvertently she mentioned your...date, when she said you'd encouraged her to sell off some troublesome cattle."

"Did she mention that our outing was strictly a business appointment that she tried to make into something else?"

"She did say it was something in the nature of a peace-keeping mission. Failed, as I understand it. What did Dad have to say about your asking her out?" Luke asked lazily.

"He understood I was trying to settle our border dispute peacefully."

"I can't remember you being so diplomatic."

Nick's eyes slanted away from Luke's, and he straightened away from the door. "Maybe I've changed."

"My word," Luke murmured.

"People do."

"Only when they're going for a new goal."

Fear flared in Nick, darkened his eyes, tightened his shoulders. Luke felt it as palpably as if he'd experienced it himself.

Suddenly, in a lightning-swift mood swing typical of Nick, he beamed a hundred-volt smile at Luke that must be a killer with the ladies. Luke was far too familiar with its volatility to be moved. Nick said, "I'm sorry I gave you such a rough time when we were growing up. Since you're leaving today, shall we part friends?" He held out his hand.

Luke might have forgotten many things about living at home, but this he remembered: Nick making nice was trouble. Luke ignored the hand. "I must say you've aroused my curiosity. Maybe I'll stay around just a little while longer."

Nick dropped his hand quickly, looking shaken.

"What's the matter, brother? Did I say something wrong?" Luke asked, his voice easy, his eyes watchful.

"I thought you were really leaving," Nick said, obviously trying to control his temper. "Your gear is all out—"

"Gear can be put away. Putting your ever-present dislike for my company aside, is there some other reason you want me gone so urgently?"

Flushed with anger, his body tense, Nick stared at Luke, and there was a hot intenseness in his eyes that bothered even Luke, who'd thought he'd seen every brand of human anger. Then, suddenly, the eyes were shuttered and the anger was tamped down. "I should have known it was too good to be true." His eyes ice-cold, his face hard, Nick turned away and headed down the hall.

Luke leaned against the door to stare after Nick, watching him walk down the stairs and disappear. "Odd little fellow, my brother."

Inside his room, while Luke stowed his duffel bag in the closet again and returned his toilet kit to its place in the top drawer of his bureau, he did as he'd always done: He relegated his difficult brother to a back corner of his mind and concentrated on something positive. There was nothing like the feel of a well-washed denim shirt, nothing like jeans that had been nicely broken in. And nothing like the thought that he would be seeing Charlotte soon. Whatever had happened between Charlotte and Nick had nothing to do with now. It was probably a mistake to stay. Still, what difference could a couple of days make? No matter how wrong or right it was, no amount of logical caution whispered by the small voice inside his head could keep his body from stinging with anticipation when he thought about what those days might bring.

The butterfly went into a clean white handkerchief, to be tucked in his shirt pocket. He could feel the padded edges of it moving against his chest as he walked down the stairs.

The kitchen sparkled with sunshine, smelled of sugar-cured bacon cooking. A stray sunbeam flicked over Athena's jet-black hair, swept up high on her head and fastened with a long wooden pick. Her bearing that of a queen, her back regally straight, she held court at the stove. Her white apron sported a perky bow, the starchiest in three counties, and too tempting for Luke. "Good morning, beautiful." He caught a crisp end strand and tugged. The bow fell loose with a cottony whisper.

Athena whirled around, her forehead wrinkled in a fierce frown, her spatula raised and ready, the apron fanning out around her hips. "Now, Mr. Luke, you stop that—unless you want me to paddle your backside with this."

"You're not big enough to push me around anymore, sweets." He snuck a kiss onto her cheek, smelled cinnamon and sugar.

She tried to look cross with him, but a smile lurked at the corner of her mouth. "My, we are feeling foxy this morning, aren't we?" She cast him one of her sternest looks. Luke responded by smiling innocently. She laid the spatula down and retied her apron bow with large hands that were deft and competent. "Now, Mr. Luke, you set down at that table, and you behave yourself, or your food is going to look like a burnt offering."

"Yes, ma'am," Luke said, his mouth quirking. "Where's Henry?"

"I don't know. Nobody tell me important things like where they are going and when they'll be back. I'm just the hired help."

"Oh, you're much more than that, woman. You're the backbone of the home, the soul of the kitchen, the heart of my hearts."

"Now, you just stop that foolish talk this minute, and eat this food before it gets cold." She ladled four strips of bacon, two scrambled eggs and four pancakes onto his plate and tried very hard to keep her stern demeanor. But she smiled at Luke as he examined his breakfast. She seemed almost to know what he was thinking, that if he started counting fat grams, he wouldn't be finished by tomorrow. What the heck? He was on vacation. He might just as well forget about fat and cholesterol and enjoy.

He did leave a pancake, a strip of bacon and half the eggs. He got a hard look from Athena, but she didn't say anything when she took his plate away. He was just rising, telling her thanks for an excellent breakfast, when Henry Steadman walked into the kitchen. He'd been out to the barn, for he still wore his sleeveless coat of red cotton above stocking feet. Athena was adamant about banning barn shoes from her kitchen.

Her silence saying more about her attitude toward Henry than any words could have, Athena reached for a pan she'd been keeping covered at the back of the stove and poured out cooked oatmeal into a bowl in front of Henry.

Henry eased himself into his chair and surveyed the lumpy mass with all the enthusiasm of a man facing a firing squad.

Luke stifled a smile. "Good morning." Still standing, Luke gripped the back of the chair he'd sat in.

"Good morning, Luke."

Not exactly encouraging, but civil enough. "I thought you didn't like oatmeal."

"I don't. That damn fool doctor, Merrill Thompson, clucked about my cholesterol the last time I went to see him, and I made the mistake of telling Athena." Henry scowled down at his cereal bowl. "Be damned if I can see how this stuff helps."

"They say it does. How high is your number?"

"I don't remember."

Wouldn't, more likely. Luke felt that niggle of concern for his father again. "If the good doctor thinks you've got a problem, you're wise to make some dietary changes."

"My only problem is him. And her." He frowned at Athena, she treated him to her placid queen's face. "I'd rather go to an early grave than eat this stuff. Take it away."

Athena's eyebrows flew up, but she clamped her lips shut, and snatched the bowl away.

"I smell eggs and bacon. Are there any left?" Henry asked Athena, in a hopeful tone that sounded strange to Luke's ears.

"No, sir," she said, scraping the remains of Luke's plate into the sink and turning on the garbage disposal with a noisy whir.

"She's trying to reform me," Henry said to Luke, "but as you can see, she has her work cut out for her."

"No doubt," Luke murmured.

"I wondered what your plans for the day were."

Caught, Luke glanced at Athena. Her eyes rolled heavenward. Then she turned her back to him and stood at the sink, humming a low tune, clearly telling him that when it came to his father, he was on his own.

"I have an errand at the Malone ranch."

"I see. Oh, come now, son, relax. You're not ten anymore. We're both adults. Where you go is your business." Henry sat back in his chair, his mouth lifted in something that might have been called good humor. "Although I must admit I'm understandably curious about your...errand."

Odd to be speaking to his father in this relaxed way. "I need to return something."

"Return something?"

"Charlotte dropped her hair ornament after the dance last night. I'm sure she's missed it by now and is anxious about its whereabouts."

"Valuable, is it?"

"No. More sentimental value, I should think." He drew it out of his pocket and unfolded the handkerchief, bringing the butterfly glittering into the light. Before he thought, he said, "I seem to remember her mother wearing it."

A stray sunbeam turned the crystal to fire. Henry's head bowed, his shoulders sagged. Athena touched Luke's elbow in alarm.

When Henry lifted his eyes to Luke's, they were opaque, expressionless. "We're leaving in a few minutes for the northwest pasture to round up calves and new mothers. I thought you might come along, but I guess you won't be able to."

"I can ride up later."

"No need. We've managed to get the job done without you for several years. We should be able to do it again."

Whatever ground Luke had gained, he lost in that instant. "I'm sure that's true," Luke said evenly, "but I will be back soon and I will ride up to help." *Even if you don't want me.*

There was a lingering essence of power in the way Henry rose, a quiet dignity in the way he slipped into his jacket and turned to face Luke. "I always thought it was the Malone boy you liked so well that you had to sneak around behind your father's back. I should have known better."

Something broke and shattered inside Luke, a thousand barriers he'd erected against his father in his mind. His father had been hurting, too. "You... knew?"

"Of course I knew. You can't really believe you could keep a secret in this small community. You were the delight

of the gossips, several of whom couldn't wait to tell me who
they'd seen you with.''

"Why didn't you . . . say something?"

"I'd said all I had to say. I told you I didn't want you be-
friending Malones, you did it anyway. What else was there
to say? You kept your nose clean and stayed out of trouble.
I was thankful enough for that.''

"I'm sorry I wasn't honest."

"So am I." Henry took the five steps to the door, and
neither Luke nor Athena moved when he turned back.
"Told any lies since?"

"None that weren't legal."

"Well, that's something, I guess."

The screen door slammed behind him, and quiet reigned
in the kitchen. "We think we're so smart when we're kids,
don't we?" Luke murmured.

"We think we're so smart when we're adults, too, and
sometimes we're even dumber," Athena replied.

The door thumped again. Startled, Luke turned to see
Henry framed in the doorway, his eyes owlish behind his
glasses, his coat and boots on. In that suspended moment,
Luke stilled, and so did Athena. If there was a clue to Henry's mood on his face, Luke couldn't see it—as usual. "Did
you forget something?"

"No, I remembered something. I remembered you are my
son.''

That had the effect of a small bombshell in the kitchen.
Athena recovered first. "About time," she muttered.

"I'm a logical man," began Henry—rather illogically, it
seemed to Luke, "and you must be, too. Have to be, to
work in your profession. You're used to dealing with evidence. Should have remembered that. Have something to
show you." Henry frowned at Luke. "Well, don't just stand
there. Get your boots on and come on."

Caught off guard by his father's sudden determination, Luke did as he was instructed, leaning against the porch wall to stamp his feet into his boots.

The barn was quiet, dark, scented with the stuff of life, alfalfa hay, corn mash, milk and animal. Like a general leading the troops into battle, Henry headed down the aisle behind the old cow stalls that had once held stanchions for milkers. As apprehensive as any buck private, Luke followed, his boots crunching on the fresh straw.

"There," Henry said. "Look there."

Two yearling steers, Hereford whitefaces, three hundred pounds each of contented cow oblivion, munched on their morning ration of hay. One was curious enough to lift his head and gaze at Luke with doe eyes. The second stood with his rump to Luke, his side glossy from indoor feeding. Emblazoned on his hip was the lazy *M* Malone brand.

"What are you doing with Charlotte's steers?"

"Look closer."

In the half light sprinkled with dancing dust motes, the Steadman flying *S* curled underneath, clearly visible.

Luke felt chilled, but he reacted as he had learned to do to unpleasant information—he went very still, controlling his mouth, his face, his eyes. "This doesn't make any sense."

He might fool a jury, but he couldn't fool his father.

"Hard to deny what you see with your own eyes, isn't it? I thought you should see these cows before you went calling. They're evidence I'm keeping for the sheriff. You're a lawyer, you know about evidence."

Yes, those blasted cows were obvious evidence. Too obvious. Too pat. And altogether too damn handy. "The most damning evidence can be circumstantial."

"Do you call two steers with her brand burned over mine circumstantial? I'd say it was *substantial* evidence, not the other kind."

Luke started the inquiry. The top brand looked as if it had been drawn with a single-line running iron. Did his dad agree? Yes. Where were they found? In her pasture. How long ago? Three weeks ago, during the last spring snowstorm. Any others missing? Wouldn't know for sure until the spring roundup.

"Clumsy job," Luke said.

"Done in a hurry, probably. Hard for a woman to handle a steer that size alone."

"Impossible, I'd say."

His father turned around to face him, his brows drawn together, his jaw set. "You still believe in those innocent blue eyes."

"I learned long ago to disregard innocent blue eyes. The physical fact is, she weighs maybe one hundred and ten pounds soaking-wet. If she did do the branding, she couldn't have done it alone."

Henry snorted. "You've been in the city too long. Cows can be roped and tied to a fence post."

"By one lightweight woman?" Luke raised a brow. "Come on, Dad, be reasonable."

"Think what you like. You will anyway. Haven't changed that much, I see." Henry turned and tromped back over the straw.

Nor have you. Pure waste of time to ask you to think reasonably about a Malone. "Dad, wait—"

His father's dark form filled the doorway. "I've got work to do, you've got an errand to run. Best we each do what we have to do."

Damn. The first time his father had reached out, and there his loving son was, giving him the hostile-witness treatment. Luke hustled over the straw to reach his father, put a hand on his shoulder. "I'd like to talk about this—" But he knew by the way his father straightened under his grasp that he was too late.

"Nothing to say. I followed my conscience, now you follow yours."

The half door slammed behind Henry. Luke stared after him, took off his hat, hit his leg with it and said a word appropriate to the barn.

The saddle creaked under Luke's weight with an old familiar rhythm. The sun beat down on his back, but the soothing warmth didn't ease Luke's mood. The wind kissed his cheek, a meadowlark warbled. He heard, and wasn't cheered.

All very well to say the logistics of branding a cow made it impossible for Charlotte to be the thief. But was she?

Had he fallen for beautiful blue eyes? Beautiful blue calculating eyes?

He raised a hand to touch his pocket. The butterfly was still there, still safe. Still a reminder of a heady, exciting night spent with a woman who provided all the intoxication. If Charlotte had played him like a fish on a line, she'd done it better than any female he'd ever known. And he'd known his share. A mocking smile lifted his lips. It wouldn't be the first time a woman had used him for personal gain. But it would damn sure be the last.

Charlotte's house had never been as impressive as Henry's, but Luke remembered it as a spanking-clean little white bungalow nestled in the oaks and cottonwoods underneath the Montana mountains. The house coming into his view under greening trees looked like its neglected cousin. The clapboard wore a coat of dull gray and an upstairs shutter dangled askew from one nail. He told himself the house's downtrodden appearance simply meant Charlotte was short of cash, and he'd already known that, but his lawyer's voice told him this was one more shred of evidence. He didn't want one more shred of evidence.

"Hello, Luke Steadman. It's good to see you again." Lettie Cochran answered his knock, her eyes shining with a friendliness that nearly matched the warmth of the sun, her smile as welcoming as her pretty face.

He tugged off his hat, knowing instinctively that he was in the presence of a generous-hearted lady. "It's good to see you, too, ma'am."

"I'll just bet you didn't ride over here to palaver with this old woman." Her eyes sparkled with good humor. "Charlotte's down at the barn with Tex."

In the presence of her graciousness, Luke felt compelled to set the record straight. "About your husband, ma'am. I never meant for one second that I thought Tex was stealing cattle..."

"Oh, don't worry about that old man. He likes to fly off the handle regularly just so he doesn't get out of practice. His bark's about eighteen times worse than his bite. Just ask me."

"Yes, ma'am," Luke answered, smiling.

"Go on down and see them both. They need some company. It'll take their mind off that horse for half a minute, anyway.

"What horse is that?"

"Our Thoroughbred mare, Lady Luck. She's trying to foal and not doing it very well, it seems. You go on down. I'm sure Charlotte and Tex will want to say hello."

"Yes, ma'am," Luke said, tipping his hat again to her, thinking she was probably wrong about Tex wanting to see him.

Luke opened the barn door and sent dust sparkles dancing in the shadowy interior. At the largest stall, at the end, Charlotte knelt beside a sorrel mare swollen with foal. A stray beam of sunshine gilded the horse's mane a burnished copper, the woman's head an iridescent black. Her head bowed, Charlotte caressed the mare with long-fingered, graceful hands. "You're all right, baby. Everything's going to be all right."

He watched—and burned with need. Damm it to hell. This wasn't the way it was supposed to be. He wasn't supposed to feel like this. He wasn't supposed to want her like this. But he couldn't take that last step on the crisp straw that would announce his presence, break the spell, and snatch away his pleasure of watching her. So he stood there and ached.

Uncannily, as if she sensed his gaze on her, she turned her head. "Luke!"

He was there, in the barn, all lean legs and broad shoulders, sexy as hell in his denim pants and plaid shirt, leaning against the wall as if he belonged there. She hadn't slept much last night, thinking he'd leave and she'd never see him again, wishing she had taken him up on his dare and kissed him a second time till he forgot who he was—and so did she.

Charlotte blazed a smile at him, as if last night hadn't happened, and shot to her feet with the ease of a gazelle. "Oh. I must be a mess—" She swatted at her neat little rear with her hands, endearingly self-conscious. "It's really... good to see you. What brings you to our neck of the woods?" While he watched with narrowed eyes, she shook out her hair wildly and uncaring, like a child might. When she finger-combed those black tresses back from her face, still missing a spear of the alfalfa, Luke's resolve left him. She might be playing him for the biggest fool in the universe, but—it no longer mattered. He wanted her. And he would have her.

Luke said, "Charlotte," and took a step toward her.

Straw crackled, and Tex appeared from the back of the stall. His red checkered shirt was darkened by sweat, his face was smeared, his mood was irritable. When he caught sight of Luke, his mouth twisted as if he'd just bit a lemon.

Luke relaxed, put on a cool face. "Hello, Tex."

Tex rasped a throaty sound packed with judgmental suspicion and turned his back to Luke. Charlotte smiled at the older man, a benign teacher with a stubborn child. Her black hair swinging loose, she returned her gaze to Luke. "Don't mind him. His bark is eighteen times worse—"

"Than his bite, yes, I know."

She said, "You spoke to Lettie."

Was she struggling to keep the conversation on an even keel, as he was? "She told me you were down here."

It took everything he had to control his voice, prevent his body from betraying him. And while he stood enthralled, her animation vanished, the smile left her lovely mouth, and he could swear the sparkle went out of her eyes, as well. He'd really blundered—but how, he didn't have a clue.

"I take it this isn't a social call."

"Not exactly." As her cheeks blossomed with that delicate rose and about a bushel of Malone pride tilted her chin at that precise angle, he realized she'd erected the old family barrier. If he had any sense, he'd leave things that way. But the need to ease her pain clawed at him. Instinctively he reached out to pluck away one last bit of hay stem from her hair, to reassure her—to touch her. "You missed one."

She dodged back from his hand, the straw crackling under her feet. "Don't touch me."

He felt as if he'd lost a world. "I'd never hurt you," he said huskily. "Never."

"I know that. I just...there's no sense in our getting things...mixed up."

He realized then that she hadn't stepped back because she was afraid, but because she felt the same sizzling excitement at his touch that he did. "What kinds of things?"

She shook her head. "I don't like being confused. I thought we settled things last night."

"You always did like everything straight and aboveboard, didn't you? A real aversion to ambiguity."

She wouldn't smile at his gentle teasing. Instead, she took another step back, bumped the stall wall. "No different than most people."

"You're not...most people."

Her eyes flicked up to him. She was going to run. Deliberately slowly, he put his left hand on the side of the stall, cutting her escape to the aisle.

"We can't do this."

"We're not doing anything. We're just talking." He braced his right palm on the other wall, and there she was, trapped in the corner. He liked her like that, her face flushed, her hair almost touching his hand, her body close to his.

"What...are you doing?"

"Just looking. I like looking at you." He tucked a finger under her chin and tilted her face up to his. "I like kissing you, too. Will Tex get the whip if I take a little taste?"

She put her palms flat against his chest. "He won't, but I should."

"Do I put you in the mood for mayhem?"

"No," she whispered, "I... No."

And like a sunflower seeking warmth, she turned her face up to him, yielding. He wrapped an arm around her slender waist and brought her up on her toes, feeling denim, seeing stars. They were in her eyes, those beautiful blue eyes that looked into his soul. He lowered his head. She watched until the touch of his mouth made her black lashes sweep down as if she needed to close her eyes to savor. He took his taste, a light brush of a kiss. One taste wasn't enough. He went back for more nectar, a hand slipping to her bottom, lifting her up a little more.

"No, Luke." With the deftness of a hummingbird, she slipped out of his grasp, her hands on his chest pushing him away. "We can't do this."

He raised an eyebrow. "Why not?"

She shook her head. "You know why not. You'd better just tell me why you came, and then . . . leave."

That was clear enough. His hand went to his pocket, and he brought out the linen-wrapped butterfly. "I came to return this." The wrap fell away, and the butterfly gleamed like a star, gathering all the light in that shadowed barn.

She drew in a sighing breath of relief. "I went out to look for it this morning. When I couldn't find it, I thought it was gone forever."

"That's why I came over as soon as I could this morning." Gently he laid it in her hand.

"I'm so glad to have it again." She glanced up at him, smiling with pleasure.

"I knew you would be."

"Thank you for bringing this back to me, Luke." The barrier went up, and her smile faded and she said, "You'd better have your handkerchief back." She went to unfold it from the butterfly, but he caught her hand and wrapped it around the ornament.

"You keep it."

Carefully she withdrew her hand from his, shaking her head. "No, I . . . No. You take it back. It's yours. I don't want your father to think I've taken to lifting the linens, too."

"Charlotte—"

A shake of her head stopped his attempt to reach back for that moment of rapport. His brows came together in a sharp frown, but he took the white square, his eyes on her as he folded it and put it in his pocket.

She looked down, as if uncertain of herself, for just a moment, then lifted her head and said, "Thank you for coming over this morning and bringing my butterfly back so quickly. I really appreciate your thoughtfulness. Now, if you'll excuse me, I have a horse to see to."

That quickly, she dismissed him, turning around, hair swinging over her denim shirt. She might accuse him of not playing fair, but neither was she. He couldn't let her end their meeting like this. "Charlotte." He reached out, caught her arm.

She turned and looked at him, and there was a flare of something in her eyes—passion or anger, he wasn't sure which. Still, she didn't twist out of his grasp as he thought she might. "What do you want?"

He wanted to grab her close and kiss her till both their heads spun, but he knew better. He was lucky she tolerated his touch. "What's the matter with your mare?"

"She's never foaled before. The trouble is, neither have I. Tex has seen several births, but they were easy ones. He isn't quite sure what to do about her."

"Lots of inexperience in one place." Luke smiled. "Mind if I go back and take a look at her?"

There was quiet in the barn in that instant. She had that determined look on her face again, as if she'd like to tell him she had no need of his help. "I'm sure you have other things to do."

Whether she knew it or not, she'd opened the door again. "I can spare a few minutes."

It didn't take a medical degree to see that the mare was almost ready to foal. "Easy, girl, easy. Let's have a look at your little one." Luke knelt between her legs and brushed his long fingers over the bulge of foal, checking the size, running his hands from the mare's shoulder to her hip. It was a large baby, possibly a colt.

When he stood up and turned to Charlotte, she had an odd look on her face, as if she'd seen something that moved her. He didn't know what it was. "I'd say you'll have your little one sometime tonight. After midnight, most likely."

"That the best you can do?" Tex roused up from behind the mare, all prickly defensiveness. "We kinda had that figured out for ourselves."

Luke said, "I'm going up in the northwest range today, but I'll be back tonight. I'll stop over this evening, if I may."

Tex muttered something, but Charlotte shook her head at him. "Mind your manners. Luke Steadman is a guest on our land." But when those blue eyes turned up to Luke, she said, "There's no need for you to come back. I'm sure Tex and I can handle things here."

"I'd like to come back, just to ease my own mind."

"I'd rather you didn't do that," said Charlotte.

He couldn't move. His eyes captured hers, held them, while he tried to think of a way to convince her that he was right, that she needed help. He couldn't think of the words. All he could do was let her believe he was leaving peacefully. "I'll say goodbye, then." He turned to go.

"Luke."

Arrested by the strange catch in her voice, he swung around. "Yes?"

"Has your father shown you the . . . steers?"

Luke nodded slowly. The silence felt heavy, laden with emotion. "I thought he would." She stood straight and tall,

all defensive pride. "I don't own a running branding iron, Luke. We haven't had one on the place for years."

"That doesn't surprise me."

"Not much does, it seems," she said crisply.

"Only you," he murmured. Then he tipped his hat to her and ducked his head to walk out of the barn.

Chapter Five

Luke's rear end was numb up to his ears from being in the saddle all day. His head must have been numb, too, making him give in to his urge to see her again, back her into the corner to steal a kiss like a teenager. Nothing like a day on the Montana range to deliver a large dose of sanity, make him realize he'd acted like a fool this morning.

He tried to stop them. He wanted to stop them. He couldn't. Pictures of Charlotte played in his mind all day long—the way she'd laughed at him over the back of her pet cow in the bar, the way her hair had swished around her shoulders out in the street and the look on her face when she'd told him of his father's persecution of her, the way she'd felt in his arms when he kissed her. Most of all, he remembered the way she made him feel. As if he'd stepped into the light after a long, dark winter.

Stupid thoughts, Steadman. Forget them. Think of a cold shower and a colder glass of beer.

He knew he shouldn't go to her ranch tonight. She doesn't want or need your help. You're pushing your way in where you don't belong. There's a simple solution. Don't see her. Hard to make love to a woman if you're not with her.

So butt out, stay out, get out. What, do you need a picture drawn for you?

Well, hell, he needed a shower after a hard day's work, didn't he? He'd take a shower whether he went over to Charlotte's or not.

Later, out riding again under a Montana sky stuffed clear full of stars, Luke knew he'd made the right choice. Though he knew he had no right to ride into Charlotte's life, he wanted to see her again. At night, when the dark and the stars were close.

The quiet beauty of the evening seeped through to his soul. He'd forgotten any place on earth could be so still, so full of wildlife, so empty of people. A coyote howled at the half moon, and a tree rustled.

Perhaps he wouldn't see her at all. Maybe Charlotte had done the sensible thing and gone to bed, and Luke would end up playing nursemaid with Tex. That would be fun. And maybe just what he deserved. His mouth tilting in a faintly self-mocking smile, Luke rode down the dusty path that led to Charlotte's barn.

She was there, all shining dark hair and long denim-sheathed legs, rising easily to her feet, looking...stunning.

"Hello, Luke." She greeted him as politely as she might a chance-come stranger. Those dark blue eyes were guarded and shielded and told him nothing of her soul.

"Hello, Charlotte." He matched her politeness with his urban brand of civility. "How's the mare?"

"We're still waiting."

"So I see." Polite words, saying nothing, revealing nothing. All so formally correct.

"What's he doing here?" Tex growled.

"He came to help," Charlotte said, not bothering to admonish Tex about courtesy this time, her eyes on Luke.

Tex made that sound in his throat that Luke was beginning to know and dislike. "This horse don't need a whole herd of people watching her. I'm gonna go home and go to bed."

Luke's eyes flickered over Charlotte's face. They'd be alone. How did she feel about that?

If Charlotte wanted to argue with Tex and keep him there, it didn't show on her face. All he could see was a cool, sophisticated woman keeping her counsel. A match for him. She said, "Go ahead, Tex. You get your rest."

Muttering that somebody around here had to be sensible, the old cowboy stomped out of the barn.

Luke's ears rang with the quiet.

"I didn't think you'd come," Charlotte said at last.

"I said I would."

"Are you always such a man of your word?"

He thought of the love-and-honor words that he'd failed to keep. "I try to be."

"That's something, I guess."

He stood there, knowing that whatever he was, whatever he'd done, she was a part of him. And always would be.

She stood there, gazing back at him, wishing she could see inside the man's heart as well as she had the boy's. And, most of all, she wished she could turn the clock back so that he'd never gone away.

The barn creaked with night wind, full of sheltered shadows in straw-laden corners. The mare groaned deep in her throat as she lay on her side and labored in birth. Her russet coat shone with perspiration. Time stretched, the mare worked—and gave a guttural cry of pain deep in her throat.

Tearing his eyes away from Charlotte, Luke stripped off his shirt and doused his hands in the bucket of disinfectant and water.

"She'll be all right?" Charlotte asked. In her anxiety, she gazed up at him.

To Luke, it seemed like the first time she'd looked at him openly and honestly. Incredible, the relief he felt. "Shh... She's doing beautifully. Look." He knelt in the straw, and so did Charlotte. He could feel her breathing behind him.

From inside the birth canal, wedged between his front hooves, the foal's black, wet nose poked out into the world for the very first time.

"Luke..." Charlotte breathed, and caught his shoulder. "Oh, Luke..."

Luke reached for one of the small legs, pulled one free, then the other. "Come on, Lady. Give your baby another push. We get those shoulders through and we're home free." Lady Luck gave another tremendous push, and the wet, slippery foal tumbled out on the straw.

"It's a colt," Luke said, his own throat feeling oddly full.

The little guy was dazed by the sudden transition from dark womb to bright world, his bronze coat soaked with birth moisture, his ears plastered to his head, his legs incredibly long for his tiny body. He lay on the straw, a wet, befuddled miniature of his mother.

Charlotte's eyes shone. She reached a slender, tentative finger out to touch the foal. "He's so incredibly... beautiful."

"He is that. We did a good job, didn't we?"

"Yes, *we* did." Charlotte flashed a brilliant smile at Luke. He answered with a slow lift of his lips that rocked her heart.

His bare shoulders gleamed in the dim light of the single bulb burning in the ceiling.

"All right, so my contribution was minimal." Luke turned his back to her and submerged his hands in the bucket of water. He came up dripping, reached for the towel she handed him and dried his hands briskly and efficiently, the way all ranch men seemed to do. His brown hair tousled, he retrieved the shirt he'd tossed on a hay bale, shrugging into it with a careless ease. He looked so wonderfully solid.

"I'm glad you came." No man should look as engaging as he did in dishabille, his jeans riding low on his hips, that flat belly exposed by the open shirt, his dark chest hair ruffled by the shirt edges. Luke's physical attributes weren't his only attraction. His personality drew Charlotte like a hummingbird to a rose. He was built of integrity, glossed with honesty. He'd never broken a promise or lied to her in his life. He might be just physically attracted to her, but she liked the look of Luke Steadman's heart and soul.

She dropped her lashes over her eyes, but not soon enough. In that dark barn, his pupils went a shade darker, a shade glossier. He'd caught her looking.

"It must be very late," she said, acutely aware of the huskiness in her voice. "I'm sure you'd like to go home and get some sleep."

In that silence, Lady Luck stirred. She pushed herself to her feet, leaned her head down, and began cleaning her youngster with long swipes of her rose tongue.

Unable to speak, her throat full, Charlotte watched the ritual bonding between mother and son and thought, crazily, that she would give her soul to be able to love another so freely.

She swallowed down the lump in her throat and tried to think rationally. "There's still coffee in the thermos. Would you like some before you go?"

Her face glowed with an inner happiness, her dark hair shone a vivid black. She looked incandescent. Coffee was not what Luke needed, but it was an excuse to stay. There hadn't been many moments in his life as moving as this one. "Sounds good."

She offered him the cup first, and he lifted it to his lips, watching her over the rim. Those deep brown eyes were so shadowed in the dark barn that Charlotte had no idea what he was thinking or feeling. He hadn't made any attempt to touch her. From the first moment he walked into the barn, he'd matched her guarded politeness.

He finished his drink of coffee and handed it back to her. She took the cup and sipped, but her throat was full and she couldn't drink it all. She offered the cup back to him, but he shook his head, his eyes still fastened on her face. She tossed the tiny bit of liquid into the straw out in the aisle.

Let him go. Don't say anything more. Don't ask him to stay, don't encourage him in any way. Above all, don't ask him into the house...where you might completely lose your head and throw yourself at him....

"There are ham-and-cheese sandwiches in the refrigerator that aren't more than a day old, and maybe even a cold hamburger in a stale bun. Are you hungry? You should be—you've worked hard, having this baby." Her lips lifted. She didn't know where she found the courage to tease him.

"How can I refuse such tempting morsels as day-old cheese and stale buns?"

The straw crackled, making them both turn. The colt scrambled to get his legs under him and, with enormous effort, struggled upward to stand on his four splayed, wobbling legs.

"Our boy's got spirit," Luke said.

Our boy. Deep inside her belly, nerves leaped and tightened. There would never be an "our boy." "You're nothing but a puffed-up, prejudiced father. Most foals get on their feet as soon as they can, you know."

"Ah, but not with the panache of my offspring."

His possessiveness filled her with her own pride. He'd been given so little love in life, and it seemed not to bother him at all. He flashed that wonderful smile at her, then turned back to gaze at the colt. "No doubt about it, our baby is the fastest, smartest, most beautiful colt in the world."

Luke's face shone in the light, wreathed with pride, all chiseled jaw and lean cheeks. He stood utterly absorbed in the new baby, utterly unselfconscious about his blatant partiality. His fingers fondled the colt's half-dry ears; the youngster cast big eyes up at Luke and promptly fell in love.

That makes two of us. "Those sandwiches aren't getting any younger." Charlotte spoke as lightly as she could manage. "If you could possibly tear yourself away from your pride and joy, we'll go on up to the house."

All that love bubbling up inside her with nowhere to go gave her feet wings. She fled from the barn, putting the tempting sight of Luke behind her, but the velvet night was just as stimulating to the senses. Frogs croaked, crickets sang. A serene, star-laden sky floated above spring-renewed earth. The full moon shone so bright that black mountain silhouettes rose against the stars.

The lone light in the kitchen window beckoned, a beacon set by Lettie. Tex's wife would be sleeping in their little house farther up in the hills, Tex beside her, by now.

Luke's long legs brought him to Charlotte's side. In that spring night pulsing with new life and promise, she yearned to reach out and catch his hand. *Forbidden.*

She couldn't have Luke, but she did have a new colt. Charlotte lifted her face to the starshine, her heart bursting with joyous thanksgiving.

"When a baby is born into this world, everything else seems fresh and new." Charlotte tilted her head back and spun around, making the constellations Hercules and the Big Dipper orbit crazily above her. "Did you know that?"

"Not till now."

His voice sounded husky. She straightened upright to scan his face, but there were two of him. She said, "Why do you look so dizzy?"

"It must be all this standing still I'm doing," he answered. Then he smiled.

That smile sent her spinning round again, revolving like an earth sprite in a ritual dance.

Luke hungered to clasp her hand and spin with her. Yet he was afraid to destroy the unearthly innocence of her. When she wobbled to a stop again, he said, "You're going to get dizzier."

"Don't be the stodgy old voice of reason. I don't want to listen to the voice of reason. I want to stay up where I am, way up, high on life." She took another turn.

"Charlotte—"

She stopped suddenly, tipsily, put her hands up in front of her as if to ward him off. "No. Don't remind me of anything. Just feel the world with me." She tried to catch his hand and missed. "Come on, Luke."

He shook his head. "I'd rather watch you."

She wouldn't listen. She caught his hand, tugged him around in a lopsided circle. He let her pull him, his mouth lifted in a tolerant smile. "Be a kid with me, Luke. Let's pretend we never lost each other." He gripped her hand to pull her close, but she anticipated his move and slipped away from his grasp. She burst into a sprint. He hustled after her, catching up to her with his long strides.

In the shadowed doorway, she swung around to him, all big shining eyes, triumphant mouth and flying hair. "Beat you."

"You cheated. You had a head start." He moved his body to trap her against the door, but she slipped away and opened it, bounding inside. He followed at a slower pace, his hands thrust in his pockets.

She had the refrigerator door open and was leaning down to look in when he came through the archway.

"Yesterday's ham-and-cheese, as promised." Two plastic bags hit the table. "One stale hamburger." Another bag came flying out and slid to the table's edge.

"I've decided I'm not hungry. At least, not for food." He moved like a cougar, all smoothness and ease, ready to pounce. He pushed the refrigerator door shut, and his hands came up to trap her.

With the grace of a child, she slid under his outstretched arm and laughed at him from the other side of the table. "I can't understand why, with such gourmet choices on the menu. I'll bet my day-old hamburger is as good as Sam's. Did you ever get anything to eat that night?"

"Yes," he said, coming around the table toward her, slowly, his eyes intent on her face. It gave him an odd feeling, chasing her like this. She'd been such a child when he knew her last. Yet here she was, this woman who electrified him with wanting her. "You've eluded me three times, Charlotte."

Quick as a wink, she shot back at him, "But who's counting?"

"I am."

She couldn't move. She felt frozen by the purpose in his dark eyes, the magnetism of his superb body. No doubt about it, he was stalking her. But she had invited the stalking.

She put out a hand and shook her head, her hair flying around her shoulders. "Luke, don't. I'm in a weakened condition."

"Good."

Her heart pounded furiously at the sound of his voice, soft, husky, darkly intimate.

"We were children for a moment—but that's all. We're all grown up now—"

"Thank God for that." He caught her hand, but he didn't draw her forward. His fingers toyed with hers, carefully, oh, so carefully. And slowly, oh, so slowly, he drew her hand to his mouth and put a kiss in her palm, folding her fingers over it for safekeeping.

She put her hand on his shoulder, inviting him into her world. He closed his eyes and moved closer, feeling as if she were the warmth he needed for life. He put an arm around her waist, gathering her into his realm. He stood there for a moment, just letting his world and hers merge. Then he gathered her closer, and she was no longer just in his world, she was his entire world.

"Yes . . ." he breathed, and brought a hand up to gather her hair into a shining ebony mass that spilled over his fingers. "Oh, yes . . ."

"I shouldn't have gotten high on the stars," she whispered.

"How do you feel now?"

One lean finger traveled the open V of her shirt, just to the bottom and back up again. Under his touch, her skin effervesced.

"Like I'm one of them, on fire, burning with heat and light."

She felt coolness on her back when her shirt lifted, and heat when his palm splayed over her supersensitive skin. He wrapped his arm around her, nearly brushing the side of her unfettered breast.

Her skin felt like silk. He wanted more. He leaned down to take a taste of her mouth, the lightest brush of a kiss. "You taste like a star, too."

His touch brought white heat under her skin, filled her with desire exploding up through her like a fountain's plume.

He eased a tiny button loose, touched the valley between her breasts. Another button gave, and he felt the first, sweet roundness of her. Aware as he had never been of the pounding of his own heart, he pushed her shirt aside and looked at her, touched her.

Coolness and dark need and heat and wanting, and wanting not to want, all careened around inside her. She needed help. She lifted her face to Luke.

His body consumed with need, he brushed her mouth again, his hand claiming her breast. And then he looked down into her eyes, into all that shining brilliance that held her soul.

Not fair. He wasn't playing fair. When the stars disappeared and the sun brought sanity after they went to bed together, she'd have to lift her chin and say she was fine. But she'd be lying. He didn't want her to have to lie to him. Ever.

"You're beautiful," he said, leaning down to brush a kiss on the sweet mound of her flesh. Then, carefully, very carefully, he closed the lowest button and then the one at the base of her throat.

To Charlotte, the dark, sweet tenderness of his beautifully chiseled face was as alluring as the feel of his hands on the small of her back as he tucked her shirt into her jeans.

"What are you doing?" She looked bedazzled.

That look of confused but utterly trusting adoration gave him the strength to do what had to be done. "Giving you time to think about this," he murmured.

"Why?" She gazed up at him, trying to read the thoughts of his heart through those darkly enchanting brown eyes.

"A gentleman doesn't take advantage of a lady's intoxication, no matter what the source." Luke captured Charlotte's hand and folded it over, reminding her of the kiss he'd put there. "Hang on to that. One of these days, when you're sober, I'll be back to give it a mate. I'll pass on the gourmet sandwiches for now. Thank you for the coffee." He walked to the door, turned. "And the stars."

"Luke— I— Are you leaving because you think I'm a thief?"

The silence stretched. She couldn't breathe, couldn't move.

"I'd trust you with my life," he said softly. "And I want you to do the same. That's why I'm leaving." He turned, his brown hair glossy in the light. The screen banged behind him, and the night took him.

Chapter Six

How quiet the house was. How lonely it was, climbing the stairs to her bedroom. How starkly white was her feminine sanctuary, ruffled curtains fluttering in the night breeze.

Drawn to the window, Charlotte pushed aside the drift of cotton and gazed out into the Montana night. The breeze flowed in over her bare arms, heavy with the soft green smell of spring.

Rebirth. The earth was stirring, and so was she.

She closed her eyes, but she could still see the stars, feel them on her skin. Her heart beat heavily, slowly, in her chest. She'd lost her mother, her father. Her brother was far away. She'd been safe in her world of work and ranch.

Now here love was again, beating at the door of her heart, clamoring for admission. She'd be such a fool to let it in.

Above her land, the Big Dipper slowly circled. She stood at the window and remembered the feel of his fingers touching her, his dark smile when he'd kissed her palm and bade her goodbye.

He'd walked away, giving her a freedom that ensnared her. Too late. Too late to be sensible. Too late for her heart to slip away unscathed. Her briar fence had been breached, her castle wall scaled.

The next morning, the sun blazed above newly green earth. Gray Mist felt the spring and begged to be let loose for a run, so Charlotte gave the gray gelding his head, and lost hers a little as she tightened her legs in the saddle and the wind tossed her hair. They scattered the birds who chittered and scolded such nonsense and left hoof cuts in the soft new grass all the way across the back pasture.

Below the mountains, under a sky as blue as topaz, cottonwoods lined the meandering creek that separated her rented pasture from Steadman's, her destination. The pines whispered, and the cattle bawled—her cattle, Steadman's cattle, mingling together to drink from the creek.

Tex, his hat pulled down hard on his head, already at the work of the day, cutting out the calves for branding, shied a cow-calf pair into the makeshift corral on their side of the creek.

Across that silver ribbon of water, the Steadman crew worked. The cattle swirled around the men and their horses, a cacophony of bawling cows punctuated by shouts from the humans. Nick worked the far side of the herd, Henry sat on his horse next to the corral.

Mounted, Luke was taller than anybody else, his hat pulled low over his dark hair, his rear end lifting in the saddle as he worked. One of the cowboys opened the corral gate and Luke whipped his hat off and beat it on his thigh, standing up on those long legs and yelling, "Hiya!" Not one but two pairs scooted in. Henry wheeled his horse around and rode to Luke's side, tilting his hat back to speak to his son. Then he smiled at Luke, and leaned forward to put a friendly hand on his shoulder. *Part of the team.*

It hurt. It shouldn't have, but it did. Charlotte lifted her head high, got a tighter grip on the reins and told herself it was good that Luke was getting along so well with his father, but the cottonwoods rustled and the pines whispered, mocking her, telling her it was time to brush the starshine out of her eyes. It was the morning after, after all.

"You gonna stand around gawking at your neighbors all day, or are you gonna work?" she asked herself.

There wasn't any answer to that. A lump in her throat, Charlotte ducked her head and whirled Gray Mist around in one of the close hauled turns he did so well, aiming him at a scrub brush a good distance away from the main action, where a cow-calf pair stood, the mother gazing at Charlotte with a big-eyed stare, trying to look casual and blend in with the landscape, as if the roundup had nothing to do with her and her daughter.

As luck would have it, the pair didn't belong to her, they wore the Steadman brand. Charlotte reined in Gray Mist, wishing life would give her a few of the easy choices this morning, instead of all the hard ones. In the years since her father's death, she'd taken a step of reconciliation on the first spring roundup she'd led and acted like a good neighbor, the way other folks did who rented open Western range where cattle got all mixed up together. When she came across Steadman cows, she'd head them out and run them into the Steadman corral. By the time she'd brought three of his calves home, Steadman gave his men orders to do the same for her.

Did she have the courage to cross the creek this year, when Henry Steadman had labeled her a thief?

Lord knew what his reaction would be if she rode onto his land. He'd probably call the sheriff and have her arrested on the spot. She had a perfect right to play it safe and leave Henry's big-eyed Hereford calves right where they stood.

But if she took the easy way out, Henry Steadman would not only have made her into a bogus thief, he'd have transformed her into a bona fide coward. Gritting her teeth, Charlotte circled the pair and drove them out of the brush, setting them on a dead run for the Steadman corral.

Nick guided his mare up next to Luke and leaned back in the saddle. "We're getting company." Nick nodded toward where Charlotte was riding hard toward them. His face bland, Nick stripped his blue bandanna free from his throat and passed it over his forehead, making a face when it came away streaked with dust and perspiration.

She looked like a gypsy with that wild mane of black hair flying free, her horse like a part of her as she worked the cattle toward the creek and into it. Luke's heart did something funny in his breast when she splashed up on the other side and, with total concentration and excellent horsemanship and not a single glance his way, drove those cattle straight into Henry's corral. He moved toward her to say good-morning, but those intensely beautiful dark blue eyes flashed his way just once, touching him with quicksilver, slicing over him. In the next instant, she reined her horse around, and all he got was a good view of her horse's backside and the flash of metal from the gelding's shoes. She moved through the trees like the wind, to safety on her side of the creek. He'd been snubbed before, but never quite so elegantly. Why wasn't she talking to him this morning?

"You look disappointed, brother. Expect her to stay and chat awhile?"

Instantly Luke composed his face. "I was just admiring her horsemanship," Luke drawled. Nodding toward the cow and calf that milled around looking confused by Charlotte's speedy delivery to confinement, he said, "Do we return the favor?"

Nick stared past Luke toward the trees where Charlotte had disappeared, his scowl disturbing his usual carefully controlled expression. "We have in the past. I don't know whether we are this year. God knows we shouldn't."

"Does He?" Luke murmured. "Isn't Charlotte innocent until proven guilty?"

"Didn't you see those cattle Dad's got stashed in the barn? What more proof do you want?" Nick was all righteous exasperation.

"Anybody with a rope and a horse could have double-branded those cattle," Luke said, his eyes giving Nick a slow, lazy scrutiny.

"Who else would have any reason to do a dumb thing like that?" Nick made a show of shaking out his neckerchief. "Why didn't she get them loaded up on the truck and get them sold? Why did she let them just stand around and get very conveniently found?"

"How the hell do I know? You think I know everything that goes on around here?"

"As a matter of fact, yes." The trees rustled in the silence while Luke kept his laser gaze trained on Nick.

A flush of color rose in Nick's cheeks, and those translucent eyes skittered away from Luke's. "What makes me such an expert on what goes on?"

"You're here, on the scene of the crime, if you will. Why wouldn't you be our resident expert?"

Nick whirled on Luke. "Don't start with your inscrutable-lawyer routine with me. Your girlfriend's guilty as hell. It's as plain as day, but for some reason, you don't want to admit it. What's the matter with you, anyway? Did the city pollution rot your brain?''

Luke said nothing, just sat on his horse and studied Nick, waiting.

Nick broke eye contact, wiped his face with his kerchief again. "Have you really got it bad for her? I feel sorry for you if you do.''

"Sweet of you to care," Luke murmured.

"It will almost be worth it to see your face when you finally have to admit the truth, that your long-lost love is a scheming little thief—and she's using you for all she's worth. What time did you get in last night, brother? You must have come home with the birds. Did she give you what you wanted?''

Luke's smile didn't change, but his eyes did. "You push fraternal loyalty way too far, brother.''

"You've never been loyal to me.''

"Oh, I was once, in my misbegotten youth. The first black eye I ever got was to protect your good name. Pretty much wasted effort, I think.''

Nick's hand dropped to his hip, to the gun belt he wore. Luke recognized the old Colt .45 that had belonged to Henry. "Going to shoot me?" Luke said mildly.

"Don't think the thought hasn't crossed my mind." Nick plucked the gun from the holster and gave it a quick and most efficient twirl. As suddenly as the sun coming out, his smile flashed, white and brilliant. He was back in control, and he liked it.

"There's a better chance you'll shoot yourself in the head, if you keep swinging it around like that," Luke said blandly.

"Oh, I'll watch out for myself," Nick said, holstering the gun.

"I'm sure you will," Luke murmured.

* * *

Charlotte was safely on her own side of the creek, breathing a little faster from the excitement and exertion, when Tex reined in next to her. "I suppose they told you thanks, real nicely," Tex growled, his mouth twisted in a sarcastic grimace.

"I didn't give them the chance."

"Umph. You're too dang nice to those people."

"If I treat them like they treat me, then they make me over to be like them and they really win. You wouldn't want that, would you?"

Tex squinted at her from under his hat, his blue eyes sparkling. "What kind of fool talk is that?"

Charlotte smiled at him. He might be crusty, but he was unfailingly loyal. Loyalty was very precious to her this morning, when certain other people seemed so changeable. "Crazy kind of fool talk, I guess."

"Speaking of fools, did you see that gun?" Tex jerked his head in Nick's direction. "Next thing you know, that dang idiot will be shooting at us."

A tiny chill feathered up Charlotte's spine. Nick was an unknown, always had been. She had never quite trusted him. But he surely wouldn't shoot anybody in plain daylight in front of half a dozen cowboys, one of whom was firmly on her side. "You know we always roust out a rattlesnake or two around the creek."

"'Pears to me we already have," Tex growled.

Charlotte didn't want to encourage Tex, but she couldn't keep a smile from lifting her lips as she clicked to Gray Mist and sent him away from the milling cattle, away from the creek, away from the sight of Luke Steadman sitting easily on his horse, carrying on a conversation with Nick that seemed to amuse him.

* * *

"You boys enjoying the scenery?" Henry's drawl came from behind Luke's shoulder, making him realize he'd been sitting there too long, gazing across the creek.

"Bird-watching," drawled Luke.

"We've got two hundred head of cattle to round up and brand."

"I'll get right at it, Dad," Nick said, and wheeled his horse around.

Henry stared after him. "He's a good man, Luke. I'd— I'd like it if you two could get along, now that you're older."

Heaven help him, he wanted to please his father. But what good would it do to raise false hopes? A new wisdom, hard learned in the past few years, made it impossible for him to put on a smooth face and pretend all was well. He opted for the kindest words he could say. "Nick's his own man. And I've learned to dance to a different drummer, somewhere along the way."

Henry gazed off toward the mountains. "I'm sorry. I thought— Well, never mind. I don't suppose you'll be here long enough for it to matter."

Luke watched his father riding away, his back straight. It was an old familiar song. But it seemed to have a different melody this time, one that cut deeper into the heart.

Slowly the sun shifted from east to west, bringing a cooler wind and lengthening shadows under the pines. They'd be done by nightfall, if Charlotte could stop the fantasies circling in her head about hot baths, cold drinks and a supine position on a bed. Wearily she reined Gray Mist around and headed out to the farthermost corner of the winter pasture, looking for those last few strays determined to hide in the scrub brush. She was beginning to dislike the sight of a white face bobbing up from behind a bush, even though every calf found was money in her pocket.

Under that big old Montana sky mellowing toward sunset, Charlotte found a last little fellow all by himself, sheltering under a scrubby pine, trembling with nerves. The calf was young, big-eyed and alone, and gone from his mother so long that he'd stopped bawling for her. Something wrong about this. A cow didn't leave her calf unattended, nor did the calf stray far from a mother's side.

She'd just herded her loner in the corral with the rest of his cohorts when Tex reined his horse up beside her. He went to say something, but then his sharp eyes fastened on the calf galloping around the pen. Quick as a wink, Tex flipped out his rope and lassoed the youngster. "Better have another look at this one."

The tone of his voice made Charlotte's heart rocket into her throat. She dismounted, the saddle creaking familiarly under her, and followed Tex's taut rope to the wriggling calf.

The calf wore her brand, the lazy *M*, all right. What she hadn't been able to see was the Flying S underneath. Her brand had been added on top of Steadman's, just like the others, but with a little less skill. She should have spotted it instantly.

The cottonwoods rattled in the late-afternoon breeze, and the wind went cold, chilling her skin. "Ear tag?"

"Theirs."

"I'm not a very smart thief, am I?"

Her voice sounded cool enough to her ears, and that cheered her a little. She ran her hand over the botched brand. The hair was still singed crisply around it, making it a new job, probably only a day or two old. Whoever was doing this to her had access not only to the running brand, but to Henry Steadman's iron, too. But he'd got a little too eager this time. He'd put his double brands on a calf that shouldn't be wearing one at all. This was just plain stupid and ridiculous. Who was going to believe she'd be that much of an idiot?

Henry Steadman would.

"I'm taking the calf over to them."

"What?" Tex lost his cool a little then, looking straight into her eyes and frowning like mad, his forehead crinkling and his mouth twisting. "Have you gone loco, girl? You want to give that mother's son of the devil another nail to hammer into your coffin?" Tex took his hat off and banged it against his leg. "And I used to think your daddy was crazy. You got him beat six ways to Sunday, gal." He jammed his hat back on his head and scowled at her so fiercely that she wanted to gather him in her arms and hug him. He cared for her, and this was his way of showing it, lashing out at her in his frustration. And to tell the truth, she'd like to hit something, too. Or someone.

"Nice calf," she said, patting the smooth little rump. "About six weeks old, I'd say. If I take him over there, he'll probably find his mother."

"Sure as shooting he'll find his mother, and you know that as dang well as I do."

"Tex, this is crazy. We haven't branded new calves yet this season, and neither has Henry. Somebody's gone to a lot of trouble to make me look guilty." Charlotte's eyes met Tex's across the calf's back. "He has to go back to his mother."

"Consarn it, I know that. But you're not going over there," he growled, looking like a thundercloud. "I'll take the dadblasted young'n over—"

"No. This isn't your responsibility. It's mine. Besides, you don't want Luke to accuse you of stealing again, do you?" At the flash of concern in Tex's eyes, Charlotte shook her head. "Lettie didn't want to tell me, but I pried it out of her. I'll bet Luke has apologized, hasn't he?"

"Don't make no difference to me what he thinks—big-city kid."

"I have a right to know who is harassing my employees, Tex. I may not be able to do all the things financially for you that I should do, but I can certainly protect you from false accusations."

"Yeah, and you can tell that young whippersnapper that I ain't no cattle rustler, either."

"I intend to," Charlotte said, smiling. "You can rest easy."

Tex got that look on his face that he always did when he was tamping down a very strong emotion. "So what's old man Steadman going to think when *you* come riding over with one of his calves?"

"He'd better think it's darn funny that this calf is wearing a brand before either of us has done spring branding."

Tex was quiet for a moment, thinking. "You could take him back up to the high pasture and leave him for them to find."

For just that one fleeting moment, it was tempting. If only she didn't have to cross that creek with that calf at the end of her rope and look into Luke Steadman's eyes. She'd do anything to avoid a confrontation, anything—except compromise her own honesty. "If Henry Steadman is going to find another calf with my brand over his, it's going to be at the end of my rope returning it to him." She ducked her head and tried not to think about Luke, tried to ignore the throb of her heart as she gave the hemp leader a turn around her wrist. "If Henry does a citizen's arrest, call my lawyer, Tom, would you?"

Tex looked like a thunderstorm brewing, but he nodded before he turned away and remounted his horse, a muscle in the side of his cheek working vigorously.

Her head high, Charlotte climbed aboard Gray Mist and dollied the rope around the saddle horn, setting off for the Steadman corral with the incriminating calf in tow, trying desperately not to feel as if she were going to her own execution. Was she totally crazy, expecting them—no, be honest with yourself, expecting Luke—to think rationally and see that there was no way she could have branded this calf?

She set a slow and steady pace to accommodate the calf, when what she really wanted to do was race over, let him loose and race back to safety. Her heart pounded in her chest and her stomach churned; the wind seemed suddenly to be ten degrees cooler, and the sun was dropping.

Charlotte crossed the creek and decided her bad luck for this day was holding, for there on the boundary sat Luke, on his horse, like the keeper of a gate, looking cool and relaxed in the saddle, his big old gray Stetson covered with a fine layer of ocher Montana dust, his boot cocked back in the stirrup.

Luke touched his hand to that hat, and when Charlotte dismounted, he did the same. She stood with her back to the creek, her chin high. The breeze loosened a strand of hair and feathered it across her cheek. She pushed it back impatiently. "Hello," she said.

Luke tipped his hat back, and his beautiful mouth turned up at the corners. "Hello yourself."

He'd spent all day in the saddle, just as she had, but he stood there as easy as silk, just . . . waiting.

"I'd—I'd like to see your father."

He smiled, a slow, lazy grin. "Are you sure that's what you'd *like?*"

Charlotte couldn't help it—she had to smile back at him. "Yes, I'm sure."

"That our calf?" Luke nodded at her baggage.

"Yes. He—" Her courage failed her. "Yes, he belongs to you."

"Is this just a neighborly call, or a ceremonial delivery of the last stray?" He pulled off his gloves and tucked them in his pockets.

The movement stretched his shirt across his shoulders, pulled his jeans across his abdomen. He was as flat as a board, and as slim-hipped as any man she'd ever seen. Those hips had fit against hers and given her a bittersweet glimpse of a rapture she hadn't yet tasted, rapture he'd denied her.... "I have something to discuss with him."

"What's going on, Luke?" Henry Steadman rode up behind his son, slid out of the saddle and put a hand on his shoulder. In all the years of her youth, Charlotte had never seen Henry lay a friendly hand on Luke. Now it had happened twice in one day. Henry was cleverly reminding Luke who was family—and who was the enemy.

"Charlotte's here to see you." Luke's tone was easy, and he had that half smile on his face that she usually loved. She was glad he was amused.

"Oh?"

How Henry could stuff so much impervious chilliness into one word, Charlotte didn't know. But his voice was warm compared to the iciness in his eyes. He stood beside a scattering of rocks that lay next to the creek, his boots planted firmly on the ground. His ground. His cattle. His son.

"One of your Hereford calves strayed onto my land."

"Indeed." Henry didn't move, and neither did Luke. From behind them, Nick rode up, his saturnine face wearing a look of amusement. He said, "What's going on here?" and climbed down off his horse to come and stand next to Charlotte, his smile brilliant.

She faced the three of them, her chin braced, her head high. "I want you to see the brand on this calf, Mr. Steadman. Actually, there are two brands."

The three men gathered around the calf, but it was Luke who first stepped forward to run his fingers over the brand.

The sight of him examining what seemed to be such damning evidence almost made Charlotte lose her courage. But she took a tight grip on herself and said, "I don't brand calves until tomorrow, and neither do you. *And I don't own a running brand.* There isn't one on my place anywhere. I've been looking for two months, since the first calf turned up. Dad never owned one—and neither do I."

"Easy enough to hide one." This from Nick, standing closest to her, his smile still in place.

"I haven't hid anything."

There was a small, cool silence while Henry examined the calf and ran his fingers over the brand. Then he stepped back, close to the rocks again. "Hard to deny the evidence that is standing here right in front of our eyes," he drawled at last. His head lifted, and he subjected Charlotte to a hard examining gaze, the sun glancing off his glasses. "I admire your nerve, young woman, but if you think I'll fall for your clever ploy, you're quite wrong. I can see how you thought I might be swayed by your bold act of returning this calf to me, but I'm afraid I don't fool quite so easily. If you hoped to get me to drop legal action against you by returning one calf you'd already stolen, you're in for a disappointment."

Charlotte told herself not to look at Luke, but her eyes betrayed her, and her gaze flickered to him for a single instant. Did he believe the things his father said? He simply stood there without a bit of expression on his face. His lawyer's face. Did he believe the evidence he could see with his own eyes? She couldn't tell. Oh, couldn't he please reserve judgment and believe in her just a little?

Luke didn't move, didn't speak. He stood farther away from her, whether by design or accident, she couldn't tell. Under that hat pulled low, his eyes met hers, but if he had any feeling of sympathy or empathy, she couldn't see it in his chiseled face. Her heart broke, there in the clearing, with the sun dropping behind the mountains and the shadows lengthening on the trampled buffalo grass, but she was just stubborn enough to try once more. "I came over here hoping to have an intelligent conversation with intelligent, *sensible* men about the impossibility of my inflicting the double brands on this animal. This is a young calf. He shouldn't be wearing your brand. I don't have a running iron, and I certainly don't have *your* brand. Someone who has access to your irons is doing this to both of us. I had hoped we might explore the possibilities. I see I was wrong. If I have acted as a less-than-gracious guest on your land, I apologize." She loosened her rope from around the calf's neck, and prepared herself to go.

"There's no need for an apology." Henry stepped toward her, his back to the creek. "I'm sorry to say it, but I think it's time I had the sheriff search your property for that iron you say you don't have."

Quick as lightning, Charlotte snatched the gun out of Nick's holster and aimed it at Henry. "Don't move," she said in a low, warning voice.

"What the hell—?" Nick growled.

"Charlotte, don't be an idiot," Luke snapped.

"Be quiet." Charlotte took aim, cocked the gun and fired at a spot on the ground just behind Henry. Before the men could move, she fired again, startling them all.

The rattlesnake that was coiled behind Henry writhed in a death dance, thrashing against the rocks, the black diamond patterns glistening in the light. Then the snake was still.

"I knew you didn't hear it rattle, because you were talking," Charlotte said to Henry. "And I didn't think you could see it from where you were," she said to Nick as she handed him back the gun. Suddenly she felt a little shaky. She thrust her hand in her jeans pocket to keep it from trembling. She hated snakes, and the darn thing had been so close to Henry.

In the stunned silence that followed, she avoided Luke's eyes. She felt cold and exhausted. She needed to go where it was warm. Where it was home. "I'm sorry if I frightened you. Now, if you all will excuse me..." She gathered Gray Mist's reins up and thrust her foot in the stirrup and mounted her horse.

"Charlotte—" Luke came to life, stepped forward, caught her arm. His eyes were dark and brilliant, alive with admiration for her. He was looking at her the way she'd dreamed of a thousand times. But it was too late. He'd thought she was capable of threatening his father with a gun—just as Nick had. He didn't know her at all. And she didn't want to know him.

"I—we thank you. If it weren't for your quick action, my father might have been bitten." Immediately Henry walked up to stand beside his son. His cheeks were pale, his eyes guarded. "My son is right. I owe you my thanks."

"You don't owe me a thing. I'll expect a visit from the sheriff as soon as you can arrange it." Charlotte let out the reins and urged Gray Mist into a high old gallop across the creek, racing to get back onto the land that belonged to her.

Chapter Seven

"Feel like you've won the lottery, Dad?" Luke asked.

"No, of course not." Henry's head came up and his shoulders were squared, but his face was pale and his mouth was colorless. Luke felt the old irritation, but with it, a sudden new adult insight. What else could Henry do in the face of trouble but put on a strong front? It was the way he had met life for years. He'd had to raise two boys without help. Luke had a sudden disturbing flash of what his own life might have been like if Henry had been weak and self-pitying.

Just when Luke was thinking his father was invincible, Henry moved to lean against his horse. The cottonwoods rustled with a passing breeze. The sun had nearly disappeared. "Let's go back to the house," Luke said gently.

Henry shook his head. "No. We need to bury...the snake. I don't want the calves nosing it out of curiosity."

Henry's first thoughts would be for the cows, Luke thought. "Where can I find a shovel?"

Henry turned to Nick, who'd been standing oddly quiet, his narrow body nearly rooted to the ground as he gazed across the creek toward Charlotte, one hand splayed on a cottonwood trunk. Now Nick came to life and walked to his father's side. He looked... thoughtful. "You know I would have shot that snake if I had seen it, Dad."

"I know that, Nick." Henry put his hand on his son's arm. "Will you go get the shovel, son?"

"Let Luke go."

Henry shook his head. "It's better if you go. You can find things easier than Luke can."

Nick frowned, obviously not wanting to be the one to run the errand. Then, suddenly, his face cleared. "Of course, Dad. You're right. I can find things better than Luke can."

Odd, Nick being so accommodating, even for his father. It seemed...incongruous. Luke's eyes narrowed, and his gaze whipped up to his brother's face, but Nick quickly gathered up the reins of his horse, reined his mount around and set his mare at a fast gallop back toward the house, disappearing below the rise of the hill.

"He's suddenly very helpful," Luke murmured.

"He puts the ranch first, just as I do."

"Does he?" Luke cocked an eyebrow, but a quick glance at his father's pale cheeks made him give up the idea of trying to play the devil's advocate. "Perhaps you should sit down."

"There's no need. I've seen a snake or two in my time."

"You were fortunate she's such a good marksman." He didn't want to think about what could have happened if Charlotte had not been so alert, so quick-thinking, so brave. She'd saved his father's life, even as Luke had been convinced she was aiming the gun at his father's head. Why was he such an all-time twenty-four-karat fool?

"It's a big one," said Henry, and there was just a tiny bit of pride in his voice. "Six foot long if it's an inch, and big around to match. Maybe that explains why the fellow was standing his ground instead of hiding like they usually do."

Luke stared at the snake, and he thought of the courage of the woman who'd calmly aimed and shot at the thing in the presence of three men. "It might be a good thing if you'd reconsider about the search warrant until we have a little more time to do some investigating. I find it hard to believe that she—"

"She's a good-looking woman. Always has been. I can see how she'd appeal to a young fellow like you."

"That has nothing to do with it," Luke said. His father's attempt at being understanding irritated the hell out of Luke. "There's just something about this that reeks."

"It all seems rather clear to me. She's stealing my cattle. Why wouldn't it work to her advantage to save my life if she saw the chance? If she could keep me from pressing charges, she could go on stealing me blind for years," said Henry heavily.

"She wouldn't do that. And somehow I think you know that as well as I do."

"I said I owe her my thanks. But that's all I owe her." He turned away and sat down rather suddenly on a rock.

"Are you all right?" Luke didn't like the bluish look around his father's mouth, the way he was holding his hand to his chest.

"I'm fine."

There was no other state of existence possible for Henry Steadman. To himself, Luke murmured, "Of course you are," and decided that he, Luke, was going to have his hands full. He was going to have to keep an eye on his father—and he would have some major fence-mending to do with Charlotte . . . if he hadn't destroyed his credibility with her altogether. His father needed him. But he needed Charlotte. He could still see in his mind's eye the hurt, the desolation, in that last look she'd given him—and how differently she'd looked at him that night under the stars. He'd lost something very, very precious. And heaven only knew if he could retrieve it.

It was the one day in his life he was glad that Charlotte Malone lived so close. He'd have to ride like a bat out of hell, but he could do it. He could retrieve the running iron from its hiding place in the old bunkhouse, ferry it over to Charlotte's and hide it in her machine shed while she was still out with her herd. It was risky, for though it was getting dark, it was not quite dark enough. Still, he liked the risk. It made his heart pound faster, made his blood throb. It made him feel alive. And very happy.

Luke decided late at night was best. They'd been branding all that next day, and so had Charlotte. He could see her across the creek, watch her working, bending over the calves, so near—and as far away as those stars she loved so much. He was forced to bide his time and wait. But when he'd eaten supper, showered and shaved, he could wait no longer. He didn't even take the time to saddle a horse, he simply threw himself in his car and drove the short distance to Charlotte's.

Charlotte must have heard the car, for she came to the door almost instantly. She, too, had showered, and she was wearing a worn, pale pink chenille robe, one that might have belonged to her mother. It shouldn't have been sexy but it was, because it fit her like a glove, outlining the sweet curve of her breasts, following the nice little roundness of her rear end to perfection. He wanted to reach out and touch the nubby material, to test its closeness to Charlotte's feminine lushness, and then he wanted to smooth away the fluffy folds and find her satiny naked skin....

The only sign she made of being aware of him was the tenseness in those long, slender fingers that held the neck of her robe closed. Her eyes were cool and clear and as impersonal as a stranger's as she invited him in to her kitchen.

Only Luke, Charlotte thought. Only Luke would have the nerve to come around again and try to do—what? Apologize? Pick up where he left off? He looked too darn tall and handsome, and what was worse, he looked endearingly unsure of himself. His brown hair was ruffled, as if he'd showered and combed it in an impatient hurry. It hurt to look at him and think of what might have been.

Luke wished to hell he didn't feel so awkward. It had all seemed so clear in his mind what he was going to say and do, but he hadn't counted on Charlotte looking at him with the same interest she might have had in an overripe side of beef.

Then the articulate, educated, intelligent lawyer opened his mouth and said, "How's it going?" He heard the words and mentally cringed.

"Wonderful. How are things going with you?"

Her voice held a new touch of irony that was unfamiliar to his ears. He was afraid it was a cynicism he'd brought to her. The thought hurt, and made him more ill at ease than ever. "As well as can be expected, I guess. The old bones and muscles have forgotten what it's like to work at physical labor for sixteen hours a day, but other than that—"

"I'm sure you'll survive," she said coolly, letting his little bid for sympathy slide right over her head.

The next thing he knew, he was looking at her back. She'd turned to the stove. That was the way she wanted things, her back to him, shutting him out. He was trying to find the words for a graceful, eloquent, moving and thoroughly self-abasing apology when she said, "Would you like some tea while you try to get your courage up to say whatever it was you came to say?"

Blunt. God, she was blunt. He folded his arms, leaned back against the door. That was as far as he'd come into the room, just the one step that brought him inside the door. "Please don't hold back on my account. Come right out and say what you mean."

He tried a half smile, thinking that if she turned around she'd enjoy sharing the amusement at his expense. Her response was to whirl around from the stove, her cheeks rosy with more than the heat from her shower. "Do you want me to say nice conciliatory things like 'Gee, it was so nice of you to drop by, Mr. Steadman? I wonder why you're here. Did you stop in to see how a lady-thief-slash-gun-slinger spends her evenings at home?"

He took a step toward her, his arm reaching out to her. "Charlotte, don't be a damn fool—"

Those blue eyes flashed eight thousand warnings at him. "No. Don't *you* be a damn fool. Don't you dare come on my land oozing your practiced Steadman charm and flashing your practiced Steadman smile and...and flinging about your practiced Steadman panache to cast your spell over me..."

"If I had practiced, I hope I'd be more successful at it."

"—and sweet-talk me and take me into your arms."

"I was three years old the last time I tried to hug a porcupine." His mouth quirked, inviting her to smile once again.

He looked so wonderful, so darkly enticing, with those brown eyes gleaming with amusement and that hard, chiseled mouth lifted in a smile that was pure tender beguilement, that she closed her eyes to block out the sight of him.

"We've been living in a dream world, Luke." He took a step forward. She heard him, and her eyes flashed open and she pushed up her hands, palms out, warning him away. "No. Excuse me. *I'm* the one who's been living in a dream world. I thought we knew each other so well that nothing could come between us, not even your father. Now I'm beginning to think it isn't the years we've been apart that have made us strangers, it's that we never really knew each other at all."

He didn't like her tone of voice. It was so flat, so solemn. So final. He knew far better than to argue with her about the depth of their old friendship. He was the one who'd just barely remembered her. "We could get reacquainted," he said, his voice husky and inviting. "I'd very much like to be your *new* friend."

She just looked at him for one silent, long moment.

"It seems to me you could use a friend right about now," he said, pressing unwisely, taking a fatal step forward.

Those blue eyes sparkled with heat. "I'd rather cozy up to the snake."

He took the hit without a sign of distress, not even a downward sweep of those long cocoa-brown lashes. "If you wanted to be his *compadre,* you probably shouldn't have shot him." Luke cocked his head to one side, studying her, remembering far too late that Charlotte's beautiful mother had had red hair and a temper to match. "Actually, I'm feeling a little bit like target practice here myself."

"I'm sure I didn't score any direct or telling hits on the invincible Luke Steadman. You should have plenty of experience in ducking by now."

The only sign that her below-the-belt hit had bothered him was in the little movement of the muscle in his cheek. "This may come as a surprise to you, but I do have a couple of vulnerable areas left that I've tried to keep protected," he said dryly. In a very low, even tone, he added, "But you've found them."

Those dark brown eyes asked for mercy. She could feel herself weakening. She pulled the belt tighter around her waist and straightened her back to come up to her full height, meeting his look head-on. "Then I suggest you do what I did yesterday. Go home and try to forget we ever knew each other."

He seemed to mull over her words, and he took his time responding. At last he said, "The going-home part is easy. The forgetting will be considerably more difficult." Luke replaced his hat, gave her a mocking salute with graceful fingers perpendicular to the brim. "If not impossible. You see, the stars come out every night." The screen door banged behind him.

A thousand stars of brilliant fire shimmered and shattered inside her. Then her body quieted, and so did the world. Into that deep silence, her thoughts tumbled, scattering.

Sit down, be calm, be cool. You haven't just made the most terrible mistake of your life.

Are you sure?

The kitchen chair felt cool and hard underneath her, sharp against the backs of her knees. Her hands were twined together in front of her, fingers icy. He'd never come back now, not after the things she'd said. Good. She didn't want to see him again. Ever.

The cat clock swished his tail in silence, ticking away the time and the night. But not the lie.

The next morning, there was no sun. It was cloudy and cool and bleak and empty in the world. There was work, of course. There was always work. For the next week and a half, she worked, doggedly, determinedly. The shimmering excitement was gone. And so was the possibility of seeing Luke.

On the 22nd of June, when she hadn't seen or heard from Luke in nearly two weeks she consoled herself with the thought that she hadn't heard from the Sheriff either. Maybe Henry had decided to drop his demand for that darn search warrant. Everyday she allowed herself to hope just a little more.

One afternoon when she had finished her book work and was feeling the need to stretch her cramped muscles she went to the barn. Inside the cool, half-shadowed building, she wrapped her hands around the business end of a shovel and set to work scooping out Lady Luck's stall, telling herself she wanted to make sure mother and baby had clean straw before she moved the cattle to the summer pasture. Nice to use work to kid yourself that way. The sight of the chestnut mare nuzzling her baby was evocative of Luke, bringing her memories of him into the barn, as clear as a moving picture—his easy smile, his bare, darkly furred arms, his disheveled hair, his seductive appeal. She would not think of Luke. Dig, toss. She would not think of Luke. Dig, toss...

"Charlotte, you in there?" Clarence Daggett's generous body filled the doorway of her barn.

"Come on back, Clarence." She thought she sounded normal. But her knees went a little shaky suddenly, and she folded her hands and rested them on top of her shovel, bracing herself. She'd known Henry Steadman was a man of his word.

The sheriff of Madison County ambled down the aisle, his hat in his hand. He was trying his best to be easy and friendly, but he had about him the look of a man on his way to the dentist. "Looks like you're working hard."

"Or hardly working. I guess you've got something for me." Charlotte put her shovel aside and rubbed her hands down the sides of her jeans.

Clarence's eyes met hers, and he gave up the attempt to pretend he wasn't bothered. "I have to tell you, Charlotte, I hate this worse than when we had to put our old collie to sleep."

"Well, thanks. I can't say as this is high on my list of things to do for a good time, either." She tried a smile, her heart going out to him for his kindness. He smiled back, but there was reserve in his gray eyes, and she remembered that while he might think he was the law and impartial, at this moment he was an active representative of Henry Steadman. She'd fought Henry for so long that she really didn't want to make it easy for Clarence to conduct his search, but it wasn't his fault they were caught in this situation. At least she'd had sense enough to call Tom Hartley and ask him how she should handle it when it happened.

"I'd like to see the warrant."

"That's your right." With obvious reluctance, Clarence drew the paper from his pocket and passed it over. She stared at it, remembering how she'd wished a miracle would happen and she wouldn't have to hold this piece of paper in her hand that gave Clarence the right to tramp all over her property looking for incriminating evidence. There were no miracles; Clarence was here with his warrant. She hadn't died; she was still breathing.

This paper was proof that she had no friends in the Steadman camp. And, to be fair, she supposed she had no right to that secret, desperate hope that Luke might find a way to intervene for her.

No right at all.

The paper was formal and correct and bore Judge Markham's signature on the bottom, which was what Tom had told her to look for. "Looks like it's legal," she said, handing it back. "Henry surely didn't waste any time, did he?"

"No, he didn't. Pretty darn mean of him, after what you did for him, shooting that snake and saving his life and all—" Clarence Daggett took one look at Charlotte's face, clapped his mouth shut, shifted his weight from one booted foot to another and looked mighty uncomfortable, for a man with a star on his chest.

"Who told you about that, Clarence? Not Henry, I bet."

His gaze skittered past her shoulder to somewhere out in the pasture. "I just heard it around town, that's all."

"You talked to Luke." The words came out before she could stop them, mostly because she was so sure they were true.

Clarence's face went a deeper shade of pink. "Well, he did drop by last week to explain a couple of things to me."

"What *kind* of things?"

"Like I said, about the snake. And about how he'd hang my hide on a nail if I wasn't polite to you. He didn't have to tell me that, no, sir. I wouldn't say or do anything to hurt you. But I guess he didn't know that. He's been gone a while."

"He had no business saying that to you." *In more ways than one. Luke must have had that conversation with Clarence the day after you so kindly sent him out of your life.*

"Well, you know Luke. He likes to do things his way. He's more like his old man than he knows." Clarence smiled at Charlotte. "So I let him think he was getting what he wanted, as long as that was what I wanted, too."

"You're a smart man, Clarence. No wonder folks keep you around." Warmth. Heat. It was hard on the heart to expand when it had been closed so tightly. Hard to get used to the idea that she wasn't quite as alone in her life as she had been before Princess's Saturday-night visit to the local bar. Hard to think that Luke had the kind of tenacity, understanding and bigheartedness that just might put this feud to rest. "Well, where do you want to start? Here in the barn?"

"I got an anonymous tip that the iron would be in the machine shed."

The warmth fled, her hands turned to ice. Yet her cheeks burned. "What kind of a tip?"

"The usual. A phone call from a guy disguising his voice."

"You knew he was disguising his voice?"

He shook his head. "You don't *know*. You guess. And, sometimes, you hope. You don't want it to be a guy you know." Clarence met her eyes clearly and openly.

"Well, let's get to that machine shed, then," she said brightly. "I'll help you look."

Clarence opened his mouth as if he wanted to argue, and Charlotte figured it was pretty unorthodox to let the searched help with the searching, but he didn't say anything as he walked along beside her.

The machine shed was really something of an overgrown shop. She kept the tractor at one end of the building. The other end had cabinets and drawers and an old anvil that looked like an iron welder's nightmare. Inside the darkened building, after they had a short discussion about where to start, Charlotte gave him the neatest side of the room, and she took the other. She made a joke about needing to clean the place out anyway, and began tossing out wire and boards with reckless abandon, unearthing rags, oil cans, a rake with a broken handle, a bicycle pump that didn't work. She worked like a woman determined to turn over the whole state of Montana in an hour. Clarence let her vent her anxiety, knowing there was little else he could do, and caring for her too much to pull rank. He simply put his energy into slowly and methodically beginning his search through old paint cans, knowing he'd probably have to go through the stuff Charlotte was unearthing, as well. He ducked when she tossed out a rag, stepped aside when she rolled an ancient tire toward the door.

"Let's see, there are more boards back here, and here's an old stamp iron." She brought it out and held it up high— and felt as if her blood suddenly stopped cold in her veins. In the shadows it had looked like a stamp iron, but held out in the light she could see clearly that it was a running branding iron.

"Great guns of Navarone. There it is, big as life, and you just put your prints on the damn thing."

Charlotte's bravado and temper collapsed. "I'm sorry, Clarence. I don't know where this thing came from. It wasn't here two weeks ago, I swear it wasn't."

"I believe you."

"You believe me?"

"I doubt you'd steal a feather from a chicken."

"Because Luke vouched for me?"

Clarence Daggett got that look on his face that men get when they have to deal with a woman and they don't have a clue about what to do. "Luke's got nothing to do with what I think." Clarence took the iron from her and strode past her quickly, moving with amazing speed for his size.

Outside the shed, in the grayish light of the cloudy day, the world hadn't suddenly collapsed. It all looked surprisingly the same, trees nearly leafed out, cloudiness still not bringing rain, house still needing a coat of paint.

But the world had changed. The long single iron Clarence stood stowing into his car was solid evidence that she was a thief. Despite the branded cattle, despite her own hostility, Luke had believed in her before. He wouldn't now.

He was a lawyer trained to put his faith in evidence, not people. This would be the end of his trust.

Charlotte lifted her head, put on a smile. Clarence had been kind. Her world was falling down around her ears, but she couldn't break the rules of country hospitality. "It's almost lunchtime. Would you like to stay? Lettie made barbecued beef yesterday and baked sourdough bread this morning."

Clarence Daggett liked his food, and his build was beginning to show it. He patted his stomach, which had begun to protrude just a little over his belt. "Barbecued beef sandwich sounds real good, but I promised Mary Lou I'd come home," he said.

"No taking bread with the enemy, right? Luke's instructions didn't extend to that."

Clarence's dark gray eyes were full of compassion under that cream-colored Stetson he wore. "Charlotte, I talked to Luke, sure I did. It didn't cost me anything to listen. But he only told me what I already knew. I liked your daddy. And your mamma was always the first one to anybody's house with that good beef stew of hers if they had trouble. I still remember how she came and helped Mary Lou after our little daughter was born. You know I'd rather eat ground glass than hurt you, don't you?"

"What happens now?"

He ran a hand around under his collar and looked as uncomfortable as one man could look. "I take the thing in and label it as evidence."

"What happens after that? Are you going to—what is the term?—run me in?" She tried to smile, but her stomach churned with nerves. This was a nightmare. It couldn't be happening.

"I don't have a warrant for your arrest. Besides, I don't figure you're going anywhere. Are you?"

"I might go into Columbia Falls for groceries."

"That's allowed." Clarence hitched at his pants and looked as if he felt awkward. "I'd better get going. Mary Lou gets a little upset if I'm later than I said I'd be." He looked as if he wanted to go, but he still stood there with his hand on his open car door.

"What kind of pie is she making you for lunch?"

"Caramel cream," he said, and looked a little sheepish because he had the right answer so quickly for her. "Try not to worry. We'll get this thing straightened out somehow." He touched his fingers to his hat.

She made another attempt to smile. It felt better this time. "I sure hope so. And make it soon, okay? Have a good lunch, Clarence."

"You take care of yourself, Charlotte. If this branding iron wasn't here two weeks ago, then somebody is sneaking around on your place who shouldn't be." He slid into his car.

"I wish you hadn't said that," Charlotte murmured as he drove away.

She had just finished eating her supper the next night when the knock came on the door. All kinds of wild thoughts went through her head, things she had to tell Tex and Lettie if she was going to be arrested. . . .

Athena stood outside under the porch light.

Charlotte swallowed once, then stepped back and smiled. She realized suddenly that she'd been dealing only with men in the past few days and she was infinitely weary of it. "How did you know I needed you?"

"I knew." Dark, deep eyes swept over Charlotte's face, cataloging every worry line, every moment of sleep lost.

Charlotte had stood up to the snake, to Clarence, to Luke. Only Athena's compassion had the ability to make her knees weak. "I'll make you some tea."

Athena shook her head. "I just came to bring you these."
She set her little wicker basket on the table and brought out
a towel-covered plate. The delicious smell of raisin-oatmeal
cookies filled the room. She must have just baked them.

Charlotte blinked several times, quickly. "You shouldn't
have."

"Yes, I should."

"Do you have to go right away?"

"Not until I've hugged you." And Athena opened her
arms.

Charlotte walked into them and buried her nose in Athena's neck. "What am I going to do? I'm going to lose everything—everything I care about."

"Have faith." Athena's arms held her tight.

"I'm afraid to hope anymore."

"Don't be. Everything will be all right."

Charlotte felt Athena's hand on her hair, smoothing it
down. She had to be strong, and she was strong, but it was
so nice to be comforted and cosseted, just this once, when
everything looked so black.

"He must despise me," Charlotte said, holding on tight
to Athena's generous waist. "I must look so guilty to him."

Athena just patted her back, wisely saying nothing, just
listening.

"He should have known I'd never shoot his father."

At that jump from worry to accusation, Athena leaned
away to look down into her face, a frown drawing her brows
together. "If somebody pointed a gun at your daddy when
he was still alive, wouldn't you yell at him?"

"I— Of course."

"Well, there you are, then." Gently she extracted herself
from Charlotte's arms. "Sometimes a woman just gotta love
a man whether he knows her or not. Sometimes a woman
gotta help a man step out on that glass staircase that he can't

see and have faith. And now, I have to go back.'' Charlotte's chin was lifted by a warm, soft hand. ''You take care of yourself, you hear? Everything's going to be all right.''

She slipped out of the door and back into the night, leaving Charlotte staring after her, almost afraid to believe she'd really been there. But the wonderful smell of the cookies lingered, and Charlotte lifted the white towel and picked one up, not sure whether she wanted to eat it, or just hold it for comfort.

Chapter Eight

The cows knew the way to the summer pasture, up past the second bend of the creek, around the grove of aspens, just past the tree festooned with blackbirds and upward along the silver ribbon of a stream that narrowed to a trickle. Gray Mist liked the slow pace, and so did Charlotte, especially on an early July day like this, when it seemed as if she could see the sky from pole to pole and the air had the warmth of a hot sweet biscuit. Even the dust was too lazy to rise. Ahead of her, Tex rode, hat in hand to scare the stragglers, his beloved tri collie nipping at the heels of wandering strays. Even Princess, the premier cow, behaved herself and followed the herd.

It had been quite a while since Athena's visit, but her spirit lingered with Charlotte. *Have faith in Luke.* She hadn't. She'd sent him away, because in that first crazy moment when she snatched up the gun, he'd acted instinctively. Athena was right, Charlotte's hackles would have flown to the moon if Luke had seemed to threaten *her* father.

I was three years old the last time I tried to hug a porcupine.

She'd been a porcupine, all right. A stubborn, thickheaded spiny pig. What were the chances he still believed in her, now that they'd found that blasted iron on her property?

Zero to none. She'd lose Luke's trust along with everything else.

She'd had time to think about what it would be like without Luke standing behind her. During these past weeks, with Luke absent from her life, the world had chilled to a bleak emptiness. Too late, she'd realized she'd learned to depend on his faith. Now, when she fell into fitful sleep and dreamed about finding the branding iron and woke shaking and afraid, all her bravado was gone. The days were long and lonely without him.

Would she be indicted, lose her ranch? Not if she could help it. This *was* her land, and she would do everything in her power to keep it, including sleeping out in the open tonight to watch the herd. Her horse was loaded down with sleeping bag, water bottle and, tucked away carefully in waxed paper, Athena's raisin-oatmeal cookies.

She'd wanted to sell the year-old calves to give Tex the money he needed, but when she called Tom Hartley to let him know, he'd advised her not to. Ordered her not to, actually. He'd said she'd better not sell even the smallest calf until this brouhaha with Henry was settled. Any new moneys in her account were bound to be suspect. She'd agreed. But she knew in her heart that it wasn't right to ask Lettie to wait, and so she'd gone to the telephone and found a buyer for the one valuable animal she had that was not part of her herd. It was like selling a part of her soul to part with Lady

Luck's colt, but Carson Dole was a good man and, most important of all, he was willing to give her the money now and wait till the foal was weaned to take him.

It had hurt to take the check from Carson that evening, but it had felt awfully good to put the money in Tex's hand the next day, after she went to the bank. He might have refused it for himself, but he loved Lettie with a secret fierceness that only Lettie and Charlotte knew, so he'd taken the money and they'd gone off to see the doctor about scheduling the operation that would give Lettie relief from her pain.

At the far border of her summer pasture, the grass was lush, and the salt blocks were strategically placed to space the cattle. Tex gave up herding, the collie sat down with pink tongue hanging, knowing his work was done. Now came the task Charlotte really dreaded. She had to tell Tex she was remaining here alone. "You ride on back to the ranch. I'm staying up here tonight."

He'd known, of course, when he saw that sleeping bag rolled behind her saddle, but he'd pretended not to notice until he was forced to. His scowl wasn't encouraging. "You've gone doggone loco on me again."

"If somebody wanted to slip some more double-branded cows into my herd, this would be a great time to do it. I want to see that it doesn't happen."

"You're a consarned fool. I'm staying and—"

"No. You know your back won't take sleeping on the ground, especially if it does finally rain. Besides, Lettie needs you. It's better if I'm here alone. I mean it, Tex. You go home."

He mumbled and grumbled and looked like a man severely torn by conflicting loyalties, but Charlotte finally told him to go or he wouldn't have a job in the morning. They both knew she was lying through her teeth, but her lie gave

Tex the face-saving push he needed to get him up on his horse and riding for home and his beloved Lettie.

Now there was just cows and tree shadows and her. A few of the older cows had already dropped their rear ends to the ground and settled in for the evening. As the sun dropped and the breeze turned cooler, the old line shack looked more inviting. She thought of the winter spiders hiding in every crack and crevice and shivered. She'd rather bed down in the open and take her chances with the cattle thief.

The moon rose over her little campfire, big, shiny, close. A coyote howled, his cry echoing against mountain granite. She popped the cap of her thermos of coffee and drank the steaming liquid to give her suddenly chilled skin warmth. She spread out her sleeping bag; her saddle would make a backrest. She wished she'd brought marshmallows to toast over the fire. Sean had never forgotten the marshmallows, or the chocolate bars, either. He'd had a relentless sweet tooth. The thought of her father hurt . . . and yet was oddly comforting, as if she weren't out there alone.

There was a bank of clouds off in the east again, but whether they would bring much-needed rain was any-body's guess. She lay there with her head tipped up enough to watch the stars wink in, one by one. Stars that twinkled with memories of tender kisses and a sweet intimacy she'd never known with anyone except him.

No. Absolutely useless, those thoughts.

Day gave way to night. The sky darkened to indigo, the trees disappeared into indefinable shapes, an owl hooted with that curious vibrating call. When it was so dark there was nothing but shadows behind her tiny fire, she heard the soft thudding steps of a horse.

Her ears ached with listening, her eyes strained to see, her nerves vibrated. Who was out there in the darkness? The thief? Or worse?

A hat came flying in, ringed on her toes.

Luke's hat, not so pristine as when he'd first come to town and tried to present it to her. The band was dark with dust and perspiration. It was a country hat now instead of a city one.

Her heart accelerated, but under the excitement she felt an ancient wisdom. The hat was hers to accept or not, and the man with it. Her body stinging with the sudden surge of adrenaline, she plucked the hat off her toes and put it on her head, tilting it over her brow and leaning back against the saddle, a woman ready for a siesta.

"May I take that as an invitation?" Luke's voice was dark with amusement. But there was a note of reserve, too.

"Take it as finders keepers," she said from under the hat, her hand possessive on the brim, hoping her voice didn't betray her excitement to his ears as much as it did to hers.

He dismounted, ground-reined his horse and strolled toward her. With one finger, she tipped up the hat to watch him. He was a dark gray figure in the dark gray night, with the longest legs, the flattest belly and the broadest shoulders in this woman's universe.

Wild excitement surged in her, but with it came that tiny shiver of fear. There was nobody she would rather see walking toward her on this earth, but there was nobody who had the power to hurt her quite like Luke had, either. Why had he come?

There was nothing of her excitement mirrored in his face. He looked utterly at ease. He might have been out for a stroll. The classic planes of his cheek and jaw were as cool as the little breeze wafting across her suddenly warm cheeks. What did he want of her?

"How did you find me?" she asked.

"Radar," he said.

"And I thought that long patrician nose was only good for imperious staring over."

"Excuse me?" He stared down at her with all the mock imperiousness at his command. "Did you say *long* nose?"

"I must have said *strong. Strong* patrician nose."

His mouth quirked. He tried to control the grin, but he couldn't. That smile was so darkly attractive that it made her toes want to curl. "Am I forgiven, then?" he asked.

"Yes. As long as you forgive me."

"Well, this was easier than I thought it would be. Mind if I share your sleeping blanket? Just to sit for a while."

Her toes did curl, and so did her nerves. She didn't want to be misunderstood. Yet how could she calmly move over to make a place for him and pretend there had been no kisses shared on a night just like this one? "As long as you take your boots off first and bring your own pillow." She wriggled her toes, glad it was dark, glad he couldn't see how just looking at him, hearing his voice, made her cheeks heat and her hands chill. He'd obviously stopped by for a talk, nothing more. She must match his light attitude, no matter how hard it was.

He tossed his saddle down opposite hers, shed his boots and settled down facing her. "This is cozy. Just us and a few hundred cows."

The slightly cynical tone made her laugh. "Not exactly the Ritz."

"A much overrated hotel."

"You've been there?"

He leaned back on his elbows and gazed at the stars. "Yeah. I'd rather be here. Not many places can compare to a night like this."

Something flitted across his face, a darkness. He was gone from her, thinking of things she'd never see or know. "You've seen so much that I haven't."

He was silent for a moment. Then he looked at her. "It's an illusion. You know that, don't you?"

"I don't know what you mean."

"When you haven't been somewhere, it seems like all you need in life is to see that new place, meet those new people. But after you do, you realize that new place and those new people are just another version of the old place and the old people, only they don't know you as well, or care about you as much. And you think maybe you've lost something you'll never get back, and you wonder if there's any place in the world that will feel right to you again."

"This place feels...right to me. It could to you, too, if you let it." She watched him, holding her breath.

"You're one of the lucky ones," he said. "You know who you are and where you belong." He reached up to brush off her hat and run his hand down the long length of her hair. "Lucky Charlotte."

She smiled, lifted her chin, struggling to keep her mind on her words when his hand kept sliding sensuously over her hair. "Lucky isn't exactly the way I think of myself these days. I may not be in my place much longer, if someone has their way. I—I suppose you heard about the branding iron."

He shrugged his shoulders, but she knew he meant yes. He gazed into the night, his hand still sliding down her hair absently.

"Who do you think is doing this to me?"

He shook his head, his concentration returning to the hand that he ran down the length of her silky tresses. He seemed to be testing the weight of her hair, the thickness. She'd never had anyone touch her with such total absorption. Yet he seemed as distant as a star. She wanted to touch him in response, but she knew it wasn't what he wanted. He wanted her to pretend that he wasn't touching her, that he wasn't lifting her hair and letting it fall against her shoulder over and over again.

She struggled to keep the conversation going. "It—it was really nice of you to speak to Clarence on my behalf."

He looked at her then, as if he had come awake. His hand fell away from her, and his face took on the look of a dark angel's. He relaxed back from her, and she felt the loss of his touch and his closeness acutely. "I'm not nice, Charlotte. I've lost the habit. Cured, shall we say, by experts?" Surprising her mightily, he reached down and picked up her stockinged foot and enclosed it in his warm palm, almost as if he had to keep touching her in whatever way he could. With a casual surety, as if he had done it for her a thousand times, he pulled her foot across his thigh and began to massage her sole, rubbing his thumbs around and around on the ball of her foot.

His hand was warm and intimate, his face cool and expressionless. She was confused, afraid to hope, and more aroused than she'd ever been in her life. "You haven't been cured of being nice, Luke. You think you have, but you haven't." The dark helped her say what she needed to say, with only the owls listening and the whisper of the cottonwoods down by the creek and her little fire throwing just enough light on his face to make him recognizable, turning his eyes into dark pools.

Luke knew he was treading in dangerous water. He just wanted to look at her, be with her, touch her. He wouldn't ask anything of her. He had no right. But when she looked up at him with those eyes shining, and that long hair draped over her shoulder where he'd left it, he felt as if his heart were going to leave his chest. He didn't like the feeling. It disturbed him, irritated him, that she had such a hold on him. She'd drawn him here. Now she was looking at him with her heart in her eyes and he knew he had nothing left of his heart to offer her. "Don't be fooled by my genial facade, darlin', or make the mistake of thinking I'm the same naive boy you once knew. There's nothing I can do to help you."

Always sensitive to his tone of voice, Charlotte shivered, chilled through and through. She moved her foot, asking for release. He opened his hands and let her go, his mouth twisting a little, as if he'd expected her withdrawal.

She wasn't finished with him. "Forgive me for being confused," she said, her voice crisp. "If you don't want to be...involved with me, why did you come?"

"Looking for the right place to be, I guess." That cynical tinge was back in his voice again. "God knows it isn't here. I guess I'll have to keep on looking."

"This is your home—"

He gave her that flash of a glance, that twist of his head. "No. Not anymore. This is your home, not mine. I don't think it ever was."

He leaned back, away from her. He wasn't touching her anywhere, and she felt the loss dreadfully. He said, "So. I tried God's country and I tried man's city and I don't like either of them. I tried ambition, living by the ten-year plan, having goals, being motivated, dressing for success, and I was an abysmal failure at all of them. Maybe I'll try sloth for a while, see how good I am at that."

"You haven't failed, Luke. You just...got another piece of your education."

He laughed; it was an amused, ironic sound. "You must be the absolute epitome of the power of positive thinking."

Quick as a wink, she shot back, "I've stood up against your father all these years, haven't I?"

"Yes, you have. And for all these years, you've believed in me. That should give you the award for optimist of the year. The worst of it is, I don't deserve your faith in me."

"Sometimes we get things whether we deserve them or not." She smiled at him, a flash of sweetness in the fire-light.

He burned to touch her again, now, quickly, before he lost his nerve. Her skin glowed, her hair was dark as coal in the little light from the fire. She sat with her knees up and her hands clasped around them, but he could see her bare throat under her shirt and the satiny skin that promised sweet curves below. He told himself it was wrong, wrong, to reach for her when he had nothing to give her in return, but his body didn't listen, and his hand doubled into a fist and he brushed his knuckles lightly over hers where they rested on her knee, once, twice. "So, having duly warned you off, I can't, as you may have noticed, keep my hands off you."

She caught his masculine hands in her smaller, feminine ones. He had lean, graceful fingers, a callus on his thumb pad. "They are nice hands. They feel very good...on me. They feel...right."

"Don't," he murmured, reaching out to brush his fingertips over her cheek, kindling a flash fire in her. His eyes claimed hers, taking them, holding them.

"Don't...what?"

"Don't be so damn wonderful."

"I'm sorry. I duly promise I'll be rotten to the core from now on." And she smiled.

"I'd better go," he said, but he was caught on her smile.

"I suppose so." Her eyes shone, and she reached for-ward and took his hand in hers. "Before you leave, I'd like...to give you a kiss like the one you gave me." And she brought his hand up to her mouth and kissed his palm, then let her eyes love his face while she folded his fingers over it. "You don't have to wait for the mate. You can have it now, if you like." She took his other hand and kissed it as she had the first. When she saw the dark gleam, the flare of excitement that at last matched hers, she knew she must seize this one chance. She must make it impossible for him to walk away from her. Her heart pounding with fear and excitement, she carried his hand to her breast, cupped his palm on her and pressed her hand on top of his. "Don't go. Stay with me, Luke. Let me be your home for just a little while."

He made a sound in his throat, a sound she'd never heard before in her life, half exultant, half agonized. Slowly she lifted her arms, letting him lean into her, taking the hard weight of him onto her soft chest. He was totally unfamiliar, yet familiar. This was what she'd wished for for so long, Luke heavy on her breasts and his brown eyes ablaze.

He tried one last time to keep her safe. "This is total insanity. You know that, don't you?"

"Yes."

"We both know better."

"I know."

At last his arms came around her and he buried his face in her hair. "You feel like my safe harbor. Maybe you always have been. Maybe that's why I was lost at sea."

His murmur was so low, she almost didn't hear him. It seemed such a part of the rustle of the cottonwoods, the whisper of the night zephyr. And so was his touch, drifting lightly over her, discovering the hollow of her throat. She wasn't afraid. She'd never been afraid of Luke. She was only afraid of herself, afraid she'd ask too much, love too much. She could not, would not, ask for more than he was willing to give. "I must have been a lighthouse in my other life."

Deliberately he unfastened her shirt, his eyes on hers as he guided his hand over the soft fullness of her, slipped his fingers under her bra strap to let his hands slide farther down on the roundness of her breast underneath the white cotton. "You don't feel like a lighthouse." When he heard her soft, sudden intake of breath, his smile disappeared and he said, soberly, seriously, "Ah. The brave lady isn't quite so brave as she thought."

She shook her head. "No. I'm ... all right."

His fingers were cool, bringing the chill of the night air to her burning skin. She wanted, really wanted, to be sophisticated about this, but every nerve cell she had was crying out with excitement, and she felt as if she were going up in flames. But just when she would have told him to wait a bit, he said softly, "Stay with me, love. You're doing beautifully," and he slipped his hand between her skin and the cloth and cupped her completely in his warm, competent hand. And, that quickly, he took her heart into his keeping.

"Better now?"

She was filled with a white heat that spiraled upward, and there was no strength in her to speak. She could only nod.

"Mmm ..." he said. "Better for me, too. But if we just did this—" His clever hands lifted her, flicked her bra loose and easily moved the fabric aside. The sensual exquisiteness of having him bare her breast, lift and settle her again in the curve of his arm, where she would be easily accessible to his mouth, made her body ache with longing, and she was full and ready for him when he found her.

It was a sensation like none she'd ever had in her life, the heat, the moistness, the slight tug at her breast, his hair brushing her naked skin. It seemed to go on and on, while he simply settled in, calling on his natural stamina and athlete's ability to pace himself. She didn't have his ability. She moved, asking for release from the exquisite torture of his mouth.

He lifted away then, a slight frown on his forehead. "Let's make you a little bit more comfortable." He pushed the saddle away and, his gaze steady on hers, he pulled her

shirt loose from her jeans and unbuttoned the last two buttons. "You need a pillow." He slid her arms out of her shirt,
folded it and tucked it under her head. When her bra was
gone, she lay there, bare in the heat of his eyes. "Beautiful," he breathed. "But, darlin'..." His eyes sparkled with
humor. "How extraordinary. You have another one." The
darkest, most sensual smile she'd ever seen curved his lips
as he leaned down over her and taught her other breast to
love his mouth, to love his tongue. She felt herself lift,
writhe, implode, under his caressing. "Luke, please—"

He lifted his head, and his mouth and eyes had the look
of a man satisfied with his work. "You could return the favor, love." She stared up at him, unable to process the
words.

"Mine aren't as nice as yours, but maybe you won't
mind." He unbuttoned his shirt, took her hand and placed
her palm against his chest. Pleasure flooded her from a new
source, his heated skin, the crisply male hair, the hard jut of
his collar-bone, the nub of his nipple rising to her touch.

The stars reeled, a coyote called, a cow mooed. Her
heightened senses heard, felt, saw. Her jeans gave, and cool
air rushed in. His hand smoothed over the flatness of her
belly and then, inevitably, down into the dark curls and the
feminine sweetness of her. She swallowed once, twice, held
on to him while he explored and caressed with a tender delicacy that swamped her senses. Luke's back was smooth and
hard with muscle, and over his shoulder the moon turned his
hair to a black silk and his face to the shadowed magnifi-
cence of a man poised on the edge of possession, his eyes
black with desire.

"Charlotte," he said softly, his mouth against her cheek,
and her name was the stuff of a thousand years of longing.

She shook her head, and he drew back. "No," she has-
tened to say. "I didn't mean that you should stop. I

152 A COWBOY IS FOREVER

meant...don't stop to ask. Don't let me think. Just...love me.''

And he gathered her up carefully, and his mouth sought hers, gently at first, and then, as he felt her bonelessness, her yearning, her yielding, he took her mouth as he would her body, filling and thrusting. She opened to him, equal to his desire, catching him and holding him. He finished undressing her with infinite care, sliding her jeans from her as easily as if they were silk. And while her body burned, he stood, stripped off his clothes and lay beside her, long, lean, naked, male. He asked her the silent question and she gave him the silent answer. His eyes dark and ancient with the primitive knowledge, the memory of primal mating, he lifted her over him, settling her on him, watching as she took him deep inside her.

''All right?'' he asked, his eyes very wise, old as the hills around him with the ancient knowledge of her.

She nodded, not wanting to meet his eyes, not wanting him to see the ecstasy in hers, the burning, the deep satisfaction, the total surrender.

But he was Luke, who would not give her quarter, and he cupped her chin and tipped her face up so that he could see her eyes. ''You feel like home,'' he breathed, and slid his hand along her thigh, making her more comfortable astride him.

He'd warned her that he wasn't the Luke she'd known, that he was no knight in shining armor, but nothing in her life had ever made her feel whole like this. She might have one night with him and nothing more, and the thought hurt desperately deep, but she would take everything this night had to give. She began to move, and Luke groaned and held her arms tight, tight, and murmured something that sounded like ''I didn't know it could be like this,'' and she sought his mouth and loved his body in ways she hadn't known she knew, ways she wanted him to remember forever.

The night turned around them, and the moon drifted higher in the sky, and the coyote cried his lonely cry, but for a little while, just a little while, she was no longer lonely, she was complete. She had Luke inside her and around her. She covered his mouth with kisses, and he returned her kisses like a man in a fever, gazing at her with the deep, vulnerable heat of man on the edge of ecstasy.

She hadn't known bliss had shades, shades of white heat and dark passion and the blazing yellow of the sun. He took her through all the shades, taught her tease and capture, taught her to kiss him in all the places her mouth would reach, taught her to love him with a wild abandon that equaled his own. Most of all, he taught her what she'd always known, that he was the only one she truly wanted to take into her body, to give all that she was. And her hair fell down around him and she loved him with her body, her heart, her life.

She was like a wildflower to Luke, and he wanted to handle her with the same sweet gentleness, but she put a fire in his bloodstream, and he demanded, and she gave, until his body burned with the need to give her as much as she had given him. He'd thought he knew everything there was to know about lovemaking, and now he discovered he'd known nothing at all. He hung poised on the edge until, with a smile like Eve's, she tossed him out onto the sea and then joined him there.

Chapter Nine

Luke's arms were hard, masculine, around her. Hard not to tremble in them, hard to look into those wonderful, languorous eyes and know that she alone had put that satisfaction there... but only for tonight. Hard to feel the deep, curled strength of his chest muscles, to absorb the wild, mountain-air scent of his body vitalized with perspiration and know that there was no turning back, that she had given everything she was to this man who wanted no tomorrow with her.

Close, so close to him that she could feel him breathe. His eyes caught hers, asked the silent question, *Are you all right?*

No, she wasn't, but she'd die before she'd let him see. Pride had carried her through so many things, pride would carry her through this. "You must be uncomfortable...."

"No," he said, "not at all." His brown eyes roved over her face with penetrating astuteness, and he caught her arms, his fingers possessively gentle, locking her to him, as if he sensed that her attempt to ease her weight away was really the need to deny him that intimacy at the end of love-making that was nearly as soul-revealing. "Stay where you are."

She fought against his subtle seduction, knowing that he wanted more, knowing that she did, too. She was greedy when it came to Luke, she'd been wanting him for so long. And so, even with her heart in jeopardy, she would take all that she could, even though he wasn't hers.

As if he sensed her retreat into modesty, he reached for the sleeping bag and covered her with it, making that considerate act a continuation of intimacy. He tugged on the end, but the corner just barely covered her.

"The Ritz has short-sheeted us," she murmured.

He chuckled, his body rippling with amusement under her. She'd meant to ease the intimacy with humor, but the feel of his laughter echoing through his body into hers brought a tingle of pleasure that reached to her toes. He seemed content to stay exactly where he was, his hand splayed on her back, holding the cover in place. She knew he didn't love her, and the sooner she eased herself away from him the better it would be for both of them, but his other hand came and pressed her head into the hollow of his shoulder, and his mouth found her forehead.

"Not only that, they've let the roof leak."

She heard the words, but with her mind and heart in turmoil, they made no sense. "What?"

"It's raining, darlin'."

"You're not serious."

"I may not be serious, but that big old cloud is. As I look past your beautiful face, I see that the stars are gone and another drop just plopped on my hand. Do you want to get up and try to keep our clothes reasonably dry while we run for the shack, or just forget the whole thing and take our cold shower as it comes?''

She didn't want the reality of rain. She wanted to drift in the world where there was just the two of them. "I suppose we'd better try for the shack." But she didn't move. And neither did he.

"Is there a problem?" His mouth found the vulnerable hollow of her throat, and the curve of his smile touched her skin.

The problem was, she didn't want to leave him, but she couldn't say that. She could only let her body stay just where it was, her breasts flattened against his chest. Needing a camouflage, she seized on the first thing that came into her head. "That place may have other...tenants."

"Ah. I remember. Spiders. You really hate spiders. Rattlesnakes are no problem, you just calmly step up and shoot them, but spiders are your deadly enemies. I seem to remember a rubber spider one Halloween finding its way into the drawer of your desk at school. We heard you scream all the way up in the chemistry lab."

Charlotte didn't know whether he was purposely lightening the mood, but she suspected he was. "That *was* you! I thought so. No one else would know so exactly how to frighten the life out of me. Thank goodness Miss Parker hated spiders, too. She told me it was perfectly all right to scream, that any normal person would do the same thing. I was only in second grade then. How could you pick on a such a little girl?"

"That's all I could do to you then, tease you. Now that you're all grown up, there are so many more interesting possibilities," he murmured, kissing her nose. "And how nicely you've grown up." His hands moved down and cupped her rear end. She felt him coming to life...along with the first cool drops of rain in her hair.

"We'd better go."

He released her arms, let his hands fall back on the earth in dramatic fashion. "It's all up to you, sweet."

His darkly masculine face was shining with mock submission, his mouth lifted at one corner with amusement. He was all charm and intelligence and complicated man, and she no longer felt self-conscious. He was hers, for whatever time they had together. She kissed that sensual mouth just long enough to tease him and then sprang to her feet. Before she had time to feel ill at ease, even in the dark, he was wrapping the sleeping blanket around her.

He helped her collect her clothes, said a graphic word when he stepped on a pebble. She laughed at him, he tugged at her sleeping blanket in retaliation. She knelt with mock ceremony and held his boots for him to step into, he steadied her while she slipped into hers. Then, with him tugging at her hand, and her laughing at him in his bareness and boots, they made their way into the shack.

He was noble and heroic, a true gentleman. He had her stand just inside the door while he used his shirt to swipe at the cobwebs in the shack. She could just barely see him in the dim light from the one window, his long length of gleaming skin shining with drops of rain, his shoulder muscles moving as he worked. There was a cot, and he turned it upside down and rapped on it sharply. When at last he was reasonably certain the cot was clean and free of visitors, he pulled her into his arms. He held her for a moment, up close, warm, with that faint smell of dust clinging to him from his labors. She nestled in his arms, thinking how very long it had been since someone had smoothed the path for her. And she loved him more, though it seemed impossible. For this was the stuff real love was made of, the tenderness after the passion, and the consideration.

"I'll leave the door open for light," he said. He reached around her to push the door back, and then carefully, his arms around her to take her with him, he sat down on the cot.

The rain patted softly on the roof, and his mouth found her temple. A little gust of a breeze rattled the tiny window-pane in the one window, bringing her the moisture and coolness of his body, like pure ozone flowing over her. She opened her sleeping bag to let Luke share her warmth, and when he felt the soft curves of her breast, he gently, so gently, eased her down. Her hands showed him how to lie on top of her without crushing her, and he showed his grati-tude by burying his nose in the side of her hair and settling himself agilely over her. She touched the moist drops cling-ing to his skin, smoothed the damp silk of his hair back from his forehead. His face changed, took on that darkly sensual look, and her heart came up into her throat.

"I need to ask a very stupid, very belated question."

She petted his hair as she might have a child's. She'd wondered why he hadn't asked, why he hadn't sought pro-tection, for himself as much as for her. It seemed very un-like Luke to act first and worry later. Luke had always been overwhelmingly responsible, even as a young man.

"Do you?" she murmured. "Maybe your question isn't...necessary."

He studied her face. "You're already protected, then?" he said.

"I...had a prescription that I had been taking for irreg-ular menses, and I...started taking it again."

She tried to hide her face from him, but he used both hands to bring her head up so that she had to look at him. "When did you do that?"

She thought about trying to keep from sharing this one last bit of soul-baring. It wasn't possible. "It was after the night we went out to the lake. I . . . knew then that if you stayed, and if you asked, I wouldn't be able to say no.''

He thought of the other women he'd known, and the prevarications he'd heard, and his heart warmed and swelled and he sought her lips with his. "Sweet, honest Charlotte. Thank you for being so quick and smart and wise. And responsible." Against her mouth, he said, "You've never known how to be anything else, have you?''

"Oh, I've known," she murmured. "I just haven't had the opportunity . . . until now.''

"You *have* rather thrown caution to the winds this night, haven't you?'' He sounded amused and more than a little pleased with himself, and his hands found new territories to explore, curves and hollows in her hips and the sweet flatness of her abdomen that he treated to careful attention. "Just how incautious will you be before this night is over, I wonder?'' And suddenly, easily, he slipped inside her, joining with her again, watching her eyes as he sheathed himself inside her.

"I seem to have lost all sense of propriety," she whispered, knowing now how to move to please him, listening to his soft intake of breath as she moved her hips.

He was vulnerable to her, so incredibly vulnerable, and he raised his head and shifted his weight to let her work her magic, his shoulders tense with exquisite pleasure, his eyes closed.

"I've fallen into the clutches of a wanton woman," he said, his eyes opened now and he looked down at her. "A fate worse than death." He was smiling the smile of a dark angel, and he looked like a man more than ready to take the fate that lay in store for him, and he loved her and she him until they both lay exhausted. They dozed then, and night crept away and day returned to claim its share of the earth.

She woke to the smell of something being wafted under her nose. "What—"

"Toothpaste." He smiled looking down at her, taking a dab from the tube he held and placing it with clinical precision in the middle of her bottom lip. "I didn't have coffee, so I thought I'd try the next best thing."

She licked. It was minty. "Why is it you have toothpaste?"

"I always carry my kit with me. I got in the habit." His eyes darkened briefly. "Don't ask why. Do you have any coffee in your thermos?"

"I might have half a cup left." She wanted to ask why she couldn't ask why he always carried his kit with him. She wanted to ask him how he could talk about mundane things like coffee and look so coolly contained in his shirt, jeans and boots, his hair slicked back, his jaw smooth from shaving, but then her heart went into that slow, well-remembered thud just from looking at him. She wanted to know how he could be the lover one moment and the teasing friend the next. Most of all, she wanted to know how he could look so wide-awake this morning, his brown eyes sparkling with good humor and alertness.

"Well, that's the end of this romance. I can't abide a woman who can't conjure up a full pot of coffee out in the middle of nowhere."

"Who do you think I am, MacGyver?" She pulled the sleeping bag up over her shoulder.

"He doesn't make coffee, he makes bombs out of two bra straps and a cigarette. We are just a little testy in the morning, aren't we?"

"No, *we* aren't, just me."

In a complete change of mood from his teasing mockery, he tapped her lightly on the hip. "Get up, woman. The sun is shining, the earth is rich from the rain, and the birds are singing.''

She groaned, huddled back under the covers and decided she didn't like this man very much, even if she did love him. "You're one of those disgusting morning people."

"Are you one of those disgusting night people? You can't be. You were out early for branding."

She couldn't tell him that she had spent most of the night awake, thinking about him. "I *can* get up early. I just don't... revel it like you seem to."

He turned on his heel and strode out of the cabin. She didn't know where he was going—maybe after her half of cup of coffee. She didn't care. She just wanted to be left alone, to drift, to remember....

"Here. Use this to wash your face. You'll feel better."

He was back, all long and lean legs and lithe body, tempting even in the morning, with the sun streaming in the door behind him, making a halo behind his hair. But he was no angel. The handkerchief he held dripped wet, cold water on her cheek.

Luke couldn't have said what was driving him. How many nights had he left Elisa's arms and felt relieved to seek the privacy of his own huge bedroom? How many times had he met her the next morning at a lavishly laid breakfast table and felt an empty loneliness that only immersion in work could drive away? And now here was Charlotte, staring up at him with the owlish look of a child, her blue eyes still drowsy from sleep and his loving, and he wanted to gather her into his arms and begin all over again.

"I very much doubt if that soggy thing will make me feel better— No, wait. Don't you dare touch me with that. If I'm to be tortured, I'll do it myself."

She held out two fingers and took it from him. He controlled the smile that wanted to lift his lips when she went up

on one elbow and stared at the cold cloth without moving.
"Take a deep breath first."

She did. The darn cloth was cold as an ice cube. She
gasped and flung it back at him.

"You didn't tell me you went to the North Pole for it."

He gathered up the handkerchief without a word of re-
proach, found the back of an old broken chair to drape it
over. "You know that creek's cold with spring runoff at this
time of year. Shall I help you get dressed?" He stood over
her, his gaze roving, bright with anticipation. "Not as much
fun as undressing you, I know, but—"

She couldn't respond to that invitation. "Go away. You're
too cheerful. Come back in three hours. I'll be awake then."

"As you wish." He bowed his head, all mock humility
and self-contained pride.

Even the thought that she might have hurt him a little was
intolerable to Charlotte. She caught his hand to stop him
from leaving her. He looked down that imperiously strong
nose at her, like a butler in an English comedy. "Does miss
wish something else from her serving man?"

He hadn't known he could playact, be frivolous. Maybe
that was Charlotte's infinite appeal for him. She made him
feel like a kid, like the world had infinite possibilities. She
looked like a child, her black hair tousled from his loving,
her cheeks warm from sleep.

"Yes," Charlotte murmured. "Miss wishes a kiss."

She was watching him with eyes that demanded honesty.
So he obliged. "Miss should be careful what she wishes for.
She may get that kiss . . . and more."

For the sake of his sanity and her body, Luke tried to ease
his hand away from hers, but she tightened her hold on his
fingers. He resisted, but in the brown depths of his eyes,
encouragement lurked. She pulled on those lean fingers.

With athletic easiness that brought them into full body contact, he sprawled across her, careful not to hurt her.

He stunned her for just a moment, the reality of him, a clean male smelling of toothpaste and sunshine and clean mountain air. The sheer weight and strength of him brought a wonderful feeling to every cell in her body.

"Now that I'm powerless in your hands, will you have your wicked way with me?"

"I might consider it, if you'd let me breathe."

"Breathe all you like." His eyes told her he liked feeling the nudge of her breasts against his. And his hands. Oh, his hands roamed under the sleeping bag, familiar now with every curve of her. He knew she liked to be stroked gently just above her breast, and he knew she liked a hand to cup her rear, and he knew she liked his tongue flicking hers, just barely coming in and then out. She leaned into him, letting her hands travel the length of his spine, impatient that there was a cloth barrier between her fingers and his skin.

"Keep on, lady, and you won't get out of bed for another two hours. Much as I'd like to see to it, there's work going wanting."

He loomed above her, so familiar, so well loved, his face almost distorted by his closeness, his chin and nose large, his eyes shining, nearly black with arousal. She said, "Just like a man to think of work at a time like this."

He brushed back her hair, his fingers light as a breeze on her forehead, but there was a coolness in his eyes.

She knew she had brought back memories of his high-powered life in New York. Instantly ready to make amends, she cupped slender fingers on his cheek. "It's not a sin to be a workaholic, Luke."

"Are you sure?"

"I can't imagine you being any other way. You were always driven to succeed, to be the best. Why would you change when it came to your life's work?"

"Right. Why would I change? Maybe when I finally realized how damn silly it is to kill yourself to impress somebody else." His gaze skittered past her head. He might have been watching a dust speck drift on a sunbeam, so remote were his eyes.

Maybe you were trying to impress yourself. "Do you miss . . . working?"

He hesitated for so long she thought he wasn't going to answer her. "At first it was like cutting out my heart. Now . . . it's hard to remember what all the fuss was about. I only know one thing. I don't ever want to be that locked in again."

Her throat ached for him, for what he'd been through, for what he'd lost. Ached for the questions she couldn't ask him. *Where will you go from here?* and *How can I bear to watch you walk away?*

"So." His attention returned to her, those brown eyes suddenly wiped clean of the seriousness. "Here you are in bed with a thirty-five-year-old societal dropout. Now that I'm thoroughly cured of thinking the world will collapse unless I'm on the job, we have this decision to make. About the day, about our time and how we'll spend it. I leave it entirely up to you. If you want to stay here for the next hour or two, I've no objection."

Put like that, as a way to spend an hour or two, it chilled her blood. "I suppose we'd better check on the stock."

He rose with lithe ease. "Right you are, then." His face cool, his eyes guarded, he strode out of the cabin.

The moment he was gone, she missed him with all her heart. If she was to have a limited time with him, why not take every moment she could get? But it was too late. That tall, lean man she'd loved as long as she remembered was gone. Nothing to do but get dressed and step out into the world, where the sun was high and her cows grazed on the range.

Yet, outside the cabin door, the lingering glow that loving Luke had given her was suffused with reality. The sky was washed clean and silky blue, the grass glowed with renewed vigor from the rain. Even the cows looked a deeper, cleaner red. The sun was warm on her face with the promise of summer, and Charlotte lifted her arms to the sky and stretched her muscles to full torsion. She felt loved, and loving.

Luke tried not to watch Charlotte as if he were starving for her all over again, but it was impossible. She was dressed in her jeans and blue plaid shirt, but in that moment, when she raised her arms, she was like a young earth goddess, giving homage. He could feel her youth, her vibrancy, her well-being, as if they were his own. In this moment, he realized he'd done something he had no right to do. He had no right to make love to any woman, least of all this one, whom he'd known and cared for since she was tiny.

Damn his soul. She was young and beautiful and she had her life ahead of her. While he...as of this moment, he had nothing of substance. He'd taken her to bed without a prospect. Without a future.

Didn't slow you down much, did it?

She came toward him slowly, not hesitantly or shyly, but as if she respected his right to return to the world of separateness. In that instant of blazing blue sky and morning warmth and the sweet, sweet smell of a rain-washed earth, he caught a glimpse of the strength of her spirit. What a woman she would be, for a man who had the guts to claim her.

The wind whipped her unfettered hair around her face like black silk. He remembered the way her hair felt sliding over his chest, and instantly he flared with the need to touch.

"Did you find the coffee?"

Mundane things, sensible things. The stuff of life, to hide behind. He shook his head, gesturing toward the horse he'd saddled, feeling the rough reins in his hands. "I didn't look."

She turned away, his flat tone dashing her good mood to bits. How could he totally put away the intimacies they had shared?

She walked away from him to search for the thermos. It was easy to find, a bright spot of red next to the stone circle of her tiny, burned-out fire. Another fire had burned out, as well, for him, obviously. But she picked up the thermos, uncapped the lid, and poured out nearly a cupful of luke warm coffee.

A determined smile on her face, she swung toward him. "You're in luck."

"You go ahead. You're the one who needs to wake up." He didn't mean it as a rejection, but he saw the color rise in her cheeks, and he cursed himself. He kept forgetting that she knew him too well. There was no hiding his thoughts from her. "Charlotte..."

"Please don't... say anything." Her head came up, and her eyes glistened; she had the grace of a queen. "I'd be very grateful if you wouldn't try to explain or say any of those things people seem compelled to say when they don't know what else to do. Please, just... have the rest of the coffee. It's not too bitter."

He took the cup, but he didn't drink. "Charlotte, please listen—"

"No, I'd rather not. You don't have to apologize or...say anything you'd rather not say. As you said, I'm grown up, now. It was...my choice, as well as yours. It may...may have been a wrong choice. Nevertheless, it's been made.''

A curse rose to his lips, and he drank the coffee to stifle it.

She saddled her horse, quickly and efficiently, with those small, deft hands he remembered lazily drifting over his body with the delicacy of fine lace.... Damn! He was like a teenager, coming to life for her that quickly all over again.

It didn't help that she was digging in her saddlebag, leaning over just enough to tighten the denim over her hips.

''I have cookies,'' she said. Her voice sounded faintly husky, as if she were thinking over other things, just as he was. ''Raisin-oatmeal. Would you like one?''

''Sounds good.''

She handed him a cookie without looking at him. Her head was turned to look out at three cows gathered around the salt block. She was shutting him out. Hell, he deserved it.

''These taste just like Athena's creations. Did she give you the recipe?''

Blue eyes like diamonds flashed over him. ''Yes.''

Charlotte told herself she wasn't lying. Athena had given her the recipe, she just hadn't used it yet.

''When do you get time to work in the kitchen? Midnight?''

''No.'' She remembered then, as she hadn't before, that there was a world out there that contained Henry Steadman and that she was talking to his son. She wouldn't betray Athena to the enemy.

''So that's where the extra tray went.''

''Sometimes Athena comes for tea. And she doesn't like to come empty-handed.''

"You don't have to protect Athena from me," he said coolly. "I'm glad she's your friend. If she brings you a sweet now and then, it's none of my business."

"I just don't want you to think that she's stealing them. She pays for a part of the ingredients with her own money...."

"I wouldn't give a damn if she stole the entire contents of the kitchen and brought it to you."

He looked and sounded angry, and Charlotte realized she hadn't seen him like this since he'd come home. He'd always had such control over his emotions that it was a revelation to see him give way to irritation.

"Well, then, I guess we've about covered the topics for the day. The only thing we haven't talked about is how you're going to face your father. But I guess that isn't any of my business."

"No," he said, sounding as if he were talking through clenched teeth. "It isn't."

She snatched up the reins and pulled her horse around to head for the creek. She wanted to be away from him, the sooner the better. Gray Mist would need a drink before he started the day's work.

Charlotte reached deep inside herself for the blankness of mind she'd sought after her parents died. She needed that numbness again. It was denial, but it was survival, too.

She heard the plodding of Luke's horse behind her. His mare would have to be watered, too, before he started down the trail back to his father's ranch.

Three bright-eyed heifers, their coats the color of brick and shiny with the rain, drank at the creek. At Charlotte's approach through the cottonwoods, their heads bobbed up. Those three pairs of big brown eyes gravely watched her approach.

"Does it taste good?" she asked them.

One heifer shook her head, the way cows did sometimes when they heard a human voice, as if they believed that if they could just rescramble their brain in a different pattern, they would understand.

Charlotte rode her horse into the stream, let Gray Mist's head drop. While he drank thirstily, Charlotte watched the cows watching her. One heifer bumped the other one, as if claiming territory, and the offended one turned and butted the aggressor, shifting a hip toward Charlotte.

The heifer wore a blotched brand.

Her blood turned cold.

There was a splash. Luke's horse, right behind her.

She turned toward him. Under his hat, his eyes flickered over her. "What's the matter?"

Anger and fear and fury at the injustice of it poured through her. She felt betrayed, and a number of other things she couldn't identify. "I shouldn't have been with you last night," her voice low and furious. "I should have been out here watching."

"What the devil are you—?"

She slid off her horse and splashed down in the creek. "I'm talking about those cows. Your father's cows. With my brand plastered over them. I'm talking about stupidity, mine and his or whoever is doing this. I'm talking about idiocy and craziness and vindictiveness and—" She reached the cow, slid a hand over the brand. "How in the heck did he do it? I thought with that running brand safely in Clarence's custody, he would give up. I should have known better." She whirled around to Luke. "I should have known a Steadman never gives up."

"What are you talking about?"

"I'm talking about— Oh, forget it. You won't believe me, anyway." She moved to lead her horse out of the creek, but

Luke dismounted and grabbed her arm before she could escape him.

She looked down at his feet. "You're ruining your fancy boots."

"Screw my fancy boots. I want to hear what you have to say."

"Oh, Luke... Why didn't you just stay in New York with the criminals and the inside traders? It would have been a lot safer for you there."

"Why isn't it safe for me here?"

She wouldn't want to be on the witness stand, facing him like this. She'd bet he was just the kind to lean into the witness box with that cool, penetrating gaze and that lean body and cajole the witness into thinking this was safe ground, just before he pounced.

Well, he could pounce all he liked. She wouldn't be intimidated by his courtroom expertise. "It's... complicated here. I can't... discuss it with you."

"I thought after last night you'd be able to discuss almost anything with me."

The switch was subtle, silky. It invited her to remember the intimacy she'd shared with him, to give in to the temptation to confide. Dangerous, that feeling. If she stayed, she'd tell him everything. She tugged on Gray Mist's reins. She had to go, before she destroyed his world, and hers along with it. But he held a firm grip on the reins, and his face had that determined look that she knew so well. "Let me go, Luke."

"Why should I? Why should I let you run away? Why do you want to run away?"

She shook her head, yanked on the reins. Gray Mist shied and would have reared, but Luke held those reins with hard, accomplished hands.

"Let's talk a little bit about trust, shall we? Let's talk about why you won't trust me enough to tell me you think my beloved brother is doing his damnedest to send you to jail."

Her head flew up, and her eyes locked with his. "What gave you such a cockeyed idea?"

"You did," he said, thinking that it was only now that it all made sense to him. "I thought it was odd when you came flying across the creek to give my father a calf that would only incriminate you further. But you did it to send Nick a message, to tell him you knew and he'd better be careful. What the hell happened to give Nick the energy to carry out such a vendetta against you?"

"Nothing," she said. "Nothing happened. And Nick isn't plotting revenge."

"You're lying, Charlotte," he said. "And you're doing it badly. Don't you know I'm trained to know when people lie to me?"

"Well, it certainly would be nice if we all had your skill."

In that silence, the sun seemed to burn into Luke's back, even as the wind caressed his face. He imagined the feel of the whip of Charlotte's hair across his skin, even though he was only gripping her hands as she tried to rip the reins away from him. "I've never lied to you."

Those blue eyes seared his soul. She seemed so cool and clean, as grounded in honesty as the mountains behind her. "Let me go."

Let her go? He didn't want to. *He didn't want to.*

An astounding thought.

He didn't deserve her. He felt very much the city lawyer at the moment, full of qualifying answers and protestations and whereases and wherefores, dances sideways around the truth. Yet he hadn't lied to her, he'd been excruciatingly honest about himself. Hadn't he? He thought he'd been fair and truthful. But maybe he hadn't. Maybe he'd lied the minute he took her in his arms. God knew he didn't know much about love. Maybe he hadn't been sure of its connection to sex. At one time, he would have said sex and love were like water and oil, better unmixed. Looking at Charlotte, with the sun streaming on her hair and the mountains at her back, he felt for the first time in his life that he had it all wrong. Now he wanted to go out and slay dragons for her. God help him. "Tell me what's going on."

"Not until I can get proof."

He noticed that she'd refrained from saying Nick was innocent. "How about reasonable doubt?"

"Suppose I'm wrong?" she cried. "That would hurt your father more than ever. For a bright man, you can be very obtuse sometimes."

"It hadn't occurred to me that you'd care about hurting my father's feelings."

Those blue eyes whipped over him like lasers, but she didn't say anything.

"Ah... He is my father, after all, isn't he? Funny how you're the one to remind me of that."

"I would appreciate it if you'd release my reins."

He didn't want to. He wanted to hold on to that horse, hold on to her, and never let her go.

There had to be a way to help her. He forced his fingers to open and, with his other hand, guided his horse around to give hers room.

"What are you going to do?" Luke asked her.

"I...don't know. I just need...you to stay out of this. Don't...get involved, Luke. You won't do me any good and you'll do yourself a lot of harm."

He looked down at her, remembered when he'd been determined not to be involved. Now wild horses couldn't keep him from helping her.

"I'm already involved," he said.

"No, you're not. I don't...I don't want you to feel obligated. I can't...accept your help, Luke. Especially not now."

"Especially not now?" he murmured, smiling. "You have a rather odd sense of the order of things."

"Don't you see what an awkward place you are in already? You've...been with me. If...*when* your father finds out, he's not going to give credence to anything you say." Color bloomed in her cheeks. "He may even disown you."

"I've given up any claim to anything my father has long ago."

Chapter Ten

Open spaces and blue skies weren't enough to keep Charlotte from getting angry. Luke's stoic acceptance of his situation made Charlotte see red. He deserved more. He deserved the world. This world, with the drift of the clouds in the wide blue Montana sky stretching over his head. He sat so easy in the saddle, long-legged and supremely male, that even as desire spiraled up inside Charlotte from just looking at him, she wanted to grab his stubborn hide and shake him till his teeth rattled.

Love rose up, a love that had her gritting her teeth with exasperation. His calm acceptance of his father's rejection tore at her optimism, her belief in the justice of life. "You deserve your father's respect."

"That isn't your concern, Charlotte."

Hearing her name said in that sober, cool tone made a rush of warmth rise in her face. He didn't want her involved in his life. It hurt like a blow to the stomach. But she wouldn't be distracted. Luke was the pigheaded one here. "Why won't you claim what's rightfully yours?"

His dark frown was quick, familiar. "Nothing in this life is 'rightfully' anyone's. My father gave me life, and shelter when I was growing up. That's all I had a right to expect."

"God forbid you should want love and kindness and understanding, too."

"I didn't have your parents," he said softly. "I'm not sure I knew what I was missing until I met you."

Charlotte knew what he was doing. She wouldn't be distracted by that dark look in his eyes, inviting her to remember what they'd had together. "Why doesn't he accept you? You're independent, stubborn, unwilling to ask for help from anyone, so darn exactly like him—"

"Nothing I like to hear more."

She tried to scowl at him, but it was hard, when he was watching her with that lift of his lips. Not laughing at her, laughing at himself. "Well, at least I didn't say looking at you makes me feel old," she shot back at him.

His smile became genuine. "We can be thankful for small blessings."

He could warn her off, ply her with charm, but darn it all, she wouldn't stand by and see Luke just...accept things. There would never be a happy ending for herself and Luke, but she'd always thought there would be a resolution to Luke's lifelong altercation with his father. She'd have grabbed that particular happy ending off a rainbow if she could. "You deserve the best of everything."

His smile twisted, turned faintly self-mocking. "Yes, well, there was the time I would have agreed with you wholeheartedly. Now I'm thankful for the simple things in life— a hot shower, a warm bed, toothpaste when I need it, and a smile from a woman's lips."

"Don't try to distract me with your flowery love talk."

Her tone was ironic, and he bowed his head in acquiescence. "It isn't flowery or lovely. It's truth. That's the way truth is. You're an eternal optimist, Charlotte, and I like that about you. Your belief that everything is going to be all right is as much a part of you as your breathing, and I wouldn't change it for the world. Unfortunately, I'm a realist. I've been one for a long time. I find that's what works for me."

She ached to tell him that being an optimist was darn hard work, when nearly everybody she loved had gone away, including him. If he really loved her, he'd want her in his future, no matter what his life had been like in the past.

She couldn't hate him for not loving her. And she couldn't hate herself for loving him. She had let him into her life, knowing full well that she could have only what he'd give her. Maybe her heart hadn't been listening. "I was wrong about you resembling your father. You've got more in common with Dad's old mule."

She sat very still in the saddle, knowing, really seeing for the first time, that she'd been foolishly naive, that despite her conscious, logical acceptance that Luke was simply passing through her life, she'd harbored that ancient woman's hope deep in her heart that making love with her would show him how good they were together, how right it was for them to be together always. Now, in the bright light of day, all the intimacy gone, dashed on the rock of her hope, she knew the truth. Luke was a sophisticated man. He'd taken what she offered. But the game, as he played it, didn't mean a thing. The loving, the laughter, the high joy, he'd given her freely, as a once-in-a-lifetime gift. And that was all it was.

Charlotte gritted her teeth and whirled Gray Mist around to send him in a dead run toward the ranch. Suicidal, this flying gallop across the range, yet she couldn't have stopped if she wanted to. Earth flew by her, sky flew by her, and the pounding of her horse's hooves seemed to beat in her brain—

A rock-solid hand whipped out from somewhere beside her, snatched up her reins and pulled hard. Those hands meant business. His will over hers. Much as she wanted to resist, Charlotte knew that if she did, Gray Mist would get the worst of it. Already her thigh and leg was scraping against Luke's and the two horses' flanks were bumping together.

Experienced old cow pony that he was, Gray Mist answered Luke's determined order and reared his head back, coming to a quick stop that nearly unseated Charlotte when Mist's rear end slid sideways.

The horses settled; still, Luke looked considerably less self-contained than he had a moment ago. "What do you think you're doing, trying to kill us both?"

She glared up into Luke's darkly beautiful face. "You didn't have to come haring after me."

"Where are you off to in such a hurry?"

"Getting on with my life. Alone. That's what you want, isn't it?"

He should have known she'd gotten the subtle message he sent. He'd thought that was what he wanted, her getting on with her life and he with his, but after seeing her flying across the grass on the way to killing herself, he'd discovered he didn't want her going off alone at all. But if he told her that now, the words would sound conciliatory and false. "I'm beginning to think you're more like that Thoroughbred horse than I thought you were."

"Well, being a mule and a Thoroughbred makes us a very mismatched pair. Good thing we weren't planning to climb into the traces together."

Climbing into the traces with her suddenly seemed like a good idea. "Yes, isn't it?" he drawled, those dark brown eyes locked with hers.

"Let go of my horse."

"Not till you tell me where you're going."

"It's no concern of yours." She threw his words back into his face, her eyes hot with defiance. When he simply sat and held on to her, she clapped her hands over his and wrestled with him for possession of the reins. He held fast and let her struggle, thinking she was a hell of a handful and he was crazy to take her on but at the moment it didn't seem like he had much choice. "You're not going anywhere until you tell me what you plan to do."

She stopped struggling, but her cheeks were rosy with her fury. "I'm not on the witness stand here. Let go of me."

Luke leaned forward a little, and sexual awareness flared like lightning and flooded every cell of Charlotte's body. He was dark and close and beautiful, and she ached to fit that hard mouth to hers, to cool the conflagration in her—or send the flames higher.

He smiled, but she didn't like the tenor of his amusement.

"You wouldn't by any chance be off to face down my brother Nick on the streets of Two Trees like something out of *High Noon,* would you?"

"Why not? I already faced down one brother and lost. Why not make it two for two?"

"You haven't lost with me, Charlotte."

"Please don't lie to me. We've always had honesty between us. Let's keep that, at least."

She moved to rein her horse away from him, but he held her mount steady and said, "Promise me you won't confront Nick."

"Don't you think I would have done it months ago if I thought it would do any good? He's too darn volatile for that. He—"

She caught a glimpse of the sudden flare of darkness in Luke's eyes, and she clamped her mouth shut. It was too late.

His face cool and very, very controlled, like his voice, he said softly, "He's always been very careful to keep that side of himself hidden from everybody. How did you find out about my brother's . . . volatility?"

"That's none of your concern."

He took the blow without flinching, thinking it was no less than he deserved. His hands tightened on hers ever so slightly. "My best guess is something happened during that ill-fated Christmas good-will-to-men peacekeeping mission of yours, and you're not going anywhere until you tell me what it was."

"Nothing happened. We just agreed to disagree, that's all."

"What else? There has to be something else."

"Well, he started to get slurpy, and it was all so fake that he made me really angry, so I waited just long enough to catch him off his guard, then I pushed him out of his car and slammed the door shut and locked it. I drove his car home and parked it at the bottom of the drive to Henry's house. I thought the walk home would do him good. It was only a couple of miles. Well, maybe three."

The light of laughter came into Luke's eyes. "I would have given up my Christmas bonus to see that." And he did see it, in his mind's eye. He saw how furious Nick would have been, how even Henry would have been aware that Charlotte had gotten the best of Nick. He knew from his long experience with Nick how avidly eager his brother would be for revenge—and to what lengths he'd go to achieve it.

Beyond Luke, back by the creek, a branch rattled, the pale green leaves vibrating in a way that had nothing to do with the tender, rain-misted breeze. A horse emerged, sashaying sideways, looking skittish and jumpy. It was the jet-black gelding that Nick rode, its saddle empty, the stirrups dangling. With a lot more thrashing and a lot less finesse, Princess burst through the brush, trotting after the black, as if her newfound, quicker-footed friend were trying to leave her behind.

"What the—?"

The bushes rattled again, and Nick came bursting through. His always flawless hair was tousled, and his face was dark with irritation. He growled something Charlotte was glad she couldn't understand, and then he pivoted around to snatch his hat back from the branch where it was caught.

Luke looked very serious, but Charlotte knew it was costing the man dearly to keep his cheek muscles under control. She could feel all her own anger dissolving in the urge to smile.

"That damn cow is the daughter of the devil." Nick smoothed his hair and settled his hat on his head.

"Speak of the devil," Luke murmured to Charlotte, "and there he is. Courtesy of the cutest little bovine bar crasher in the West." He raised his voice to speak to Nick. "She flushed your horse out of that bush like quail. What were you doing . . . standing in the bushes spying on us?" Luke leaned back in the saddle, his eyes half-closed. He looked as if he weren't interested in much of anything, but Charlotte bet he'd noticed that Nick's horse's legs were dark with damp.

Nick's face cleared, and he looked very sure of himself, as if denial after getting caught red-handed was an old game for him. "I didn't even know you were here," Nick said, very evenly, swinging himself into the saddle, looking much happier to be able to meet their eyes on the same level. "I was checking on our cattle. Taking care of the ranch's busi-ness." Nick's gaze wandered to Charlotte, and his mouth took an unpleasant tilt. "A concept that seems to be foreign to you, brother. What have you been doing? Or do I need to ask? You didn't come home last night. Hard to believe you stayed out in the rain all night. Did you find shelter somewhere?"

"Aren't you on the wrong side of the creek?" Charlotte asked coldly.

"I wouldn't be, if your damn cow hadn't startled my horse and chased him over here."

"I'll have to buy Princess another beer the next time we're in town together," Luke murmured. "Turns out she's got more class than I thought."

"I'll throw in a glass of champagne." For Charlotte, it was hard to look at Nick's saturnine face and remember he was related to Luke. And yet there was a family resemblance in the shape of Nick's jaw, the brown depth of his eyes, the coffee-brown hair. That resemblance had fooled her into thinking that Nick could be talked out of this insanity. Now, watching Nick stare at Luke, his eyes hot with jealousy, Charlotte realized she had confused resemblance with likeness.

She'd make Nick think about something other than his hatred for Luke.

"We found the cattle you cut out last night, Nick."

Out of the corner of her eye, she saw Luke's horse move, as if he were directing his mount to come between Charlotte and Nick.

"Charlotte—"

She ignored Luke. Her concentration was on Nick. "But then, I suppose you wanted us to find them."

Nick's face took on that blank, innocent look he could do so well. "I don't know what you're talking about."

"The new cattle you branded with my brand. Where did you get the second branding iron?"

"You must be crazy." He moved to ride off.

"You're the one who's crazy," Luke said, "if you think you can get away with more of this stupidity." Luke's eyes were so cold that even Charlotte was taken aback by the damped-down force, the cold control.

Nick lifted his head and managed to look nearly as cold as Luke, with an added measure of contempt. "I always knew you never really thought of yourself as my brother. This proves it. If you're willing to side with a two-bit hustler like her—"

"I warned you once before to watch what you said about Charlotte in my presence." Luke moved his horse closer to Nick's. "Now I'm warning you again. Don't push me, brother. When I think about those two cows you botch-branded last night, I find I'm not exactly filled with fraternal charity for you."

"When did you ever feel charitable toward me? You're no brother of mine." Nick wheeled his horse around and, with a yank on the reins, skirted Princess and sent the black flying back across the grass toward the creek.

When Nick reached the safety of the trees, he slowed the black down and turned him around quietly. He wanted to see what they were doing, his traitorous brother and the little cheat. They were still sitting there talking, looking all cozy and close. Well, he'd give them something to talk about, all right, and real soon.

"I want to know what *slurpy* means, Charlotte. Tell me exactly what happened between you and Nick."

She shook her head. "It was nothing."

"I thought you said you wanted the truth between us."

He sat in the saddle, very straight, his eyes shielded by his hat. His face was cool and emotionless, but she knew she'd hurt him. "Oh, Luke. You must know your brother better than that. He'd parked on the side of the road, and by the time he put the car in neutral, I was braced. He just pulled me over to his side of the car and tried to kiss me. I resisted, and when he wouldn't stop, I leaned on the car horn. He jumped off that seat sky-high, and I reached across, opened the door and pushed him out. He got to his feet, but when he came toward the car, I just shoved it in gear and drove off. The only possible damage he could have suffered was to his ego. I didn't tell anyone about it, not even Lettie or Athena. The one person who might have guessed what happened was his father. I didn't think it was anything, at least not then. What's new about a Steadman and a Malone having a brawl? It was only afterward, when he looked at me in church or in town, with that—look he has, like he was envisioning me frying in a pot of hot oil and he liked what he saw, that I realized his reaction was rather... strange, more intense than it should have been. I suppose if I had thought about it, I should have known Nick doesn't suffer insult lightly. It just didn't occur to me at the time."

Luke lifted his hand, trailed a finger down her cheek. "You'd better be telling me the truth. You'd better not be making this sound like less than it really was to keep me from hurting my brother."

She lifted her head, her hair blowing wild and free in the breeze. "I wouldn't lie to you, Luke."

"I know that."

He dropped his hand, and Charlotte felt the cooling of her skin where he'd touched her, followed by the longing for more touching racket through her system. She wanted to ask whether she would see him again, but her pride wouldn't let her.

Her eyes betrayed her.

"I'm sorry it's daylight, too," he said, and cupped her chin with a firm, warm hand, as if he needed to touch, too. "Unfortunately, there's something I need to tend to."

"What—what are you going to do?"

"I think I'll pay a visit to the local constable. While I'm gone, behave yourself, hmmm? Stay on your side of the creek."

She struggled to follow the shift of mood with him. "Don't worry. I'm not going to play the Lone Ranger without my Tonto."

He caught her fingers. "Don't put me off with that good humor of yours. Promise me, Charlotte." He studied her face. "And no crossed fingers, either."

"Promise. With no crossed fingers. Now you promise me something. Promise you'll come and tell me about your talk with Clarence." She said the words lightly enough, but her heart was in her throat.

"Done. I'll come by later this evening." He said the words lightly, too, but there was a promise in his eyes.

She watched him ride away, tall and easy in the saddle, and she knew he was taking all her heart with him.

"I don't know how you practiced law in the big city, but we're real careful here before we accuse anybody of anything without solid proof." Clarence Daggett pulled a booted foot off his desk, where it had been resting, and let the front legs of his chair drop to the floor.

"That's how we practice it in the big city, Clarence. That's why I want you with me—"

"As for staking out that mountain country, if you think I can do that single-handed, all I got to say is, you been away too long, old friend. Too damn much territory for one man to cover. Be crazy to try. Besides, it wouldn't do any good. We both know whoever is doing this is local. If I went out like that, everybody in five counties would know it before I got halfway up that dang mountain."

Luke sat with a hip on Clarence's desk, looking coolly relaxed, but feeling frustrated. He knew there were advantages to keeping the law in a small town, but there were disadvantages, too, dammit. "We're in a gridlock here, Clarence. The hell of it is, it's all been done with smoke and mirrors, like magic. Somebody is creating the illusion of theft without actually taking anything."

"Hell, I knew that. Why do you think I haven't hauled Charlotte in?"

"So what are our alternatives?"

"Sit. Wait. That's about all we can do until we get something concrete." Clarence slanted a look up at Luke, and his chair creaked under his weight. Sitting and waiting was something Clarence did well. It wasn't Luke's forte.

"Sometimes that works, sometimes it doesn't. I keep wondering what's going to happen when our ersatz thief decides to escalate." Luke picked up a paperweight from Clarence's desk, shook it, watched snow scatter over a perpetually smiling kid with a sled and a dog.

"How would he do that?"

Luke set the paperweight down carefully. "How do you know it's a he?"

"Don't try your fancy-dance word shufflin' with me. We both know it's a he. And we both know who the he is."

"Do we? I thought we needed evidence."

"I don't need evidence to know," Clarence snorted. "I need evidence to arrest. You think he's going to do something worse?"

"That's what bothers me. I don't know."

"Something to hurt Charlotte?"

"It's possible."

"Hell, Luke, I don't even have a deputy."

"You could swear me in."

Clarence moved in his chair, looked uncomfortable. "I'd rather not."

"Why not?"

"I know you're a big-city lawyer and all that, but you've been away awhile, Luke. Suppose I deputize you and—"

"And I turn out to somehow be involved."

Clarence turned a little pink around the cheeks, but he held his ground. "Let's wait a little bit to see how this all shakes out."

Luke slid off the desk, gathered up his hat. He didn't say a word, just headed for the door.

"Luke!"

He turned back, waited, silent, watching. Clarence wriggled his rear end, looked disconcerted. "Don't do anything I wouldn't do. I'd hate like hell to haul you in." He looked sheepish. "Mary Lou would give me what-for."

Luke remembered Mary Lou; she'd been a pretty girl growing up, a cheerleader. "Give Mary Lou my regards, and tell her she's married to Montana's finest." Luke gave Clarence a salute and sauntered out the door.

Luke levered himself into his car, his hands gripping the steering wheel. He was damn sure tired of running into brick walls. Funny. He'd lived here all his life, and he couldn't think of a way to proceed. Maybe the technique for setting up one's own brother didn't come easily to anybody, even a man like himself, who had no special love for Nick. Heaven knew he was reluctant to turn his mind to the task. Nick was his brother, for God's sake. His own flesh and blood. And for just a moment, Luke felt a blinding flash of insight.

That must be how his father had felt all these years.

Then, of course, there was that other promise he'd made to himself. He'd decided long ago that he'd never get in an altercation with his nearest and dearest again. Luke rapped the heel of his hand against the steering wheel of the car. Charlotte was right. He should have stayed in New York with the inside traders and the carjackers.

Chapter Eleven

"I was looking for you."

For Charlotte, the heat in the barn suddenly intensified. At the sound of Luke's voice, low and controlled, like satin rasping over sandpaper, the colt she held moved restlessly in Charlotte's arms. "You found me."

That wonderfully sensual smile lifted his lips as Luke came toward her in an easy walk. "Not yet, but I will," he murmured.

"Behave yourself. I'm working here." Charlotte ducked her head and returned her attention to the colt, who'd had the misfortune to poke his nose at a porcupine, but she was suddenly and acutely aware of the heavy scent of new hay drifting in the air, mingled with the scent of clean man. Fresh from his shower, Luke smelled like the air after rain. His shirt was open at the throat, a beige cotton shirt that looked as if it had gone to the office once but now was old and comfortable from many washings. His jeans still had that new look, but they fit him well. Very well. Her mouth went dry. Her unruly mind would remember what it had been like to be so alone with him that it seemed as if they were the only two people on the planet.

She hadn't wanted to fall in love. But it had happened so long ago, she had no defense against Luke's charm then. She had even less now. The sensitive, savvy little colt felt her tension and shifted restlessly in her grip. "Easy, sweetheart."

In a whisper of denim, Luke knelt down, tightening the legs of his jeans over his muscular thighs. "I see our baby poked his nose where it didn't belong."

"He's too curious for his own good. Like most other babies, I guess."

"You can't possibly be suggesting that our wonderful, unique baby is just like other babies." His eyes gleamed with amusement.

"I'm sorry. I lost my head." Her heart did that little flip-flop that it always did when she thought about "our baby." There would never be an "our baby," but it was still a heart-wrenching idea. Charlotte wrapped careful, gentle fingers around the last quill, to extract it with as little hurt to the colt as possible.

Without being asked, Luke handed her the unguent in its flat container, his fingers long and lean against the black-and-red cover.

The colt didn't like the idea of someone touching his nose with salve. In an instant, Luke was there to lean over the back end of the colt and hold him steady for Charlotte's ministrations, all the time keeping an eye out for those sharp little hooves that shot out instinctively.

Funny how just having Luke there sent sensations rocketing through her. Being a smart, loving partner in bed was natural enough for Luke, but she'd forgotten that city life hadn't taken the country out of him. Working together with the animals for the corporate good of the ranch and family was like being a husband and wife. It was far too evocative of every dream she'd ever had in her life, and as arousing as the memory of those long-fingered hands on her breasts. Working with him in easy concert like this would be painful to remember once he was gone.

"You put one more swipe of that salve on his nose and he's going to drown in it."

"Oh, right, sorry, I wasn't thinking—" The trouble was, she had been thinking, but not about the colt.

He handed her the towel, his eyes warm, questioning. She wouldn't let him probe for answers. She took the darn towel, wiped her hands, turned her back to those brown eyes that had suddenly gone three shades darker, taking her time draping the towel over the stall. She said, "Thank you for your help."

"You're welcome." Still watching her as if he had her on the witness stand, he said, "We're a good team."

She shook her head, then turned to leave the stall. Luke caught her arm, his fingers warm on her wrist.

The colt bobbed his head nervously, whickering low in his throat for his mother. He didn't want to be alone anymore. And, darn it all, neither did Charlotte.

Lady Luck responded with an answering whicker, but she couldn't get to the colt, tied as she was across the aisle in another stall.

"Want to tell me what's bothering you?"

Best to get it over with quickly. "I sold the colt to Carson Dole."

Luke didn't flicker an eyelash. "I would ask why, but the answer is obvious. You need the money."

"Yes."

"He's yours to do with as you wish, of course." He looked like a man with a face stripped clean of emotion. It was for the best, Charlotte knew, but it hurt to think that

Luke could suspect her even for a moment. Then, as if his mind had ticked over with the answer, he said, "You needed the money for Tex and Lettie."

His shoulders relaxed and his face took on a more normal look even before she said yes. She turned away, reached for the lid of the unguent container. For just a moment there, he hadn't believed in her. But what did it matter? There was no future in his believing in her. "I might have needed the money for a new hay baler, or repairs to the barn roof. Would that make a difference?"

"Charlotte." He took the container from her, set it down on a hay bale and reached up to smooth her hair back. Suddenly, all the doubts, the sad emotions, were gone. He was here, and he was touching her. Luke always could do that to her, make her feel as if nothing mattered but this moment with him. "I want to offer to help you financially, but I know if I did you'd throw me right out of this barn."

Of course, she smiled. "You're learning, Mr. Steadman."

"I like the teacher." He leaned forward to brush his lips over hers, once, twice, lightly, so lightly. Just that easily, they progressed beyond being first-time lovers and became, somehow, lovers who were friends. There was choice for her in the touch of his mouth, and yet there was male determination to take more, if she was willing to give. She answered him by going up on tiptoe and wrapping her hands around his shoulders.

Her scent drifted to his nose, clean and fresh, like June strawberries growing wild in a pasture. He released her, murmuring, "Don't you know I'd give you the moon if I could?" When it hit him what he'd said, he felt stunned. He'd said those very words to Richard so long ago about this wonderful female, who'd been nothing more than a child then. He hadn't known he would be the man to worship at her feet. Or maybe, in some deep part of him, he had known.

The deep hunger clawed at him to bring her close. Luke lifted her to align her breast, hip and thigh to his and lowered his head to taste her mouth once more.

If he kept holding her as if she were life and breath and air to him, they wouldn't have a prayer of making it to the house. "I have a whole field of hay to bale this afternoon."

He didn't miss a beat. "There's real sex talk."

"Would you rather I tossed you down in the hay and had my wicked way with you?" She smiled, and her eyes sparkled and caught all the light available in that dark barn, burning into his heart.

He raised an eyebrow. "It's been my opinion that rolling around in the hay is a much overrated activity. Hay is dusty and full of sharp ends. I much prefer a bed."

"A man after my own heart. Now if— Hey!"

He dragged her outside the stall and took her down to sit with him on the bale, catching her in his lap, wrapping his arms around her, taking her back with him until his shoulders bumped up against the stall wall, making a lie out of every word he'd just said.

"What are you doing?" She made a token protest, but it was starting all over again, that high joy.

"Finding a new position." His voice was full of humor and sexual arousal, and his mouth was lifted in a seductive smile. Her breasts pressed against him, and she sat half in and half out of his lap, her legs over his, denim rasping against denim. "This one isn't too bad. With a little improvement, it just might work—"

"You're incorrigible."

He was also earthy and real—and a liar. He had that look in his eyes that a man gets when he knows the woman he wants is surrendering. He laid his hand above her breast.

"And you're delectable." He reached up to pluck a hay stem from her hair. "My own little hayseed."

The colt had shied away from them when Charlotte cried out, but now he came nuzzling to see what was going on.

"You've come to protect her honor, have you?" Luke asked the colt. "Good fellow." And, catching Charlotte's hand, he guided her fingers over the back of the colt's ear.

It was so like Luke to put his own needs and interests aside and give the colt what he needed at the moment.

She watched him, dark and lean and strong, and wondered at the miracle of sitting in his lap, being a part of his world, when for so long she'd circled the periphery. "I promised Tex I'd help him this afternoon."

Without batting an eye, Luke straightened his legs and dumped her off his lap. She let out a yelp, the colt started backward, bobbing his head, thinking he didn't understand these unpredictable humans.

From the floor, she sat staring up at him. "Was it something I said?"

"You bet."

"What—what did I say?"

"I'd rather get a rattlesnake mad at me than be the cause of Tex's further disappointment." His mouth still controlled in that droll expression, he reached for her hand to help her up.

"Coward."

"Yes, ma'am. No doubt about it."

She tried to brush at her rear, but was hampered in her efforts by his pulling her close. "I can help you do that."

She sheared off, away from him. "Thank you, but no thank you. You've proven you can't be trusted."

He cast a shrewd look at her, wondering if she was serious, deciding she wasn't. "You like being caught off guard. If I were a totally predictable man, you wouldn't give me the time of day."

"What makes you think that?" She wasn't looking at him, she was very busy brushing her backside and restoring her dignity.

"The guys you haven't married. There are quite a few of them around who'd like to be your partner. You haven't given them a look."

She kept her head bent, briskly busy with those capable hands, so damned feminine in her jeans and blue denim shirt and her dark hair falling over her shoulder when she finally straightened and met his eyes. "Maybe I was waiting for you."

There was a blast of honesty. *Deal with that, Steadman, you of the facile mind and quick mouth.* "You really are an optimist," he said. He tried to pretend her words had no effect on him, tried to shunt aside the curling in his gut that told him no woman had ever loved him the way this woman did, but the fire was there, burning, incessant. Gently he reached for her and wrapped his arms around her, breathing in her scent, hearing that slight intake of breath she made whenever he held her close. She yielded beautifully, all softness and slim pliancy, her wild-strawberry scent making him think of the night stars and laughter and toothpaste and rain. He buried his face in her hair, soaking his soul in her. "How are you today?" he asked softly. He'd been worrying about her, wondering whether she was regretting their night together, wondering if he could be with her tonight, wondering whether he was making things worse for her with his father.

"I'm...fine. Have...have you talked to your father?"

Had she taken up mind reading? "Uh-uh. Haven't been home. I'll stay and help with the hay, if that meets with your approval."

She was quiet for a moment. He found himself holding his breath. Then she said, "Oh, I don't know. That's a big favor to ask. But if you're a really good guy, maybe I'll let you go out there and get all hot and sweaty and full of hay stems.''

"You're such a generous woman." He tilted his head down to her, found her mouth. He felt her come up on tiptoe, press her breasts against his chest. Her mouth was sweet and generous under his. Nothing held back. If time and circumstances were different, he would take her with him down into the hay, stems be damned, and love her until neither of them could think straight.

He could feel her beginning to burn in his arms. He knew her well enough now to know the signs, the slight acceleration of her breathing, the tension under the surface of her skin. He fit her to his body, knowing she'd feel his desire. He didn't care. With Charlotte, he felt the need to be as honest and generous with her as she was with him.

"Luke—"

"I know," he murmured. But he held her still.

Lady Luck whickered low in her throat, and a mourning dove cooed somewhere in the eaves of the barn, and Luke thought how peaceful it was to stand here like this with Charlotte in his arms.

"I wish we could stay like this forever," she murmured.

"Yes," he said.

"Luke, I have to go."

"No," he said, but he forced his hands to loosen and release her.

She stood there, looking delectably aroused, her hand fussing with the shirt button at the top of her throat. "Were you serious about helping me with the hay?"

"Yes."

Charlotte liked the look in his eyes, clear and open, as if he had nothing to hide from her.

"We'll be in the field next to your father's fence. Perhaps you should go talk to him. Nick will probably have told him about seeing us together. You could explain—"

''There's nothing to explain.'' Now he shuttered his eyes, closing her off. ''Let's go make hay while the sun shines, shall we? Where's your hat?''

He escorted her out of the barn into her house and bullied her into digging through the clothes hanging on her back porch to find a hat. He plopped it on her head and pushed it down tight. ''You're trading me a sunburn for a headache. I hate hats.''

In answer, he swatted her rear end and pushed her out the door.

''What's he doing here?'' Out in the hay field, Tex stomped around from the front of the tractor and favored Luke with a good old scowl.

''He's helping.''

Tex mumbled an expressive word that articulated his opinion succinctly, and turned away to climb up into the tractor seat.

Six hours later, inside Charlotte's house, after they dined on an omelet Charlotte had made, she sat across the table from Luke and tried not to drink him in with her eyes, but she couldn't seem to stop. He sat sprawled back in the chair, his long legs stretched out to the side of the chair, which was too small for him. His eyes were dark with tiredness, and his mouth had trouble trying to smile at her, but he did it anyway. ''I wish you'd have let me tell Tex to slow that tractor down so the bales wouldn't come out of the baler that fast.''

''Couldn't do it. Test of male strength, horns locked and all that. He'd think I was a wimp for sure, if I'd let you intercede for me.''

''He gets a little carried away—''

''Don't apologize for Tex. We need a thousand more people on the planet like him. He's stood by you through tough times, and that makes him golden as far as I'm concerned.'' His eyes caught hers, held. He might be tired, but he had enough energy to turn her heart over. "I'm glad he was there for you, Charlotte. I do...care about you."

Funny how those words, those simple words that sounded so loving, weren't enough. She rose, turned her back to him and leaned on the stove, trying to keep her insides from churning. She'd promised she wouldn't ask for more.

Reaching for a strength she hadn't known she had, she turned around. "Would you like to stretch out on the couch and take a nap before you go home?"

"Does that mean I'm not invited to stay the night?"

Her hesitation was very brief, but he saw it. "Do you think it's wise for you to consort with the enemy so...consistently?"

"You mean, Henry might forgive me for one lapse, but two nights puts me beyond the pale? I don't give a damn what Henry thinks. Will you come lie down with me? Just for a little while."

Her heart leaped, her blood sang. She knew how her face must look—illuminated. *He needed her. But just for a little while.* "I'm going back up into the mountains tonight."

"Not without me, you're not."

She didn't argue with him. She guided him up the stairs and into her little bedroom under the eaves. He looked darkly masculine there in her feminine retreat, the pale twilight flooding the room with windows dressed in white cotton ruffles. He looked even more masculine lying stretched out on her bed, whipcord-lean and muscled, his stockinged feet nudging the edge of the foot rail.

He flopped an arm away from his body. "Come here," he said. She tugged her boots off and slipped into the hollow of his body that open arm created. He rolled toward her, fitting her into his hard leanness.

"Wake me when you're ready to go."

He dozed off, breathing deeply. She lay with the feel of his body pressed against hers, his weight and warmness so exhilarating, so strange yet so familiar.

The ruffled curtains fluttered in the breeze wafting into the room, bringing coolness and the smell of new green grass and wild plum trees exploding in blossom. She would always remember this moment when he lay beside her in that vulnerable state of sleep.

When the light had turned from the golden to soft gray to dark, she slipped out of his arms and sat up to pull her boots on. It was a measure of his fatigue that he didn't waken. She stood up to turn and look at him. Heaven knew he hadn't gotten much sleep last night. The sight of him sleeping in the soft twilight made her mouth lift in a tender smile.

Charlotte rode out under the stars slowly, deciding that this once she wouldn't try to solve unsolvable problems or think about Luke, his father and her place in the tangle. She would just stretch out in her sleeping bag, watch the stars progress across the heavens, listen to the rustle of the leaves and the murmur of the water and hope she didn't hear any other sounds that night.

He watched her the whole time she rode up, chose her spot, laid out her sleeping bag. He could feel his body burn with excitement, because she was totally unaware of his presence. She was asleep now, completely vulnerable to him. He could do anything to her that he wanted to do. But he was cleverer than that, smarter, more powerful.

He knew how to hurt her.

Did she think she'd stop him by sleeping there on the ground? She was a damn fool if she did. He was going to win. He knew it. He had such a surprise for her. She'd be so sorry she'd tangled with him. Oh, yes, he'd win. He always did.

*   *   *

She came awake too suddenly, her skin crawling, as if she'd been touched by an enemy. Around her the night was filled with night music, the sighing of the wind, the hoot of an owl, the bawl of a calf. She didn't want to be alone. She wanted Luke. It struck her suddenly that she'd been alone all her life, and in only one night with him she'd learned to yearn for his presence. But he was in her room, sleeping, supremely at ease, as only Luke could be.

The room was filled with light glowing a pale gold when Luke awoke. He'd been interviewing witnesses in his sleep, taking depositions, one from Charlotte, one from Nick. Now he thrust a hand up through his hair, remembering, lying there in the soft, sweet darkness of dawn with the breeze blowing across his bare chest, knowing he was alone in the bed and wondering why. Beside him, the sheet was empty and cool. Was she in the bathroom or the kitchen? Odd, how lonely this bed felt without her, when he hadn't spent more than a few hours with her.

He rose and headed for the bathroom. He'd have a quick shower, shave, brush his teeth, get into his clothes and find her.

Fifteen minutes later, fully dressed, Luke strode into the kitchen, saw that the stove was cold. The only thing alive in the room was the swish of that silly cat clock's tail. The sun was a little higher now, and the coolness was giving way to a summer's warmth. The light streamed across the scarred maple table. There was nothing on it—no dish, no spoon, to indicate that she'd had breakfast and gone out to see about her animals.

Out in the barn, Gray Mist's stall was empty. He knew then where she was. Muttering several incisive words, Luke strode to his car. He'd have to go home to get the mare and ride up into the high country. Then he'd give in to the distinct urge he had to wring her neck.

Charlotte was kneeling by the stream when Luke dismounted and walked toward her. She was dressed in her usual faded jeans and a blue-and-white-striped cotton shirt, and she was splashing water over her face with abandoned enjoyment. Unaware of him, she lifted her face to the sky and let the water glide down her cheeks. Caught in the half shade of the cottonwoods, she had the elfin beauty of a water sprite paying homage to the purity of the brook. She heard him and turned, her blue eyes dark with a joy that made him go weak in the knees. It was damn hard to be irritated with a woman who looked like a black-haired Lorelei after sleeping out on the range, but he'd give it a go.

"I told you to wake me."

"You needed a good rest." She rose to her feet and came toward him, with that slow, graceful walk that tore his guts out. She was a naturally sexy woman, young and alive with good health. He thought of how he'd have felt if anything happened to her out here alone while he was tucked up cozy in her bed sleeping, and he really wanted to wring that pretty neck of hers.

"You're too damned independent for your own good."

He was a male in a bad humor, and bound to make his displeasure known. A lesser woman might have quailed at the sight of six feet two inches and one hundred and ninety pounds of angry masculinity. Not Charlotte. She just looked bright and full of sass. "I thought I was the one who woke up grumpy."

"What the hell do you think you're doing, coming out here alone?"

"Protecting my land," she said, and her words carried to him on the Montana wind.

He made a sound in his throat, turned back to his horse and flipped the reins over the horse's neck to ground-rein him. When he faced her, he felt a little more in control. "Don't come out here again without me."

About a hundred replies jumped into her mind, but she looked up into his darkly beautiful face and knew she couldn't say any of them. He was concerned for her. No one had been concerned for her for a long, long time.

"Nothing happened, Luke."

"That's no guarantee you'll be so lucky the next time."

"I'll be careful." And then, gently, "I've been looking out for myself for quite a while now."

Slowly, Luke's temper eased. She was all right. Nothing had happened to her. And at last, finally, none too soon, his training kicked in. If there was no agreement, it was best to change the subject. "So you didn't find any more cattle?"

"No."

"Then it was a waste of time staying out here."

"Of course it wasn't. He may have seen me, decided the risk wasn't worth it and gone away."

"Oh, there's a cheering thought."

She tilted her head, looking at him as if he were a child to appease. "Let's agree to disagree, shall we?"

Luke wasn't in the mood to be conciliated. "Nothing new about a Malone and a Steadman having an altercation." Deliberately he pulled back the cuff of his shirt and looked at his watch.

"What are you doing?" she asked.

"Wondering just how late in the day it has to be before I can have a civilized conversation with you."

"How do you feel about midnight?" she shot back at him.

"Yes, nighttime does seem to work out rather better for us."

She thought of about a thousand replies to that one, and was opening her mouth to deliver one or two when he strode to his horse, gathered up the reins and mounted.

"You're not going to run away just when it's getting good, are you?"

"I've decided it's time for me to go home and face the music," Luke said.

She sobered instantly. "Let me go with you."

All he did was look at her and shake his head.

"You're too damned independent for your own good," she said to him.

He tilted his hat to her. "One more thing we have in common."

She stood watching him ride away, torn between a longing to be with him and the sure knowledge that if she stepped into the Steadman house at Luke's side, she could very possibly set Luke's deteriorating relationship with his father in a cement that would never crack.

The tack room smelled of leather when Luke stepped inside. His father had a lamp on, with the light shining on the piece of tack he was repairing. His father had great skill working with leather, and he enjoyed the task, something few other ranchers did. He had the strip of rawhide clamped to a wooden board while he worked with his knife peeling off a thin edge.

Luke knew all about preparing a case to manipulate a witness. He didn't want to do that with his father. He wanted honesty, and a not-so-simple truth. His father was a great lover of logic and truth. It wouldn't be easy to talk to Henry, but he had a stronger reason to try again than he'd ever had in his life. "I'd like to speak with you for a moment, if I may."

"So you decided to come home, did you?" Henry raised his head, and his eyes met Luke's. If there was any reaction

at the sight of his son, Luke didn't know what it was. "You
might have done better to stay where you were."

Luke had known it wasn't going to be easy. He'd always
had a predilection for the jugular, and now he knew at
whose knee he'd learned that preference. Henry was ever the
gentleman, but he knew how to place the rapier with precision. "I wonder if, just for a moment, you could put aside
your opinion of me and we could talk about something
that's very important."

"I can't see that we have much to say to each other."
Henry went on cutting the leather with a sure and steady
hand. That evidence of his father's detachment disturbed
Luke more than his cold face.

Luke wanted to turn on his heel and walk away. He'd
beaten his head against this particular stone wall too many
times, and when he left the ranch that last time, he'd vowed
never to try again. Now here he was. Here he had to be. For
Charlotte.

"I'm afraid something is going to happen to Charlotte."

"Yes, something is going to happen to her. She's going to
go to jail."

"I don't mean that way. I mean . . . someone is going to
hurt her."

Henry stopped cutting his leather. "Who would want to
hurt her?"

"I'm . . . not sure."

"You're not sure? What kind of an answer is that?"

"It's the only answer I can give you right now. I just
wanted, needed, your assurance that you wished Charlotte
no harm."

"I wouldn't have a hair on that girl's head hurt. I only
want what the law says is my right—protection from theft.
If it takes putting Charlotte Malone in jail to stop the thefts,
that's what I want. Nothing less, but certainly nothing
more."

"Suppose she isn't the thief?"

Henry shook his head, went back to cutting his leather.

"Suppose she isn't the thief," Luke said again, determined to have his father listen to him just this once.

"Doesn't make any sense."

"Think about that, Dad. Think about how it doesn't make any sense."

"You've . . . taken up with her, haven't you?"

He was used to shunting off attacks, by a witness, by a district attorney, by a disappointed woman. Still, his father's blunt words hit him squarely in the solar plexus. "An archaic term, but yes, I suppose it describes the situation accurately enough. Just let me ask you this. If you were going to steal your neighbor's cattle—"

"I don't steal my neighbor's cattle. Or anybody else's."

Luke took a hard grip on his patience. "But if you were going to do a little judicious rustling, wouldn't you make sure you shipped them off before anybody found them?"

"Maybe she didn't have the chance."

"One, yes. But how many cattle do you have in the barn now? Five, six? She's not a dumb woman." He knew he should stop. He knew he shouldn't play dirty. But Charlotte's life could be at stake. "She's too bright to do something so crazy. She's Maureen Malone's daughter."

The knife slipped. A bright bead of blood appeared on the fleshy part of Henry's thumb. Wordlessly Luke handed Henry his white handkerchief. Those glasses flashed at Luke. He thought his father might refuse the offer of the handkerchief, but Henry took the white cloth and wrapped it around the wound.

Luke had intended to give his father an emotional jolt, but he was sorry Henry had cut himself. "You'd better put some disinfectant on that. Do you want me to—"

"I don't need any help from you."

"No, I don't suppose you do," Luke said steadily. "You never did. Just let me ask you one more question. Who found the first double-branded cattle?"

"Nick did. He was out in the north pasture when he saw them and brought them in."

"Don't you find that a little strange?"

"Not at all. He's out on the range, seeing to business. We work on this cattle ranch."

Luke felt the heat, the flare of emotion. His father knew exactly which buttons to push. "Then I'd better not keep you from it." He turned to walk out of the tack barn.

"Are you planning on marrying her?"

He thought about ignoring his father's question as if he hadn't heard. He couldn't do it. Luke stopped, pivoted slowly to face the man who was his father. Henry stood there with the handkerchief wrapped around his hand like a wounded warrior throwing the last lance. "I don't plan on marrying anyone just now."

"Then ask yourself this. How honest are you?"

"Charlotte knows I'll be leaving soon."

"I've tried to teach you to be a good man. I've tried to show you that the whole world wouldn't bow down to you just because you carried a little ball down a field better than anybody else. I tried to keep that praise they heaped on you from turning your head and show that a man's real worth in the world is his ability to get a job done." He shook his head slowly. "I guess I didn't do a very good job. Nothing I ever said or did had much effect on you."

Luke bowed his head in a mocking obeisance, his mouth twisted in a bleak smile. "You'd be surprised, Father."

Chapter Twelve

The steering wheel of the car felt smooth and familiar under Luke's hand. The quiet twilight filled the air with the sweetness of a summer's evening, making the harsh words he'd exchanged with his father seem as if they'd been uttered in another lifetime. Charlotte's house sheltered under the mountains; the jut and thrust of those purple peaks was once again as familiar to Luke as his own name, as familiar as the dust cloud that enveloped his car as he pulled up and shut off the engine. The muted peace of the evening was shattered by the sharp burr of her outside telephone bell.

He remained sitting in the car to give Charlotte a chance to answer the phone. Quiet drifted over him, and in the softly enfolding mystery of day slipping into night, Luke remembered an old line, something about home being the place where they had to take you in. He'd been fool enough to believe that. No more. Everything he owned was packed in the trunk of the car. He'd left his father's house, knowing he'd never return.

He wouldn't move in with Charlotte. That would make him the liar his father thought him to be. He was a man without a place to hang his hat, but he couldn't leave, not with Charlotte in danger. He'd let her know that he was heading to a motel, and then he'd leave. Because she deserved a man who could give her his life.

He sat waiting in the car for Charlotte to finish her call, until he could wait no longer. He ached for the sight of her face, for the warmth of her smile.

The kitchen felt like her, smelled like her, clean and fresh with bleach and lemon and a hint of the lavender scent he hadn't identified until just this minute. There was the aroma of coffee too, and when he heard Charlotte's voice, low, throaty, teasing, coming from the living room, he walked to the cupboard and rummaged around for a cup. He was helping himself from the coffeepot on the stove when Charlotte came around the corner, the phone to her ear. He leaned back against the counter and brought the cup to his lips, his eyes on her face.

Her eyes blazed with that look he lived for. She tried to reach him, but her phone cord wouldn't quite reach. She beckoned for him to come closer, but he stayed where he was, his back against the counter, the coffee cup in his hand.

"No, you're not catching me at a bad time. Luke just walked in the door, that's all. No, of course you're still my favorite fella. You always will be."

The sudden knife of possessiveness hit him on a blind side. He'd never been possessive, not of Elisa, not of any woman. So she was talking to a guy, sweet as all hell in her jeans, her crisp white shirt and her bare feet with those nicely shaped toes. For some reason known only to the laughing gods of irony, she was holding the phone out to him, her smile beaming.

"Want to say hello to an old friend?"

"I don't have any old friends."

Her smile faded just a little. "It's Richard. Go on, say hi to him. He's got a part, and he's dying to tell as many people as he can about it."

He took the phone from Charlotte's hand and decided that *jackass* was too good a name for him. Need and hunger burning inside him, he grasped her around the waist and headed for the living room couch, where he sat down with her, dragging her into his lap in one smooth movement. She seemed startled, but she settled in quickly, with that way she had of fitting his hardness to her softness that both soothed and aroused the hell out of him.

The phone was still warm from her hand. Her hair was silk against his cheek and smelled like strawberries. Luke shifted her closer and tucked her head in under his chin and thought about how he'd felt when he believed she was talking to another man on the phone and knew that somehow, somewhere, all his plans to be cool, to be easy, to take things as they came, had gone very much awry. He leaned back with her, feeling that hungry edginess ease out of his gut, only to be replaced by another more basic hunger. In his ear, Richard rambled on about his part in a TV detective series, about how he was the second banana and the part was a real breakthrough for him. It was good to hear his old friend's voice, and Luke was glad Richard was at last finding some success in pursuing his dream, but he could feel Charlotte's cheek against his as she fit into him like a kitten, and Luke could feel her breathe and smell her skin, and he wanted to throw the phone away and bury his hands in her hair and his body in hers. Instead, he had to content himself with rubbing his hand up and down her arm, as if he weren't really thinking about her at all. He realized then that he was doing what he had done most of his life, escaping from the harsh storms of his father's repressiveness into the safe harbor of Richard and Charlotte's life. He'd taken from the two of them all his life. Had he ever given back anything?

The man was taking too much for granted, coming into her house, sitting down on her couch with her in his lap, letting his hand drift from her arm to her thigh in a careless embrace. Yet he felt so hard and solid and endearing. In his black shirt with the tiny stripes, a cotton city shirt, too dressy for the country with its button-down collar, but decidedly sexy with the front open to expose Luke's throat and the shirtsleeves rolled up, exposing his tanned, muscled arms. And darn that man, his black denim jeans went beyond sexy to downright dangerous, especially with his spit-and-polish-clean black boots. He looked dressed for trouble, ready to do some bar cruising in a city. She wondered what he'd said to his father, what abuse he'd taken for her sake.

When Luke finally handed her the phone, she asked, "What did he say?"

"He wanted me to know that if I didn't act like a gentleman and take care of you, he'd come home and knock me flat."

"I'll bet you're scared to death." Richard was five-ten and weighed a slim one hundred and fifty pounds.

"Shaking in my boots."

"Did you tell him it was too late for you to be a gentleman?"

"No. There's an old Steadman rule. Never destroy anyone's good opinion of you, even if it's undeserved."

"That sounds like a great rule."

"Right up there with clean your teeth every night." Now was the time to tell her he was on his way. Now was the time. But he could smell the perfume of her hair and feel the silkiness of those soft black strands against his cheek. The words wouldn't come. He wanted a little more time. Just a few minutes more with her, with the peace of her, and the hunger of her.

Charlotte lay in his arms, aware of the hand that lay splayed at her throat above her breasts, his fingertips heavy and warm against the bare skin under her blouse collar. He was all coolness and calm, but those eyes were dark as midnight, and he was watching her as if his life would end if he took his eyes from hers. But he wasn't making a move toward her.

"Do you have to take my brother's instructions quite so literally?" She tried a smile, hoped for an answering smile, was disappointed. Exasperated, she leaned forward and kissed him. His mouth was cool, uninvolved. She didn't know what was eating him, but she could guess. Henry.

"You could help me out here," she said.

"Help you do what?"

She couldn't read his eyes, but she knew his soul. He was spoiling for a fight. He needed her help in putting back that high wall that protected him from loving, from intimacy. He couldn't do it by himself anymore. The thought cheered her immensely. If he could be obtuse, so could she. She smiled at him, as if she missed the point altogether. "You must be deadly in the courtroom."

"I do what's necessary."

He wasn't going to give an inch. She lost a bit of her courage. Maybe she had read him wrong. No, she couldn't have. He was here. And he was holding her. "You look ... drained."

"Thank you very much." He bowed his head in mock gratitude.

"It didn't go well with your father, did it?" She lifted a hand to his cheek, felt the fine, dark stubble of his night face. She wanted to give him the world. He looked at this moment as if he didn't want it. Or her.

"No, it didn't go well."

She felt full, suddenly, of things she wanted to say, things she wanted to give him. Full of love. She reached for the silk of his hair and ran her palm over it, loving the feel of his hair under her hand, the curve of his head.

His eyes darkened, flashed. "You give sympathy so well."

She felt the anger surge within her, but she knew him too well to give way to it. He needed her desperately, but he'd die before he'd admit it to her. Or to himself.

Charlotte shifted a little, and then more, till suddenly she was straddling him. "Perhaps I can give you something you like better than sympathy."

He might have put other people off with his stoic act, other women, but he wouldn't fool her with that idiotic nonsense. She dragged her hand around to the rim of his ear, found the tiny hairs there. "Have you ever thought about all the different kinds of hair there are on the human body?" Her other hand was splayed against his chest, to help her hold her body away from his. "Tiny little ones here." She teased along his ear, up and down, gently, so gently, her eyes fastened on his. He looked completely in control, but she knew he wasn't, felt the evidence of it beneath her. He'd hardened instantly. Smiling, she leaned closer, let her hand drift to the back of his neck, where she found a whorl of hair that seemed promising. "Stronger ones here, but embedded in very sensitive skin. Did you know the back of your neck is sensitive as a primitive survival defense?" She made forays there for a bit, all the while watching him. She thought she saw the muscle move on the side of his jaw that betrayed his teeth clenching. She was getting under his skin, all right, but he was determined to keep control as long as he could. Spurred on by evidence that victory would be hers, she let her hand move to his chest, where she slowly unbuttoned his shirt. Her eyes dark with laughter, she said, "If you want to say no to this scientific exploration, Luke, you'd better do it now."

His mouth twitched with a sudden dark amusement, but he didn't smile. "Far be it from me to stand in the way of scientific advancement."

His dark pelt exposed, she took her time exploring it, careful not to catch her nails in the darkly springing curls. "This hair is coarse and springy, again contributing to the survival of the male animal by providing defense." She shattered his defense by finding a nipple under those curls, rubbing it against her palm. She discovered the other with her left palm and, just for good measure, rubbed them both, first one way, then the other.

His hands had been open, but now she could see them closing, as if he needed to keep his hands clenched to keep them away from her. She pulled the snap loose on his jeans. The sound of the zipper rasping open filled the entire room. Steeling herself to keep from losing her nerve, she slid her warm fingers against his even warmer flesh, feeling the path of curls down, down.... "And this hair also conceals and protects—"

"And I thought country girls were shy."

He relaxed back against the cushions, his mouth curved in a darkly sensual look, his eyes nearly black with arousal, his body as ready for pleasure as an indulged pasha's.

"You've got a lot to learn about country girls. Would you like to continue this lesson upstairs, where we both would be more comfortable? I know you like your comfort."

"I find," said Luke, reaching for her hand to let her help him up, "that I have this insatiable thirst for learning—in the proper atmosphere."

Warm and dark was her room in the twilight, with a cool breeze rustling the curtains. Hot and cold danced together on her skin. The coverlet on her bed whispered as she drew it back. The bed gave as Luke lay down and drew her on top of him. He held her for a moment, just held her. She could feel her heart beating, and his, too, the slow, steady rhythm under her ear confirming his life, his reality. But still it must be a dream to be with Luke like this on her childhood bed, wrapped in the ultimate freedom of sensual intimacy.

"Charlotte."

He said her name, just her name, but she knew that in that moment he, too, was savoring the dark, cool world that sheltered them and the particular closeness that only a man and a woman about to make love could share.

He seemed to know that she needed quiet in this serious act of joining with him. He lay still, not breaking the mood, still only holding her, his hands quiet on her back. And in that moment, she knew she would never again in her life love anyone as she loved this man.

Slowly, carefully, she rose up over him and began to undo his lower shirt buttons.

When at last she was cool and bare in his arms, Luke dragged his hand over her back in a silken, ragged caress, but Charlotte knew what she needed. She needed him inside her, and she wanted him now, before she began to think, before she began to doubt the wisdom of loving him so thoroughly, before she began to remember that he would never be hers. She clutched his back and rolled with him, taking him into her, tightening around him, his sharp intake of breath sending a ripple of pleasure through her that echoed in their joining.

"Charlotte—"

Her name was a breath, a song, a sigh. "Shh..." She moved to take him deeper. He held his weight on his hands above her, and now he threw his shoulders back in a spasm of pleasure.

She watched the cords and muscles in his shoulders tighten, watched his eyes close in that acute pleasure that was nearly pain, saw the sleek line of his neck as he lifted his head in a futile effort to contain and shape his pleasure.

She would not let him. She knew she must make him feel the chilliness of the breeze, the warmth of her body, the tightness with which she held him, now, quickly, before he remembered to raise his guard again and shut her and the world out. She danced light fingertips over his bare back, and he dragged in a tortured breath. She cupped his muscled rear, explored, felt his rising tension. And, in concert, her own.

He sought her mouth hungrily, and she felt him trying to hold on to sanity, but, ruthlessly, she pushed him over the edge. And went with him.

They slept and woke in the absolute darkness of night before dawn, and Luke took his revenge on Charlotte, treating her to a long, slow loving that had her writhing beneath him in a twisting need that was heightened by the path of his mouth on her ear, her neck, her breast. Oh, yes, a Steadman could be depended on to take his revenge quite, quite thoroughly.

Charlotte came awake slowly, curled into Luke's side. She looked up into his face. He was lying there on his back, his arm protectively around her, his brown eyes wide open, staring into the gray light.

"You have the loudest birds in the world."

"I'm sorry."

He rolled, taking her with him, and he was all smooth-muscled grace, her lover, his skin golden in the early-morning light, his dark, sleek head hers to touch. She felt heady with sweet abandonment, both sated and hungry. When he gazed down at her and threaded a hand through her tangled hair, his languid possessiveness matched her mood completely.

"No, you're not. You're the most unrepentant woman I've ever seen in my life, as well as seductive, shameless and beautiful—"

Her beauty was the kind a man didn't forget—the wild blackness of her hair against the white of the pillow, the ivory perfection of her skin, her eyes nearly black with arousal and surrender. He wondered at his insatiable need for her.

He gazed down into that lovely face, knowing he was being selfish, but he was too close to heaven to retreat. Still, he could try to be a gentleman. "Is there something you need to do first?"

She stretched her arms up, and then, as if it were an accident, let them fall on his shoulders. "Not yet."

He found her with his hand, discovered she was moist and ready for him. He eased his body into hers, felt that instant stab of pleasure that was the delightful prelude. He loved her, and in the loving he discovered yet another facet of the jewel that was Charlotte.

The room glowed in the light of a sun fully risen when Luke woke the second time. He felt Charlotte stirring beside him, warm and sleek and content. He was feeling rather content himself as he leaned forward to brush his mouth against the hollow of her throat. She opened her eyes, looked at him and smiled. He laid back against his pillow, feeling her smile warm him. "And I thought you were a morning grouch."

"Just shows how wrong you can be."

Her voice was early-morning husky, infinitely attractive. He felt that need to touch her, to claim her, and leaned over her again, telling himself he'd take just a small taste.

"Luke."

"Umm..."

"I do have to get up now."

He pulled away from her instantly, a smile tilting his lips.

She thought about him as she scooted to the bathroom, thought about his touch when she had showered and was pulling on the terry robe. Her skin was sensitive to the looped cotton. Little wonder. She'd felt the rasp of his fingertips, the smoothness of his lips, over most of her body in the past twelve hours. He'd entered her world most thoroughly, and she knew that for her there would be no forgetting. She could only savor each moment as it came and not look too far into the future. For there was no future.

But she wanted one. Oh, how she wanted one, especially when she emerged from the bathroom and saw him lying on his side in her bed, the sheet draped over the curve of his hip, his dark head turned as he gazed out the window. She wanted to know what he was thinking. Was he thinking about the night they'd had together, about the touches, the kisses, the murmured words? Was he thinking he'd remember her? She knew she'd remember him always like this, long, lean and easy in her bed.

He heard her, turned his head. Those dark brown eyes flashed over her, bringing heat to her skin all over again.

"Are you hungry?" she asked, reaching for the mundane.

"For food?" His lips curved in a sensual smile as he held out his hand to her.

She came and sat beside him, feeling the warmth of his fingers on hers, the heat of his gaze roving over her face. She wanted to hold on to this moment for just a little longer, to keep the picture of Luke nestled in the muss of sheets, his face relaxed, no longer wreathed in the tension he'd carried into the house with him after he talked to his father. She wished they could always be like this, locked away from the rest of the world. "Yes, for food, my fuzzy-faced friend." She brushed her fingertips down his cheek, felt the morning bristle on his chin.

Gently he eased her robe open just enough to see her throat. "I didn't hurt you, did I?"

Not yet. She shook her head, unable to speak, for he was drawing his hand down between her breasts carefully, as if soothing her. She felt the sting, the rise, of desire all over again.

"What do you have to do today?" A glance at her face, and he brought the hand he was holding to his chest, played her fingers over the crisp dark hair.

"I'm—I have to go to church. I have to make the coffee for the social hour that follows church. I promised Margaret Murchison."

"Ah, yes. That inveterate organizer of dances has stretched herself to do church coffee hours, I take it."

Charlotte smiled back at him. How could she help it? He was being Luke—charming, deferential. "I suppose our little social gatherings seem silly to you—"

He swiftly pulled her down onto the bed. "Most social events in the country make sense. They're given by people who actually enjoy seeing each other. I can't say the same for several outings I attended in the city. There it was a case of see and be seen, or further the career." He brought the hand entwined with hers up to his jaw and rasped her palm against his beard. "My shaving kit is out in the car. I suppose if I go outside like this, I might give Lettie a bit of a start."

"You'd positively make her day. But rather than let my man show his charms to the neighborhood, I'll get your kit for you and then start the coffee."

"Woman of my dreams." He didn't seem to object to her calling him her man. Instead, he pulled her head down and kissed her, giving her a taste of what she'd hungered for more than coffee. When he released her, she let her eyes travel around his face, wishing she could find the answer to the complexity in his dark brown eyes. She said, "Will you wait here at the house for me while I'm gone?"

"You'd rather I didn't go with you?" He said it easily.

"I'd love to have you go with me. I just didn't think you'd want to go."

"If I show up with you, I'll make you the object of all kinds of gossip and speculation."

"It's probably too late for that," she said dryly. "Marris Hollis has already driven by the ranch three times this morning, just to check and see if your car was still here."

His eyes darkened, and he shook his head, his expression wry. "Charlotte, I'm sorry—"

"Don't be. I'm not." She gave him a clear, cool look. "Marris Hollis can look all he likes. Which he will do, whether you come to church with me or not."

"Well, if you're going to throw yourself to the Christians, I'd better come with you."

Luke liked the way Charlotte looked in a dress, all legs and small waist and eyes. The navy jacket was snubbed and came just below her breasts, and the rest of the dress was a color between green and blue that made him think of a lake on a summer day. The skirt swirled long and full around her knees as she walked out to his car and lifted those nice legs inside.

He put the car in gear, the thought of those elegant and meaningless Sunday mornings when he'd attended church with Elisa playing in the back of his mind. Now, that lifetime seemed to belong to another world, almost as if he'd never lived it. This morning, with the Montana sun heating the car and turning the soil to dust, was like a thousand others he remembered from his boyhood.

Charlotte moved, and a drift of her perfume wafted to his nose, a delicate lavender scent. Then she turned and smiled at him, and it was a smile that was both brave and slightly uneasy. She might be having second thoughts, but she'd die before she'd let him see.

He found himself flooded with admiration for her. Admiration. That was it. That was the thing he felt for Charlotte that was new to him, that he'd not felt for another woman . . . along with a few other deeply sensual things he couldn't put a name to.

They drove into town, where Sunday-morning quiet lay in the shadows of the trees, in the quietness of the street. Everything was closed; the light was off above Sam's Silver Branch Saloon.

"How *was* your hamburger that night, Luke?"

She looked as if she needed talk to distract her. He smiled. "Let's just say I think it's too bad the old cafe is closed," said Luke. "The old brick structure has held up pretty well. I'm surprised there aren't more broken windows."

"I try to keep them repaired."

"You own that building?"

"My aunt Carol left it to my dad. Through his will, it came to me. Every spring and fall, Tex and I take a walk through and try to plug up any cracks in the ceiling. So far, we've been lucky. The building is pretty sound."

He was surprised. He realized then that he'd assumed that her financial cupboard was bare, that she was without assets. Maybe he could help her get someone in there to open it up. Even a little rent revenue would help. "What are you going to do with it?"

"Sell it, I suppose, if anybody ever comes along who's foolish enough to buy it."

"Umm."

"Luke, you have that funny tone in your voice."

"You can hear a funny tone in 'Umm'?"

"Yes, I can."

"You have extremely sensitive ears." His voice dropped to a low, intimate tone. "But then, I should have remembered that from last night."

She wanted to give him back as good as he gave, but they were pulling up in front of the low-slung new church building, and as usual a gaggle of young singles stood outside under the cool shade of a cottonwood tree, waiting until the last minute to go into the warm church. Charlotte had hoped they'd be late enough so she wouldn't have to walk the gauntlet of curious eyes, but no, there they all stood, heads turned to stare at Luke's expensive car.

"I miss the old church and the steeple," Luke murmured.

She dragged her attention away from the crowd, which suddenly seemed to hold the county's entire population. "That's right, this is the first time you've seen the new church. This one is handicapped-accessible."

"Progress," he said, his mouth quirking. "Well, here we are at the ring of fire. Are you ready to walk over the coals?"

"Umm," she said.

"Definitely a funny tone in *that* 'Umm.'"

He reached across her to open the door, then made sure he was out of the car as she was stepping out. Marris Hollis's eyes were ready to pop out of his head. Tim had a sheepish smile on his face, while Tom Hartley, her lawyer, was scowling at them.

Marris pursed his lips to whistle.

"Put a sock in it, Hollis," Charlotte said. The would-be whistler turned a mottled red, right down to the top of his knotted paisley tie, but he faced the challenge with all the courage he could muster. "I was just admiring the view. It isn't every day we get to see those legs, Malone. I wasn't sure you had any."

Everybody laughed except Tom. Luke gave Marris that half smile that was just this side of dangerous.

"Oh, sorry, Luke."

"Like Charlotte said, put a sock in it, Hollis."

While his attention was on Hollis, Tom Hartley took Charlotte's arm and walked her away from the group, saying something to her in a low tone. Luke wanted to follow and rip Hartley's hand from Charlotte's arm, but he contented himself with standing and waiting, casting a look at Hollis that made that worthy man toss his cigarette away and turn to disappear in the church.

"Trouble?" Luke murmured when Charlotte returned to him and deliberately slipped her arm through his.

"He says that under the circumstances, he'd rather not represent me."

"What circumstances?"

"I believe it falls in the category of consorting with the enemy."

"Maybe he'd like a punch in his circumstances."

"Luke, no. We're in church, remember?" She looked anxious, agitated, adorable.

"We're not in the door yet."

"Please, don't alienate anybody else on my behalf. It's bad enough that your father is angry with you—"

They were alone in the summer heat and the Montana breeze. Everyone else had discovered discretion to be the greater part of valor and gone in. "Are you sure you want me to go in there with you?"

"More so now than ever." She looked like a soldier preparing for battle, a defiant hand flicking that long hair back.

"All right," he said. "Armor up and at the ready? Then in we go." He held out his hand at his side for her to grasp. She shot him one of those killer smiles that cheered him immensely—just as Henry Steadman and Nick stepped out of Henry's old white Cadillac. Instinctively Luke moved to shield Charlotte and send her forward, but she stood her ground.

"I won't be rude to your father, Luke."

Under his breath, Luke murmured, "Let's hope he has the same penchant for good manners."

A breeze displaced a strand of Henry's white hair, and his father immediately lifted his hand to smooth it back into place. His white shirt was crisp and traditional; Nick wore a dark shirt and tie that was as city-sleek as Luke's own. Nick extended an arm to his father. Henry took it, surprising Luke.

Nick slowed to accommodate his father's slower pace. As they came closer, Charlotte faced the two men squarely and lifted her chin. "Good morning, Mr. Steadman, Nick."

Henry glanced ahead of him, as if mindful that he was about to enter church. His eyes strayed back to Charlotte, to the hand Luke was holding. For a moment that seemed like an eternity to Luke, Henry studied Charlotte, from the high color in her cheeks to the silky flutter of her dress skirt. At last he murmured, "Miss Malone. A good morning to you." His gaze flashed to Luke's face.

Henry moved as if to walk past without acknowledging Luke.

Daringly Charlotte caught his arm. "You haven't said good-morning to your son."

Nick smiled, his lift of the mouth strangely reminiscent of Luke's a moment ago, sure that his father would rebuff Charlotte and cut Luke.

The silence stretched. At last, the essence of a smile played around Henry's lips. To Charlotte he said, "You remind me of a banty hen I once had. All ruffled feathers and spunk, with the tenacity of a bulldog. You're entirely right to remind me of my manners as I approach God's house. Good morning, Luke." And to Charlotte, Henry made a polite gesture with his arm, indicating that she should precede him into the church. "Beauty before age," he said, with that ghost of a smile.

Suddenly, hauntingly, Charlotte caught a glimpse of the man Henry had once been, a man as charming and as lethal as Luke. And for the first time, she wondered how her mother had made the choice between her father and Henry. Just as suddenly, she caught the expression on Nick's face. He looked . . . furious.

Every head turned their way as the four of them walked down the aisle. Luke stopped at the first empty pew to the right, but Charlotte shook her head and slipped into the next pew up on the other side, taking him with her. When Henry and Nick came in and sat exactly where Luke had wanted her to sit, he understood. He'd somehow gone, with unerring accuracy, to his family's pew.

The chatting that had been filling the room with the sound of friendly voices died away into a stunned silence. Even Sharon Reece, the organist and music teacher, seemed rattled. She reached for a sheaf of music, sent it skittering to the floor. Her face a bright shade of pink, she recovered the music and began to play "How Great Thou Art," hitting a sudden, jarring wrong note. Someone in the back tittered.

Luke glanced at Charlotte. Her color was high, but so was her chin. He reached for her hand. Her fingers curled around his and she tossed him a quick smile. He felt better then.

The minister came in, a young, sincere man who was easy with his pulpit and his flock. Blessedly, he seemed not to recognize Luke, and after recognition of birthdays and anniversaries, the service began. Luke bowed his head. Saying a prayer seemed like an extraordinarily good idea.

Well, if this didn't just tear it. His father was softening toward both of them, he knew it. He could feel it in his bones. They wouldn't get by with this. He'd let enough days go by. Tomorrow was the Fourth of July. In the evening, everyone would be in town, watching the fireworks. He'd act then.

Chapter Thirteen

Charlotte was lying beside Luke, loving him with her eyes, when he stirred. She didn't want him to wake up just yet. She treasured those first few sparkles of time when he slept beside her, his body relaxed.

"Good morning, sunshine."

He was awake now. Dark and husky and late-morning sleepy, Luke's voice sent that first warmth of arousal to the tips of Charlotte's toes. And there were his eyes, too, making little forays on her face, her hair, her body covered by the sheet. His hand moved, found her bare hip, and every nerve in her body leaped to life.

"What's on the schedule for today?"

That low murmur sent chills down her spine. Couldn't let the man know he had such an effect on her. She lifted an eyebrow and slanted a sage look at him. "Getting out of bed?"

"Wiseacre woman. What time is it?"

"Eleven o'clock in the morning."

"Decadent. Don't you know every good rancher gets up at the crack of the rooster's crow?"

"I think you've got your metaphors mixed."

He didn't seem to care. Dark and muscled and beautiful, Luke lay sprawled with that consummate ease that characterized a good athlete at rest. Under that sleek brown mat of curling chest hair, his skin had a golden glow from his time outdoors—and from the light that filled the room.

This is more than love. It was intimacy, and the stuff memories were made of. When she was ninety years old and people thought she was dotty, she'd close her eyes and remember Luke like this: a thousand little vistas of male flesh, a thousand evocative scents of skin and hair. And under her own pretense of lazy relaxation, a thousand pulses of heat vibrated that told Charlotte she was with the man who should have been hers—the man she'd have fought tooth and nail to keep if he had any other last name.

"I don't see you jumping out of bed."

"Are you telling me in your polite, not-so-subtle way that I'm as lazy as you?" he asked her chidingly. "Where's your big move toward the state of uprightness?"

"Umm... Too nice here." She'd spent the night watching the herd with Luke under the stars and talking to him, mostly, while Tex caught some sleep. Owlish, but awake, Tex had ridden out to relieve them from watch duty around six. They'd stumbled up to Charlotte's bed, too tired to think of anything but sleep.

"So what do we have to do today?"

She liked the "we." She liked the hand on her hip, too, making slow circles that seemed to be getting wider with each revolution, making her forget work, forget everything but the sublime pleasure of that light, teasing touch. "We have to feed Lady Luck, check on the colt, work on the tractor, repair harness, check on the salt blocks...."

"What are we doing after lunch?"

"*After lunch,* we're going to the Fourth of July celebration in town. Can you stand that much excitement?"

His eyes darkened, and his hand splayed over her abdomen. "I should be used to it by now, after all you've given me."

I love you. She wanted to say it, ached to say it. But she couldn't. It would make him uncomfortable to hear her say words that he couldn't reciprocate. Still, she would tell him before he left. Somehow, she'd find a way to tell him that she loved him without strings, without obligations. Before he left Montana, he'd know there was one person in his life who'd truly loved him. She wanted him to take that with him, wherever he went. *You are loved, Luke.*

"I'm glad you haven't been bored," she said lightly.

He got that dark, serious look on his face. "Your job isn't to amuse me."

"Oh?" She lifted herself up, leaned over him and deliberately flicked her tongue over the small nub of his nipple, nestled in his chest hair.

"On the other hand, I might be, that is there is that remote possibility that I . . . well, it's hard to believe it, but I could be wrong. . . ."

He let her have her fun for a bit, but then when her tongue explored lower and found him, he swooped, grasped her arms and lifted her over him.

The summer heat lingered. The lake sang a siren song of invitation with its cool, shimmering reflection under a twilight Montana sky, while the park beside the lake resounded with the shouts of children screaming from the highest chair in the Ferris wheel. Cotton-candy scent and the smell of popcorn permeated the still early-evening air.

Charlotte strolled beside Luke, thinking that heaven was really an amusement park by a lake in the twilight.

"We have to have popcorn while we watch the fireworks," Charlotte told Luke.

"Does it say that in the manual?"

"It's a Malone family tradition. You buy the popcorn, then you go look for a good picnic bench and you sit on top of the table, not the benches, and—" Her voice caught.

His face looked dark and warm and real, and he reached for her hand. It was so sweet to be understood, to be *known* this well. He was a wonderful lover, this Luke of hers, but he was just as wonderful a human being.

"Far be it from me to stand in the way of a family tradition."

Clasping her hand lightly in his, Luke took her strolling along the grassy pathway toward the popcorn stand. A fractious, tired child cried out, was shushed by his mother. Tex and Lettie passed, Lettie said hello, Tex grumped at Charlotte, scowled at Luke.

"She's going in the hospital tomorrow," Charlotte told Luke when the couple was out of earshot.

He clasped her hand a little tighter. "I'm glad something good has come out of all this."

At the popcorn stand, Luke purchased the requisite bag of popcorn and, carefully balancing it in one hand, caught Charlotte's up again in his other, bringing the warmth back to her skin. "When was the last time you came here with your parents?"

She had to think, to add, to subtract. "It would be six years ago this year."

"Want to talk about it?"

He looked easy and cool, and she remembered then that he had long experience in dealing with people in the throes of life's crises. She couldn't do that to him, not tonight when the breeze smelled of summer and a half-moon hung over the water. "No, please, I...no." She didn't want sympathy. She wanted to do as she had been doing, run the ranch, work, survive.

His face was cool when he gave her a hand to help her climb up on the picnic table, and stayed cool as he settled on the tabletop beside her. She didn't know whether Marris Hollis picked the table next to hers on purpose, but it didn't make any difference. Not even Marris could spoil the beauty of the night, the aching closeness of the stars.

Luke's arm came softly, warmly, around her waist. He held the popcorn within her easy reach.

"I have some cousins in Virginia," his low voice murmured in her ear. "They need a trainer for their Arabians. I'm thinking about going there when we get this thing settled between you and my father. I'd ask you to come with me, if I thought I wouldn't be ripping out a part of your soul—"

Going with Luke to Virginia. Being with him, being a part of his life. The thought was so tempting. All it required was a betrayal of her father's and mother's memory.

Charlotte shook her head, bumped the popcorn bag, made kernels fly. "You're right, Luke. I can't do that. I can't go... and you can't stay."

A rocket sizzled, red stars blossomed in the air, their sparkle reflected in the water. The crowd aahed and applauded at the first explosion of color, as crowds always did. Another swish, blue stars blossomed, and in quick succession green and yellow. A firebomb exploded with a boom and echoed across the lake to reverberate against the mountains. It wasn't Charlotte's heart breaking, but it felt as if it were.

His arm tightened around her waist, his mouth found her hair. "I want you to be all right."

"I will be," she said, but she knew she was lying.

He didn't want to hurt her, but it would hurt when he left, he knew that. He'd tried to protect her from gossip, but he'd done a lousy job of it. He was here, in public with her, because it was what she wanted. It was what he wanted, too, he thought suddenly, amazed. He wanted a public relationship with her, where he could hold her close in full view and it was his right but he also wanted the secret relationship he had with Charlotte that no one else could share, that wonderful secret bond between lovers.

He wanted marriage.

Luke loosened his arm from around Charlotte so suddenly that she turned around to look at him.

Color blossomed again in the sky, this time a fountain plume of pure silver light. He felt as if that light were inside him, exploding. He'd been thinking about her, not wanting to hurt her. It had never occurred to him that when he went, he'd leave behind the best part of him.

"Luke? What is it?"

He shook his head. "Going for a walk," he said. He had to escape the perfume of her hair, the softness of her body pressed against his side.

He felt her concern as he slid off the table, but he kept on walking, climbing the hill that divided the lake from the rest of the horizon. He looked away from the fireworks, back over the town—and saw red flames dancing against the black sky.

His heart thudded in his chest. He shook his head, turned around to look at the sky behind him. Was it a mirage, a crazy reflection of the fireworks? No. There were no fireworks just now. The fire he saw was coming from the direction of Charlotte's ranch.

His mind going at warp speed, he raced back to Charlotte, plucked her off the picnic table, ignoring her startled gasp.

"What is it—?"

"Don't talk, just move."

He dragged her with him to the rise of the hill, and she saw it then. He felt her sway, felt her tremble. "It can't be."

"We'll call the fire truck from my car."

He took her with him, nearly lifting her off the ground in his haste. He could feel her fighting him, fighting the panic. He stuffed her in the car, grabbed up his car phone and dialed the emergency number, even as he maneuvered his car out of the space in the grassy field and roared out onto the highway.

"They're on their way," he said tersely, and reseated the telephone.

Charlotte sat frozen beside him, unmoving. He reached over, grasped her hand, clamping her fingers tightly in his even as he shifted gears and gunned the motor up to a speed that had gravel pinging against the undercarriage of the car. A hose. She'd have a hose. He'd get it going, and they'd save something. . . .

But when he pulled into the drive and they scrambled out of the car, Luke knew no hose in the world could save either the house or the barn. Both were enveloped in flames. Wood crackled and popped, accepting the fire greedily, the sparks flaring obscenely against the sky in a horrible parody of the fireworks they had watched only a moment ago.

"Thank God the horses are out," Luke growled.

Lady Luck neighed in an endless high-pitched protest, and the colt echoed her cries and raced after his mother around the perimeter of the corral, but they were both far enough away from the flames to be out of danger.

"Yes," Charlotte replied. The word seemed unreal, echoing inside her head. Nothing seemed real, not Luke's hand around her waist, not the fire that lit the sky. She wanted to cry, but the tears wouldn't come. She felt stripped of emotion, as if all thought and feeling inside her head had vanished.

The one thing she could feel was Luke's hand, gripping hers tightly, warm, hard, solid.

"If you can think of anything I could do to—"

"There's . . . nothing."

The sky burned red in every direction. Luke could feel the heat, feel the power of fire having its own way with wood, brick, straw, hay. Fury rose inside him, fury at Charlotte's loss, at his own helplessness. He should have seen this coming. But he hadn't. Once again, he'd underestimated Nick.

There wasn't a doubt in his mind that Nick was responsible—and, in his own way, so was he. It had been Luke's return, and his continuing presence, that escalated Nick's desire to harm Charlotte—and caused her to lose her home.

A crowd began to gather. Marris Hollis asked Charlotte if he could do anything, organize a bucket brigade, get a shovel, pull down timbers. Charlotte smiled then. It was a faint smile that must have cost her the world in effort. "No, Marris, but thank you very much. It's . . . kind of you."

"You know I really am ready to give you a hand if you need it," he said shamefacedly. "I'm really sorry I—"

Charlotte put her hand on Marris's arm. "Don't be sorry for anything. I know you're my friend. I've always known it."

If Luke hadn't already been head over heels in love with Charlotte, he would have fallen then. To watch Charlotte being considerate of Marris Hollis at a time when her world was falling apart made his heart want to jump out of his chest.

The sheriff arrived; people made way for Clarence Daggett instinctively. Behind him, the fire truck roared in, and two men jumped to the ground and began dragging out the hoses.

"Any idea how it started?" Clarence asked Charlotte gently. Charlotte shook her head. She turned toward Luke, as if the strain of acting normally with Marris and Clarence had drained away her last bit of strength. Luke sheltered her in his arms, holding her close, taking in her hurt, her desolation.

"Miss Malone."

Charlotte made a movement asking for release. Luke held her for a moment, resisting. He didn't want Charlotte to turn and face his father. But Charlotte pushed, and so Luke had to let her go. But he swore that if his father subjected her to one more test of courage, he would pick her up and carry her away.

Henry Steadman's face was darkly wreathed in concern. "This is a terrible thing to have happen. I'm very sorry—"

The fire-borne wind lifted Charlotte's hair, swirled it around her shoulders. She raised her head and straightened that long neck of hers, and Luke thought she had never looked more beautiful. "I'm surprised to hear you say that. I would have thought you'd be pleased."

At Charlotte's side, Luke clasped her hand tightly and faced his father. Luke was aware that for the first time, he and Charlotte were confronting Henry Steadman as a team. He wanted to feel sorry for his father, knew he should, but it was difficult. He didn't care that Henry had shut him out over the years, but his father's constant championing of Nick and his refusal to see the truth about his eldest brother had brought them to this night.

Henry Steadman looked drained, older and, Luke thought, infinitely more aware. "I know we've had our differences. But you surely can't believe I'd wish anything like this on you. You should know me better than that." His glance shifted to Luke. "Both of you."

Charlotte was not so easily appeased. "What else can I think? You and your son have done everything to drive me out—"

In the flickering firelight, Henry lost color. He looked like a man who had been stripped of an essential part of his being. "Luke wouldn't have any part in this."

"I'm not talking about Luke. I'm talking about your other son." The shouts of the men and the crackle and the hiss of the fire behind her gave her the strength to do what she had to do. "I'm talking about Nick, Mr. Steadman."

"Nick had nothing to do with this—"

"Did I hear my name mentioned?" Nick strolled up casually, his hands in his pockets, graceful in his jeans and black shirt with that smile on his face that would have done the devil proud, while behind him the night sky was lit with flames and noise, shouts of men and the pop of wood giving way to the greedy flames.

Charlotte felt her weariness and shock give way to cleansing anger. He'd come to gloat. She'd see to it that he wouldn't get the chance. "You won't win," Charlotte said. "I won't be driven away by your despicable capacity for destruction. I'm staying, Nick, no matter how many times you try to burn me out."

"Whoa, now, wait a minute. Who says I'm responsible for this?"

"I do," Charlotte said. The wind whipped her hair around her face again, and she pushed it back furiously. She had tried for so long to strive for peace, but now she had lost everything, and she was no longer in the mood for peace. She wanted desperately to state the truth in front of Henry and Luke. "I know you set this fire, Nick."

"How could you possibly *know* such a thing? Think my hands smell of gasoline, do you? Want to take a sniff?" He held them up, but no one moved.

"What makes you think the fire was set with gasoline?" asked Luke coolly.

Nick dropped his hands and shot Luke a dark look. Recovering, he said, "What else would it be?"

Nick's cool denial sent Charlotte's temper flaring. And the anger felt good. It took away the pain. "You'd be too clever to walk in here smelling of anything incriminating. That's not to say you don't smell. You stink to high heaven." Nick smiled at Charlotte's words, but she wasn't finished. "Well, listen to this, *Mr.* Steadman. I won't give up, and I won't go away. This is my land, and I'll stay on it if I have to pitch a tent!"

Nick's smile vanished. He took a step toward Charlotte, his mouth curled. "No, you won't. You'll go away, and the sooner the better. My father and I want you off that land, and you'll go if we have to drag you away kicking and screaming."

Henry whitened with shock. "Nick, you don't mean that. You can't mean that. It was never my intent to drive Charlotte off her land forcibly."

Nick whirled around to his father. "What difference does it make how she goes? The important thing is that she does go, preferably tonight." Turning to Charlotte, he continued, "We'll make you an offer for your land. It's not worth as much without the house, but—"

"Son! A man doesn't take advantage of a woman like this—"

"What do you want to do?" Nick cried. "Wait another twenty years before we get more land? Maybe you have the patience for that. I don't."

Only the fire snapped in the sudden silence. At last, Henry said, "Are you saying you had...some part in this?"

Nick recovered immediately. "Of course not. Just because I want to see Charlotte Malone out of here, that doesn't mean I've done anything criminal."

"But you have," Charlotte cried. "You've been taking your own cattle and branding them to implicate me and put me off my land. When that didn't work, you decided to burn my house down."

Henry breathed in sharply. He looked like a man who'd taken a blow to the solar plexus. "That can't be true."

"Don't be ridiculous, Charlotte," Luke drawled. "Nick doesn't have the courage or the brains to pull off a scheme like that." His voice echoed eerily in a night snapping with the sound of destruction, and the fire highlighted his face.

She could bear no more. She'd lost everything, and now she'd lost Luke, too. She flew at him, pounding her fists on his chest. "Don't defend him! Don't, don't, don't!"

He caught her arms and turned her around so that she had to face Nick. "Look at him. How could you think an innocent face like that hid a brain capable of such duplicity?"

She felt his arms, hard, holding her. She felt him breathing. She'd loved this man. And now he was defending his brother against her. "Let go of me." She heard her voice, cold, lifeless.

"And look at the fire. Look how cleverly it's been set, so that both buildings were too far gone by the time it was discovered to save anything, how nicely it's burning. Nick isn't that...resourceful. Don't you agree, Charlotte?"

She couldn't think, couldn't breathe. The heat of the fire burned on her face, but her skin felt ice-cold. Like her soul. "I'm beginning to think that a Steadman is capable of almost anything."

"Be reasonable, Charlotte." He sounded so cool, so self-contained.

He won't give up, Charlotte thought dazedly. The man is demented.

"Of course Nick didn't do this. He *was* at the fireworks with you, wasn't he, Father?"

Henry's face looked bloodless in the light of the fire. "He stayed behind at the ranch. He...said he had something he wanted to do."

"There, you see. He was at the ranch all the time. Inno-cence established." Luke smiled at Charlotte, all charm, his hand biting into her arm.

And then, through the heat and the ice and the agonized pain, a tiny light burned inside her soul. Luke was a law-yer. Luke knew how to make a witness feel comfortable, just before he went in for the kill. Charlotte understood—and knew she'd failed to play her part. "Of course, you're right, Luke. Nick couldn't possibly have been responsible for such a clever and diabolical scheme. He isn't smart enough to carry it out—"

Nick's smile vanished. He took a step toward Charlotte. "What do you know? What do you know about me and clever schemes? What do you know about who I am and what I think?"

"I know you aren't clever enough for this—"

"What do you know about clever? I'm smarter than any of you—"

"What are you saying, son?"

Henry caught Nick's arm, as if he needed his son's sup-port to stay upright. Nick turned on Henry, his eyes blaz-ing, his face red with heat. He wrenched his arm lose. Henry was knocked off balance, and only Luke's quick reaction saved his father from stumbling.

"You can't be telling us you did this terrible thing, Nick."

Nick's face was white with rage. "Why not? Somebody had to do something, or she'd be here forever, her with her tumbledown house and her broken-down ranch. I wanted her out. And so did you. You've wanted it for years—"

Henry's sharp intake of breath stopped Nick's tirade. "You admit that you deliberately set fire to this woman's house?"

Nick's eyes turned brilliant, pleading, eerily reflecting the firelight. "I did it for you. You wanted her land—"

"Yes, I wanted her land, but only if she was willing to sell it to me of her own free will. I could never condone destruction of property. It's against everything I believe. She has a right to live on her land, as long as she doesn't steal my cattle, which it appears she never did." Henry reached out to Nick, caught his shoulders. It hurt Luke to see his father's struggle to absorb the truth. "What have you been doing all these years? Where is your head? Haven't you been listening to me? I've given you everything, my work and my life. I've tried to teach you the right way to live in this world. I've tried to give you my time to make up for the mother you didn't have, for the woman I married who wasn't fond of you. I didn't want you to suffer for my foolishness. I thought you...knew what your place was, what you meant to me." He shook Nick, as if desperate to change him and undo the things he had done.

His face drawn into a contemptuous sneer, Nick shook off Henry's grip on him. "Give me? What could you give me to make up for making me the joke of the world? Henry's little mistake, that's what they used to call me."

Henry turned away, his face ashen.

"You've had every opportunity," Luke said softly. "There's only one person responsible for your troubles, and that's you."

"What the hell do you know about anything?"

"You'd better speak to the sheriff, Luke," said Henry.

"Nobody's going to lock me up." Nick looked wildly about, whirled around and took off running. Luke was after him in a flash. At Luke's car, Nick swiveled around, a .45 gleaming in his hand. In the face of the lethal weapon pointed at him, Luke jerked to a stop at arm's length.

"I need your keys, brother," Nick said, his voice low and threatening. "Give them to me."

"That's not what you need."

Coolly and calmly, Nick pointed the gun at Luke. "I can't miss at this range, and you know it."

Charlotte stifled a scream and stepped toward Luke. "Stay away," Luke ordered her. To Nick he said, in a low, very calm tone, "Shooting me won't get you the keys."

"Oh, yes, it will. If I shoot you, everybody else will know I mean business, and they'll stay away. Hand them over, Luke."

Luke shook his head slowly.

Nick smiled that unearthly smile of his and took aim at Luke's midsection. "I'm going to enjoy this."

"Son, no!" Henry's voice was a tortured cry.

But Nick's smile widened, and he cocked the gun. Just as Charlotte tensed to throw herself in front of Luke, a shot rang out.

A look of surprise flickered across Nick's face, and blood bloomed just below his shoulder. "Drop the gun, Nick." Clarence stepped out from behind Charlotte. Nick held on to the gun, a strange smile on his face.

"Don't make me shoot you again, Nick."

Nick shook his head. "Strange. I can't feel...anything."

His knees buckled, and his fingers scraped the side of the car as he slid to the ground. "Feel very strange—" And he lost consciousness.

Henry swayed backward, and Luke steadied him. "Easy, Dad."

"So much damage. Tried to give him what he...lacked. Tried to give him what I lacked. Didn't think you needed anything. You had it all. I've been stupid. So stupid, and now..." Henry's eyes were on Nick. He moved as if to go to Nick, but Luke held him back. Clarence had called Elsie Brown, a paramedic, out of the crowd. She'd already made Nick more comfortable on the ground, loosened his clothes, found a blanket to pillow his head.

Luke helped Henry walk to Nick then. He wasn't sure which face was more ashen, his father's or his brother's. Henry asked, "Is he—"

"He's passed out just now, Mr. Steadman," Elsie said with calm briskness. "It's a shoulder wound. I'd say he has a good chance of surviving."

"He'll have to stand trial, Dad," Luke said gently. "He'll probably go to prison. Too many people heard him admit to stealing and arson."

"Will you defend him?" His father looked hopeful.

Luke shook his head. "No."

"Suppose I shouldn't have asked. Just wanted the best for him. Always wanted the best for him." Henry raised his eyes to Charlotte, and Luke thought this must be what a surrendering general must look like, shaken, defeated, gathering tattered remnants of pride around him. "I'll compensate you for your losses, of course."

Charlotte's chin came up, and the Montana wind whipped her dark hair across her cheek. "I don't want your money . . . or your help."

Henry took the blow stoically. "I'll send over ten head of cattle in the morning."

"I'll send them right back again."

"Well, the least we can do is offer you the hospitality of the ranch while you rebuild. . . ."

"No." Charlotte looked proud, unbowed. "I couldn't set one foot on your land."

"Charlotte, you've no place to go." Luke reached for her but she eluded him.

"I'll stay in town, at the apartment above the cafe." She turned away from Luke, as if she meant to walk to town by herself.

"Will . . . will you be coming home?" Henry asked.

Luke shook his head, his eyes on his father's.

"So I've lost you both, then." He put out a hand, his eyes glazed. "I have...nothing now. Nothing. Just like Charlotte." He shook himself, as if trying desperately to regain his equilibrium. "I'll...I'll be at home, if you need me for anything."

"We...won't need you."

Henry looked stricken, but he nodded his head. "No, I suppose not. You never did."

Luke went to turn away, but Henry caught his arm. "Tell Charlotte that I'm...I'm sorry. My hands aren't too steady these days, but if she needs them to help her rebuild her house, they are at her disposal. I want...I have to do something to make up for what my son has done. I must do something. Help her to understand that, will you, son?" And then, as if he didn't quite know how to say the word: "Please?"

"I'll see to it," said Luke, thinking it was the first time in a long while that he'd met his father's eyes and understood what he saw there.

"I... That is, if you..." Henry shook his head. He looked old, shaken, stripped of his pride and his spirit. "I'd appreciate it if after awhile you might think about trying to forgive me a little. He raised his eyes, and there was pleading in them, a look of supplication that Luke had never seen there before.

His father wanted him to stay. But he wouldn't ask. He'd hope...but he wouldn't ask. And so Luke had his own victory, but the ashes of it had a bitter taste. "There's nothing to forgive."

His father straightened. "I'm...proud of you, son. Proud of the man you've become." And with that, he turned away, as if he could say no more.

Luke watched him go, thinking that those words had cost him dearly. But he'd liked hearing them.

Charlotte was striding down the lane, her head high, her boots hitting the ground methodically, when he pulled up next to her and reached across to open the car door. "Get in."

She shook her head and kept walking. He trailed along slowly with the car, the open door just a few feet ahead of her. "Charlotte, my father gave up on a considerable amount of his pigheaded pride tonight. Now it's your turn."

"Who said so?" She came to an abrupt stop; he slammed on the brakes.

"I did."

"Well, who are you to tell me what to do?"

"The man who loves you."

She got in and slammed the door.

"You've inhaled too much smoke," she said in a truculent tone.

"Have I?" He threw the car into gear and roared down the dirt road.

Outside the little brick cafe, Charlotte got out of the car, and when she turned around to face him, the wind tangled her hair and the moon went behind a cloud sending her face into the shadow. "I'd ask you to stay, but there's only one small cot to sleep on."

"We'll manage." He reached into the backseat to grab his shaving kit.

When he straightened, he saw that she hadn't moved. She simply stood looking at him.

He dropped his hand and kept his face cool, but he felt . . . desolate.

"I think . . . I'd rather not be with you, tonight, Luke."

"All right. I don't blame you for not wanting to be with somebody named Steadman on this night." He tried to tell himself that it was all right, that she was in shock, that his brother had destroyed her home and she had a perfect right to shut him out, but some irrational part of him asked why she didn't need him on this night, more than ever. God knew he needed her. "I'll see you in the morning, then."

She shook her head. "I'd rather you didn't...come around again."

He felt anger surge through him, but he controlled it sharply. "Mind telling me why?"

"I can't...I can't bear to lose anything more. If you're going away, go now, tonight. And don't come back. Don't—" her chin came up, and he looked into her eyes for the first time "—don't make me hope again. I can't...hope anymore."

It hurt to see her like this, his eternal optimist. He wanted to give her back her hope, now, when she needed it. He knew it was colossally bad timing. But for the first time in his life, he was afraid. If he let his mind rule his heart and let her walk away from him, he might never have the chance to give her back the hope she needed.

Luke looked up at the sky and prayed for the eloquence he was supposed to have. "Charlotte, let me stay with you tonight."

She shook her head again, dark hair flying every which way.

Driven to desperation, he said, "Let me stay with you...always."

"Always? What does that mean?"

"Weren't you listening back there? I love you. I want to marry you. I want to be with you, see you in the morning, work with you, have children with you—"

She stared at him for a moment, her blue eyes brilliant in the hazy, smoke-scented night. Then she flew at him, banging her fists on his chest, with little effect.

"Charlotte—"

"Don't do this to me! Don't, don't, *don't!*"

"What is it—?"

She reared back to glare up into his eyes, and hers were alive with fury. "You don't like sympathy—well, I like it even less."

"Charlotte, I'm not feeling sorry for you. I'm trying to propose here, and I've chosen a lousy time to do it, but I want you to know that you're not alone in this. We'll rebuild your house—"

"Stop, just stop. You're too darn late. You're just . . . too late. Now, go away."

She turned and went to the door of the cafe. Luke watched her, knowing there hadn't been many times in his life when he felt like this, and he hoped there wouldn't be any ever again.

Suddenly, Charlotte cried out and thumped her fists against the door, crying desperately.

He ran to her, caught her up and enveloped her in his arms. "What is it?"

"The key. The key to this door is—was—in the house."

He held her for a moment, let her wet his shirt with her tears. Then he went to the car to get his tire iron and broke the windowpane above the doorknob for her, reached in and opened the door. The air smelled hot and close as he followed her up the stairs. Inside the upstairs room, he pulled open a window and let in the cool night air. She turned on a small lamp on a table by the bed, he searched for the bathroom, found it behind the door. There was a wrench on the floor; in minutes, he had the water flowing through the taps. He found a towel, soaked it and brought it in to her. She was sitting on the edge of the cot, hunting through her jeans pocket for a tissue. He sat down on the cot beside her and tenderly cleaned her face.

"I thought I told you to go away."

"Yes, you did," he said in a calm, low voice.

"I won't marry you."

"Then we'll live in sin instead."

"It would be bad for the children."

"Extremely bad." He knelt to pull off her boots, then lifted her feet onto the cot. "Do you want anything to drink? I could run over to Sam's and get you ice water, or a cola."

She shook her head. "Don't think you can just be nice to me and make me change my mind about marrying you."

"I wouldn't dream of peddling influence—unless it works."

"Sometimes I don't understand you. I know you so well, and I love you, but I don't understand you."

"I don't understand you, and I love you, too."

"You're not going to stay, are you?"

"Wouldn't dream of it." He lay down on the cot, took her in his arms and turned her back to him. She lay against him easily, knowing it was the place she belonged, the place she had always belonged.

"You're a liar, Luke Steadman. What's worse, you're a sneaky liar."

"Yes, ma'am." He smoothed her hair back from her face. She could call him every name in the book, if it took that bleak sound out of her voice.

"A sneaky, polite liar. They're the worst kind."

"Yes, ma'am, they are."

"I want to cry, Luke."

"Go ahead. You're entitled."

"I'd rather sleep."

"That sounds like an excellent idea."

"I want to sleep with you, but we'll have to be very close. Practically on top of each other."

"I'll try to put up with the inconvenience." Amusement lurked in his deep rumble.

"When I wake up, you'll be here?" And she reached for his hand. He knew Charlotte well enough to know he had his answer to his proposal.

"I'll be here," he said. And when he thought of what the morning would bring, and how she would wake grouchy and adorable, and how they would make plans to build a new house on the ranch and they'd live there together and raise children who were both high-strung and spirited and sturdy and rock-dependable, his mouth curled in a smile and his eyes closed.

Epilogue

"He hasn't asked to hold the baby yet."

Charlotte looked so wonderful to Luke, all blue eyes and black hair blown every which way by the mischievous morning wind, anxious love sparkling deep in the dark blue depths of her eyes, the white lacy blanket that their son didn't need on this warm morning spread over her arms.

"He will, darlin'. Relax."

He wasn't at all sure that he could predict his father's reaction, but he couldn't bear for Charlotte to be disappointed. His wife read him far too well, for she shot him a glance that he was beginning to recognize, a glance filled with Charlotte's particular blend of love and the exasperation that he seemed to elicit from her so easily, a glance that said, *I know you.*

She held Mark tenderly in her arms, making tiny swivels of her body to keep him quiet and amused. At six weeks of age, her son had already shown a lively curiosity about the world and an ever-ready store of energy. Now he looked up at her with big blue eyes so like her own. Luke gazed at the two people who were his world, knowing he must have a foolish look of awe and love on his face. He didn't care. They were his, these two precious people, and every day they seemed to call forth more love from a well deep within him that he'd discovered was limitless.

Charlotte and Luke stood in the back of the church, keeping the baby in the children's crying room, in case he made a noise, which he hadn't yet, being the most perfect baby in the world that he was. Henry stood close by in the entryway of the church, hat in hand. He'd agreed to come and take part in the baptismal service, but he'd wanted to drive in his own car. Luke had been disappointed about that, but he'd decided that he'd take whatever Henry could give and not ask for more. Charlotte wanted harmony on this day, and he'd have moved the earth to give it to her.

Henry stood a few feet away, distancing himself from Luke and Charlotte. His father's aloofness was the only thing that had dampened Luke's happiness at the birth of his son. His father still had not spoken to the child, asked to hold him or, indeed, shown much interest at all.

"And now I have the great privilege of accepting a child into our Christian fellowship," the minister said from the sanctuary. "Will the parents and grandparent, as well as the child's sponsors, come forward please?"

Mike and Delores Hallorhan rose from the pews, Delores looking very stylish in her white summer dress, Mike's face flushed and his smile wide. They waited to let Charlotte and the baby and Henry and Luke pass, and then they followed the family up to the altar.

The minister introduced Charlotte and Luke to the congregation, even though they were well-known by nearly everyone there, and reminded those seated in the pews that they were soon to become a larger family to this baby.

Then the minister took the baby into his arms and, turning to Charlotte, he asked, ''What name shall be given to this child?''

''Mark Henry Sean Steadman,'' Charlotte said, in a voice that was soft and not quite steady.

Luke wanted to look at his father's face then, but he was afraid to. It was easier just to say his own little prayer that this day would go as Charlotte wished, and keep his focus on his son, who peered up at the minister with owlish eyes as the pastor put his wet hand on the boy's dark hair. The baby took the shock very well. He was going to be brave, strong and adaptable, all the characteristics he needed in the ambiguous and confusing world he'd come into. Of course, how could the baby be anything but wonderful, when he had a mother with Charlotte's courage and determination? Luke couldn't keep his hand from creeping around Charlotte's waist, needing to touch her, to claim just a little ownership of the amazing woman at his side.

When the ritual was over, the minister kept the baby in his arms and took Mark for a little trip up and down the aisles of the small church so that everyone in the congregation could see the new addition to their church family. Several women, all too familiar with the long feud between the families, looked on the blue-eyed little boy in his white blanket nestled against the minister's black robe and began digging in their purses for tissues.

When the minister returned Mark to Charlotte's arms, she was glad, for she could see her son's lip coming out and she knew they had almost exhausted his patience with this strange business. She was so proud of him for having taken it all in his stride.

Later, when the service was over, and everyone had crowded around to ooh and aah at the baby and say all the silly things adults say to babies, like ''Isn't he just the most adorable boy you've ever seen!'' and ''Oh, he looks like his mother!'' "No, of course he doesn't look like his mother, he's the spitting image of Luke." And from one woman named Lucille to another woman named Lucille, "Oh, and of course you'd remember!''

"Never mind what I remember," said the second Lucille.

Even Tex looked down into the baby's face and then up at Luke. "Well, you've finally done something worthwhile," he said, grudgingly, while Lettie chided him for his bluntness and poked at his arm, telling him to hush.

Everyone filed out the big double doors of the church to gather under the cool shade of the cottonwood, leaving Luke, Charlotte and Henry standing inside.

Henry stood at the open door, an errant breeze lifting a strand of his straight, white hair, poised to say goodbye and walk away. Luke felt a stab of disappointment that was sharp and deep.

Henry turned his hat in his hand, looked out the church door and then back, not at Luke but at Charlotte.

"Was it your idea to name the boy after me?"

Charlotte lifted her chin. Luke felt his heart sink. Nothing had changed after all. Charlotte said, "It was a mutual decision. Luke and I agreed that it was what we both wanted."

"You are...a good woman. You have a forgiving heart."

"I'm glad you think so."

"I'm glad you and Luke are settled in your new home. It helps me...to forget...." His courage failed him. "I thank you for asking me to be a part of...things here today. Well, I guess I'd better be going." Henry turned away, his shoulders sagging. He looked very old. He smoothed his hair back and put on his hat.

In that silence, that long silence, Charlotte felt as if she'd lost her ability to breathe. Even the baby was still, sensing her tenseness. If she let this moment go by, she would regret it for the rest of her life. She couldn't wait for Henry to ask for the baby. He never would. He would think he didn't have the right, that he had lost his privileges as a grandfather. A Steadman man was never easy, but he was well worth the battle. Quickly, before she lost her nerve, she said huskily, "Wouldn't you like to hold your namesake?"

Henry stood stock-still, as if her words had shocked him. At last, he moved, shaking his head. "It's been too long. I might...drop him."

"Of course you won't drop him," Charlotte said quickly. "Here, we'll help you." With brisk determination, she walked to Henry and put his grandson into his arms. Luke felt as if the breath he'd been holding would explode inside him.

Henry frowned, as if he were genuinely afraid he might drop his grandson. The baby looked up at Henry, smiled and kicked his feet. Henry gazed down at the boy as if he were looking at heaven. "He doesn't mind my holding him."

Luke felt so...strange. He felt as if he wanted to tease his father. "He knows a soft touch when he sees one. Watch out for him. He's a schemer."

"He's a fine-looking boy."

"We didn't think so. We thought he looked a lot like you, Dad. He's certainly got your nose."

Henry glanced up at his son, looking very taken aback. Then his smile came, a little rusty, but a smile, nevertheless. "I believe he does have my nose, at that." Another hesitation. "He has his mother's eyes."

"Maybe he'll dazzle the girls with those and they'll forget to look at his nose." Luke put his hand on his father's arm. "He has a lot to learn. We'll need help teaching him."

"Oh, I'm sure you'll do a fine job." Henry looked up, saw the quick flash of disappointment in Luke's eyes. "But on the other hand, there are probably a lot of things a grandfather can teach his grandson. Like how to cast a fly rod, and how to turn a cow, and how to tell if a girl likes you by putting a dandelion under her chin. If you'll let me take him out occasionally—"

"He's your grandson," Luke said softly. "You can see him as often as you like."

Henry gazed at his son. In a choked voice, he said, "Generosity seems to run in this family."

Charlotte smiled through her tears. She'd been given her rainbow, and it had so many pretty colors in it.

Henry raised his eyes to Luke. "I'd like to get to know my grandson. Maybe I'll do a better job of being a grandparent than I was a father." And still holding the baby in his arms, Henry turned and walked out the church door into a June morning brimming with the promise of summer.

* * * * *

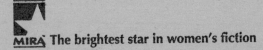

MILLION DOLLAR SWEEPSTAKES
AND EXTRA BONUS PRIZE DRAWING

No purchase necessary. To enter the sweepstakes, follow the directions published and complete and mail your Official Entry Form. If your Official Entry Form is missing, or you wish to obtain an additional one (limit: one Official Entry Form per request, one request per outer mailing envelope) send a separate, stamped, self-addressed #10 envelope (4 1/8" x 9 1/2") via first class mail to: Million Dollar Sweepstakes and Extra Bonus Prize Drawing Entry Form, P.O. Box 1867, Buffalo, NY 14269-1867. Request must be received no later than January 15, 1998. For eligibility into the sweepstakes, entries must be received no later than March 31, 1998. No liability is assumed for printing errors, lost, late, non-delivered or misdirected entries. Odds of winning are determined by the number of eligible entries distributed and received.

Sweepstakes open to residents of the U.S. (except Puerto Rico), Canada and Europe who are 18 years of age or older. All applicable laws and regulations apply. Sweepstakes offer void wherever prohibited by law. Values of all prizes are in U.S. currency. This sweepstakes is presented by Torstar Corp., its subsidiaries and affiliates, in conjunction with book, merchandise and/or product offerings. For a copy of the Official Rules governing this sweepstakes, send a self-addressed, stamped envelope (WA residents need not affix return postage) to: MILLION DOLLAR SWEEP-STAKES AND EXTRA BONUS PRIZE DRAWING Rules, P.O. Box 4470, Blair, NE 68009-4470, USA.

As seen on TV!
Free Gift Offer

With a Free Gift proof-of-purchase from any Silhouette® book,
you can receive a beautiful cubic zirconia pendant.

This gorgeous marquise-shaped stone is a genuine cubic
zirconia—accented by an 18" gold tone necklace.

(Approximate retail value $19.95)

Send for yours today...
compliments of ▼ *Silhouette*®
TM

To receive your free gift, a cubic zirconia pendant, send us one original proof-of-purchase, photocopies not accepted, from the back of any Silhouette Romance™, Silhouette Desire®, Silhouette Special Edition®, Silhouette Intimate Moments® or Silhouette Yours Truly™ title available in August, September or October at your favorite retail outlet, together with the Free Gift Certificate, plus a check or money order for $1.65 U.S./$2.15 CAN. (do not send cash) to cover postage and handling, payable to Silhouette Free Gift Offer. We will send you the specified gift. Allow 6 to 8 weeks for delivery. Offer good until October 31, 1996 or while quantities last. Offer valid in the U.S. and Canada only.

Free Gift Certificate

Name: _____

Address: _____

City: _____ State/Province: _____ Zip/Postal Code: _____

Mail this certificate, one proof-of-purchase and a check or money order for postage and handling to: SILHOUETTE FREE GIFT OFFER 1996. In the U.S.: 3010 Walden Avenue, P.O. Box 9077, Buffalo NY 14269-9077. In Canada: P.O. Box 613, Fort Erie, Ontario L2Z 5X3.

FREE GIFT OFFER   084-KMD
ONE PROOF-OF-PURCHASE
To collect your fabulous FREE GIFT, a cubic zirconia pendant, you must include this original proof-of-purchase for each gift with the properly completed Free Gift Certificate.

084-KMD

Who can resist a Texan...or a Calloway?

This September, award-winning author
ANNETTE BROADRICK
returns to Texas, with a brand-new
story about the Calloways...

SONS
→OF←
TEXAS

Rogues and Ranchers

CLINT: The brave leader. Used to keeping secrets.

CADE: The Lone Star Stud. Used to having women
fall at his feet...

MATT: The family guardian. Used to handling
trouble...

They must discover the identity of the mystery
woman with Calloway eyes—and uncover a
conspiracy that threatens their family....

Look for **SONS OF TEXAS:** Rogues and Ranchers
in September 1996!

Only from Silhouette...where passion lives.

Silhouette®

You're About to Become a *Privileged Woman*

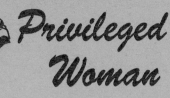

Reap the rewards of fabulous free gifts and benefits with proofs-of-purchase from Silhouette and Harlequin books

Pages & Privileges™

It's our way of thanking you for buying our books at your favorite retail stores.

Harlequin and Silhouette— the most privileged readers in the world!

For more information about Harlequin and Silhouette's PAGES & PRIVILEGES program call the Pages & Privileges Benefits Desk: 1-503-794-2499

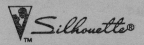